HOSTILE TERRITORY

JERRY AUTIERI

1

Varro drew a deep breath and closed his eyes against the midday sun. The enemy had at least chosen the correct ground for their attack, if the wrong opponent. He listened to the Iberian barbarians' distant jeers and curses and contrasted them with the silent discipline of his troops. The padding of his mount's hooves on the dirt and the creak of leather were all the sounds he made, and the blocks of infantry dared not even this much.

Opening his eyes again, the dark ranks of barbarians had drawn closer. He credited their bravery. Consul Cato had broken the main rebellion earlier in the year and had been crushing anyone else who raised a sword against Rome. These Iberians marched toward their deaths, but their swagger betrayed no fear of it.

Tribune Galenus stroked the neck of his brown horse, his narrow, ever-angry eyes scanning the same line of barbarians. The tendons in his jaw twitched as if the promise of battle irritated him. Dressed in his muscled bronze chest plate and wearing a deep red sash, he cut the figure of a Roman god leading his men to battle. This was also a stunning contrast to the irritable, small-minded man that Varro knew him to be. He was no Jupiter ready to hurl a lightning bolt, as much as he tried to dress the part.

"You're impatient," he said, his narrow eyes never leaving the forming battle.

"Sorry, sir." Varro felt his cheeks warm. He hated to be so easily read. "I feel as if I should do more."

A thin smile reached Galenus's lips, but he remained fixed on the barbarians spreading from their massed ranks.

"They'll be in range of our velites soon enough." The tribune offered a final pat to his horse's neck, then sat back in the saddle. "Whoever reaches the hastati after that will learn regret. Like all the other rebels before them, they will be rolled up and defeated before anything interesting happens. You couldn't join your friends before the battle ended. Not that I would allow it, in any case."

Galenus finally turned his thin smile on Varro, who nodded and looked back to the forming battle.

His appointment as Galenus's adjutant was a promotion, even if it did not come with any actual pay increase. It was also a far safer appointment than Curio and Falco, who both had to lead their hastati centuries from the front. He looked to them now, finding both in the tenth maniple.

Falco's height made Curio seem all the shorter. Both men were capable in battle and could be counted on to survive until the last. Varro wished he could be with them, meeting the enemy face-to-face and driving the line forward. His many citations for bravery proved he was the right man for that role.

But Consul Cato recommended him to the tribune under some pretense that he should learn the art of command firsthand. To Varro, it felt more shameful to let others take risks he would not share.

"They have no fear of death?" Galenus asked, breaking into his thoughts. "Or are they just misinformed? What motivates a man to throw his life away for a mere skirmish?"

Varro did not answer, since Galenus had an unsettling habit of talking to himself. But on the tribune's other side, his Iberian interpreter offered his thoughts in strained Latin.

"They fight for their homes, sir. To them, every battle is a chance to restore their land and kill a Roman. Wouldn't any man do the same?"

Galenus tilted his head. "But the conclusion is foregone. Defeat and death for them, and the continuation of Roman authority. Your kinsmen are not as wise as you are, Aulus."

"Maybe not, sir." Aulus laughed.

He was armored as a Roman, but the faded blue tattoos of his tribe still decorated his face. Out on the frontier, he could pretend to be a citizen, but he would never be accepted in Rome. Varro was grateful for Aulus's language skills and understood the need for such men, but did not like them. He preferred his friends among the Ilegertes who had adopted Roman speech and manners. They had no intentions to become Romans themselves and simply learned to integrate a better way of life into their traditions.

The Iberian line now gathered into a rough formation. Their leaders and the bolder among them capered before their lines, daring the velites in their wolf skins to cast their javelins early. But even the lowest rank of the Legion maintained greater discipline than their foes. They waited for the signal to begin the attack.

It came with a curt nod from the tribune. The tubicen, who sat on his horse to the left, now raised the bronze bucina to his lips and sounded the command. Varro watched as the velites raised their javelins and let out a joyous cry. They then surged forward at the brash Iberians who tempered their antics when they realized the fight had begun. These tribesmen carried larger shields and wore heavier armor than Varro was accustomed to seeing. Even so, some did not trust their armor alone but attempted to retreat out of javelin range.

The velites' javelins arced across the gap at the bold—or foolish—who defied them. Yet even the most audacious of them cowered when the javelins stitched into their ranks. Their screams echoed across the fields to reach Varro at the back of the Roman lines. As satisfying as it was to hear the death knell of an enemy, neither he nor any other soldier responded. The Romans watched in silence as the youngest and poorest of their fellows dared the Iberians to battle.

Tribune Galenus stretched forward to observe the initial attack. His horse snorted as if eager to charge. Varro's mount—recently acquired at great expense—side-stepped and challenged to keep him reined in place.

Velites seeking rewards for glory and daring battled those Iberians still forward from their lines. The rest cast their lot of javelins and then sensibly retreated from the fight. Such battles inspired Varro, particularly to see the lightly armored and poorly armed velite dare the superior Iberian. It pained him to watch them taken down by falcata and spear. But in places, the lucky velite plucked victory from his enemy's lifeblood and stole away with a trophy for proof.

"They'll come now," Galenus said. "Order the hastati forward."

The tubicen sounded a new series of notes. To hear them so close confused Varro. He was accustomed to listening for that tune at the front of the line, and he nearly kicked his horse forward in response. Indeed, had he not been mounted he might have started.

Instead, he watched the lines of hastati advance as the velites raced through the spaces between the infantry blocks. Galenus sat higher on his horse, having selected the best vantage point to observe the battle. He had over a thousand infantry on this patrol with thirty cavalrymen in support. These waited on the left wing for an opportunity to roll up the barbarian line. Like his tribune, Varro was to study the entire battle line and be a second set of eyes for Galenus.

But he found himself drawn to the right, where the tenth maniple of hastati anchored the flank against a row of trees. Varro stared hard into those dark woods, aware that ambushers might lurk in their purple-shadowed depths. He had seen it before, and it was a good tactic, if a predictable one.

Yet Falco and Curio led their maniple in pace with the main advance. Varro focused on them as they called for the light pila cast. As they reached a jog, all across the line the hastati raised their pila. The iron heads gleamed above their feathered helmets as the centurions led them closer to the enemy lines.

The barbarians broke into a dash at this, probably having learned from experience they could not linger in front of a Roman line. They raised their shields as they screamed in defiance.

The air filled with pila, faded yellow streaks that arced overhead and plunged into the barbarians. Varro had never seen the pila cast from this distance. It was as if a wave of iron and wood had exploded from the Roman line and washed away the front rank of Iberians. Scores of them fell aside, maimed or killed, and caused their comrades to skip around them or else tumble over bodies.

Heavy pila formed the second volley, a stronger weapon designed to break armor and shield at a close distance. Varro was certain he heard Falco's command to throw even from his rear position.

The shuddering thud of these heavy weapons filled the air and mingled with the screams and curses of the barbarian warriors. They eschewed slings and javelins in favor of heavy swords and armor. To them, Varro had learned, such weapons were for the weak and a disgrace to real warriors. But as another line of barbarians collapsed bleeding into the dirt, Varro was glad the Romans were more practical.

"An impressive sight," Galenus said. "The barbarians are already defeated and just need to realize it. We'll let the hastati explain it to them. I don't expect we'll need to move up the principes."

"What about the cavalry, sir?" Varro pulled his eyes from where Falco's century had advanced into contact while Curio's remained back to both guard the flank and relieve them when needed. The cavalry sat on their proud mounts, their armor unsullied and the plumes of their helmets waving in the breeze. "They will not want to miss an opportunity for glory."

"Spoken like an infantryman," Galenus said. "When you command, Varro, you cannot have a favorite. Both cavalry and infantry have their place. I will use the cavalry if the need arises. But this is nothing other than a skirmish."

Chastened, Varro turned to watch the battle. His horse again tested his control, and he tugged the animal back into place. He had learned to ride from the best horsemen in the world, the Numidians. But he found little admiration for his techniques among the Roman cavalry. This did not bother him, since he merely had to ride beside the tribune. But he was new to this horse, and still had to learn its personality. If he had to battle from the saddle now, he might find himself dismounted in short order.

The thunderous clamor of battle rang to the sky. The barbarians had piled in, but Galenus still preserved lines of both principes and triarii. These soldiers shouted encouragement to the hastati in combat. This was another tradition Varro had not seen before. He was always a hastatus and always in the front of the battle. He rarely heard anything from behind other than the shouting of his optio.

The forces were evenly matched, but it seemed Galenus's predictions were accurate. The Iberian line already buckled at the center as the hastati plowed forward, sheltering behind body-length shields and stabbing with their short swords. These Iberians seemed to favor the heavy falcata, and as such, they suffered in close combat without the space to bring the weapon's full force to bear.

"Send in the cavalry," Galenus said, seeming to purposely avoid looking at Varro. The tubicen played a new series of notes, and Varro watched the wedge of horsemen lunge into action.

The horses swept out and around the barbarian line and crashed into its left flank. It was as if a great boulder plowed through their ranks and scattered the barbarians. With this jolt to the Iberian line, the hastati pushed harder, and soon the Iberians at the rear peeled away and ran for the trees where they had emerged earlier.

Victory shouts followed them, but the throaty commands of centurions held the hastati in place.

"Advance and pursue," Galenus said.

More notes sounded and centurions across all lines belted out the command as the order raced forward to the front lines. Varro shook his head.

"Sir, the consul's orders were—"

"Hold your tongue," Galenus said, gazing ahead as if leading all the legions against Hannibal rather than the thousand-strong scouting force that they were.

The Iberians were in full retreat now and in complete disarray. Varro agreed they would be easily run down and destroyed. But they were simply to find the enemy, engage if needed, and return to Cato with their report as soon as possible. Varro feared the pursuit might extend into the woods, and thereby sacrifice their advantage of formation combat.

All lines began to advance, and the hastati raced forward. Varro flicked the reins to keep his horse in step with the rest of the command group. He watched as Curio brought up his century while Falco let his fade back to rest. A secret smile reached Varro's lips. He imagined how eager the men were to join the glory of victory. Curio would be pressed to keep them in order. Varro imagined the small man's struggles against the surging, youthful confidence of the hastati.

He wished he were up there with them.

The advancing Romans stamped their feet as they marched after the fleeing Iberians. It created a fearsome thrumming through the earth so that the enemy would know that death pursued them. The principes and even the triarii banged their weapons on their shields as they advanced, generating more noise than the battle had done.

The tribune did not increase his pace even as all his lines surged ahead after the frantic barbarians. Instead, he smiled like a doting uncle letting the children have some fun before their evening chores.

Varro had only served the tribune for a handful of similar skirmishes. He hesitated to say he had fought in any of them, and Falco had rightfully teased that he had been a mere observer. Today he was beginning to feel almost cowardly. Why not draw closer? Why linger behind when the battle was won? Was Galenus so averse to drawing his sword?

He bit back on the foolish thought, for of course tribunes hardly ever fought. If they did, it meant the battle was lost. It was nothing he had ever given much thought to since he was always concerned about the pike or sword thrust at his face. Now to be in the command group he found the experience lacking. Perhaps he would feel otherwise once he was in a proper battle and not a skirmish.

As he trotted forward, he felt something zip past him. It might have been a large bee and for a moment he dismissed it. But then he realized a bee would have passed him from the front. This had come from the rear.

Pulling his horse around, he faced a mob of Iberian slingers emerging from where the Roman cavalry had been posted. They came running from the trees, young men with small shields and bare chests. But they stopped to fit stones into their slings while others spun them overhead.

"Slingers to the rear!" he shouted, then turned his horse to face them.

They moved fast, being lightly armored and young. They seemed to lack cohesion, as a number of them chased the triarii line. But enough had marked the lagging command group that Varro was certain they would be swamped in minutes. There could be no fatter prize than a tribune and his staff, and even the simplest Iberian farmer knew it.

Galenus started shouting orders, but Varro did not wait to hear what they were. He kicked his mount's flanks and drove it toward the triarii line. The horse seemed relieved to at last be freed to run and bolted forward.

Now that Varro was essentially a cavalryman, he no longer carried his gladius and scutum. Instead, he hauled up a long wicker shield covered with heavy hide and reinforced with an iron crossbar and boss. He drew his long Greek-style sword and pointed to the danger as triarii turned to his call.

"Intercept them before they reach the tribune!"

A stone shattered the edge of his shield and he expertly tuned his horse to face the slingers. By cutting down his profile, the hasty shots went wide of him.

He now galloped forward, confident that the triarii centurions and optiones were turning their formations to face this new threat. Some Iberians stood in place to load more shots, others drew clubs, spears, and swords, and still others turned to flee.

Their faces were fresh and youthful, and some might not have been old enough to stand beside the youngest velite. But Varro did not care. They could kill him just as dead as any veteran.

His charge broke up the leading groups of new arrivals. The beat of his horse's hooves was enough to send them running. But he caught up with one and hacked down with his long sword. It took the man on his shoulder and sprawled him out. Varro's horse screamed and jolted to the side.

Another stone crashed off his shield.

But another somehow shot under his helmet, striking him behind his ear.

He howled in pain, but the helmet brim had dispersed the force of it. His shock and his mount's pain combined to destabilize him.

Then someone grabbed his leg and yanked.

The horse bucked as it kicked. Varro heard a wet crack and a short scream. But then he flew over the horse's neck, dragged by his momentum. He had barely enough time to twist so that he landed on his back rather than his neck. His chain shirt crunched against the dirt.

Above him, the great shadow of his horse reared up alongside the shadows of enemies gathering over him.

He had still gripped his sword but had lost his shield. He thrust it upward with a scream and prayed he could get off his back before either his horse or his enemies killed him.

2

Varro's ears rang with the clamor of battle, shouting, screaming horses, and the clang of metal. Above him, his horse reared up as sling stones pelted it. He had been the first to reach the newly arrived Iberian slingers and so suffered from being their closest and best target. Fortunately for him, his mount's flailing protected him from the enemy attempting to get past it and end his life.

He held his sword upright, hoping that if his horse struck down he would dart away from the pain. As hard as his crash had been, and as breathless as it left him, he still scrambled up. He found his wicker shield had skidded out of reach.

A stone slammed into his shoulder, and a bright pain exploded as white light in his eyes. He staggered back from it, the mail absorbing the worst of the force, and sought to hide behind his horse. But the mount had regained its senses and now fled from the danger.

The Iberians shouted with triumph and raced to surround him. Varro swept his long sword in a warding arc as he backed away. They were boys with a few reedy men interspersed. He cursed himself for having rushed ahead. The triarii had followed him, but their mail shirts were just heavy enough to make rescuing him uncertain.

Then to his great fortune, one of the Iberians rushed him and blocked the more practical-minded of his enemies who would have rather killed with sling stones.

He heard Tribune Galenus and the triarii closing in from behind.

For the moment, he was blessed with a one-on-one battle and he sneered at his enemy.

"I owe you my life, boy," he said. "Too bad I'll take yours."

His sword clanged against the Iberian's round shield. The slinger's short sword flashed as he struck with a frantic passion. But the Iberian's attack lacked skill and cunning, as if he had only learned swordplay this day. Varro parried and evade the flurry of strikes. He was fine to let this whelp exhaust himself. His companions could have overwhelmed Varro, but they now stared past him at what must be the arriving triarii.

Varro slammed his sword against the Iberian's and threw his body weight forward. The slinger staggered back, and Varro's sword slipped under his guard to cut a long gash in the boy's shoulder.

To his credit, the boy did not falter but lunged forward with his sword, determined to avenge himself. Varro danced aside from the blow and retaliated with a fierce stroke to the boy's cheek. Yet now the gods looked after the boy, for the strike left a superficial line of red blood for what should have been a beheading stroke. The pain caused the Iberian to drop his guard.

Something held Varro's sword, and he did not know what. Nothing physically arrested his arm, but a weak voice deep in his mind warned he was about to cut down a boy. He had done so before—many times to his own regret. He could not indulge a debate with that voice on a battlefield, and so instead swept inside the boy's reach and then pummeled him flat with the butt of his sword.

A shout rose from behind and the formerly bold slingers now fled toward the trees. Varro glanced to see Galenus with a contingent of the triarii now in pursuit. The tribune and his staff pulled up their horses before Varro and his dazed opponent.

"What did you intend, Centurion Varro? You're fortunate those slingers did not shatter your skull, as thick as it must be."

"They ambushed us, sir. I acted to counter their advantage."

Galenus's frown deepened. Aulus, the Iberian interpreter, shouted at the boy on the ground. They had a brief exchange, then made his report.

"The boy says they were acting alone. Just village children too young to join their brothers in this battle."

Varro looked again at the prostrate and bleeding body at his feet. In the heat of battle, he had acted like a man. But now he was just a child of maybe twelve years. He had dark hair and pale eyes, with a spiraling tattoo on his shoulder which Varro had sliced open.

Galenus snorted. "Well, now he'll never see another battle. We'll take him prisoner, along with whoever else we find fit enough. Otherwise, the seriously wounded will be finished here and left to rot. Let these barbarians know what happens when they dare the might of Rome."

The triarii thundered past, chasing off the final threat into the woods. To the fore the rest of the scouting force had reached the trees. But wise centurions prevented their men from following. The battle was done.

Only now did Varro realize the dull ache in his shoulder where the sling stone had struck. He reached for it, increasing the terrible pain as he did.

"You're hurt?" Galenus peered down from his horse. "And you lost your mount?"

"I'll find him again, sir." Varro winced at the incredible pain now blooming under his awareness of the injury. "This isn't the worst I've felt."

"You're to go to the hospital when we return to camp. The gods preserve the lives of fools, but they don't always keep them from injury. You're holding that shoulder oddly. Have it examined and report to me later."

Varro acknowledged his order, then hefted his defeated foe off the ground. He squirmed at the pain of his gashed shoulder and Varro smirked.

"We both feel it in the same place. But I'll wager you'll feel it much longer than me. We're both of us fools, lucky to have survived ourselves."

The boy also bled from a cut under his matted hair where Varro had struck him. His eyes were wide with fear, but they focused on Varro as he spoke. He seemed to struggle to understand, but Varro just shook his head and nodded to the sheeting blood from his shoulder.

"You can still die. I've seen that happen before. Come on, if you're going to live to become a slave, you'll need that cut mended."

Galenus dismissed him with a frown of disgust. The others of the command group ignored him, except for Aulus who stared after the boy as Varro led him to the rear. A collection point for prisoners was already forming with velites surrounding them. Varro led his captive there, then looked him over before releasing him to the guards.

"I know you hoped to kill me, but you instead saved my life. The tribune was right. My skull should be broken. I have you to thank for it remaining intact. So I spare you now. Even if it's to slavery, it is still life. You might even be sold to someone back in Rome and you can buy your freedom one day. It doesn't have to be all bad."

The boy glared at him as his lips trembled and he tried not to paw at the cut on his shoulder. A velite guard gave Varro a skeptical look.

"Just a moment," Varro said. He then produced a bandage from his kit and wrapped the boy's shoulder as best he could. Red bloomed in the white cloth, but it was a slow oozing. If he could keep it clean, he would live.

Satisfied he had done his best for his erstwhile foe, he handed the boy over to the bemused velite.

"This one wanted to play warrior like his brothers," Varro said. "He's just a child. Don't make it worse on him than it is already going to be."

"We'll keep special watch on him, sir." The velite took the boy by his other arm then shoved him into the ring of defeated Iberians. A dozen huddled on the ground, each one staring listlessly into the dirt. The boy crashed beside one of them, then offered Varro a final glare before turning aside.

He found his horse hiding amongst the trees at the far end of the battle. The beast had only a grudging trust with Varro, both being new to each other. Dark blood clotted on its rear left flank where a stone had broken its skin. But Varro approached warily even if it was his horse. While he did not know this particular horse well, he had learned enough about horses in Numidia to know this one was upset with him.

"I know, you trusted me and I got you hurt. It's understandable that you're mad. But let me get you to someone who can see to that wound. Come on, let's get you to your friends. I think you're in love with the tubicen's horse, aren't you? Don't be shy with me. We've got to work together now."

His Numidian mentor, Baku, told him that you bonded with a horse when both of you could speak to each other with or without words. The horse would understand you and you the horse. Right now, Varro felt as if his mount were asking him to go around to his rear so that he could kick Varro's head off.

But the calm speech and soft approach allowed him to get closer and to stroke the horse's neck. Then he gently gathered the reins and they were once more walking toward the battle lines. When he purchased the horse, the wry cavalryman had told him it was customary not to name the animal until it survived three battles. Varro was beginning to think the cavalry had played some sort of joke on him. So he discussed name possibilities with the horse as they crossed back to the others. The horse seemed to have no opinion, but at least Varro was satisfied his mount listened.

The final tally of the skirmish was entirely lopsided to the Roman. Galenus was pleased to count over three hundred dead Iberians with half as many taken captive. In turn, Galenus boasted no casualties other than normal injuries. A score or so of the men would be out with their wounds for a while. As they marched back to camp, Varro's shoulder grew stiffer and more painful, and he began to wonder if he might be among that number of wounded.

On return to the marching camp, Varro was relieved to see the doctors at the hospital tents. The Greek doctors and their orderlies were overworked even in times of peace, for there was no end to sickness, training accidents, overzealous punishments, and all manner of physical complications. But after a fight, they would be pushed to their limits. So Varro was sure to arrive before the rest of the wounded did.

Nevertheless, the doctors were not fooled and followed a strict triage system. When the casualties entered, Varro felt shame for seeking advantage. As if to further shame him, he found himself seated across from a man who had taken a spear to his eye. It was wrapped in bloody cloth and the young soldier was clearly in shock, still chatting about the great fight they just had. By sunset, he would be screaming, Varro was certain. His own shoulder was not as bad as losing an eye.

So he waited as men groaned through their stitches, held down by strong orderlies as the Greek doctors sewed them up. They had prodded him a few times and asked how much his shoulder hurt. His answers never generated a better response than grunts from his examiners. But after a few hours of waiting, a doctor arrived to treat him.

Getting out of his armor had been the hardest part, for raising his arm overhead felt like fire poured down his shoulder and neck. But they removed it without cutting. Varro had money, but it was all sitting in a place called a bank back in Rome. He could hardly afford to pay for his promotion, and still owed money on his horse.

"Well, I imagine the bone is chipped or bruised," the doctor said after poking him and watching his reactions. "So, we'll wrap it up and put it in a sling. You'll not be fighting for a few weeks."

"No argument from me, Doctor." He paused and looked around. It was a nervous tick, not that he expected to find anyone listening. The tent was filled with men laid out under sheets and wrapped in bandages, orderlies bending over them to treat their ills. Moaning and muttered curses would cover his whispers.

The doctor noted the silence and raised a brow to Varro.

"I don't suppose you'll treat the prisoners?"

The doctor's eruption of laughter was out of place in the grim confines of the hospital tent. Orderlies glanced up from their work with irritated frowns.

"Have a look around, Centurion. Do you imagine I have nothing better to do with my time? Tomorrow morning some of these boys will die and others will wish they had. That's what I have to focus on. And no doubt you careless soldiers will deliver a fresh lot of wounded tomorrow. So what do you think?"

"I know." Varro raised his hands in surrender. "But if I bought you one, a boy, could you help him? He just needs a wound cleaned and some stitches."

The doctor's smile vanished. "Did you hear me? I need sleep

too, Centurion. I'm busy the rest of the night and busy from dawn tomorrow. We're on the march and I have to get these men on their feet again."

"I can pay you." Varro lowered his voice. "Or if you need another favor, I can consider what can be done."

"Why?" The doctor's question hung between them, and Varro did not have a suitable answer.

"Because I'm claiming this prisoner as my slave. And I can't have him die from an infection while he needs to carry my gear."

The doctor sighed. "Bring him by before we march. If it's not too big of a cut, I'll clean and stitch him. But if I'm busy, then he'll have to wait."

Varro left the hospital tent with his left arm in a fresh white sling and his chain shirt slung over his other arm. The fresh air outside was a relief from the scent of unguents and blood inside the hospital. The camp hummed with activity. Men crisscrossed the breadth of it with their heads down.

All of Cato's legions were marching south at the request of the praetors in Far Iberia. Another massive rebel army threatened the stability of the province and they needed the legions to put it down. Along the way, they fought skirmishes as they had today, and each time delivered defeat to the Iberians. Looking now at a camp too big to see end to end, he expected victory in the south as well. But with his injured shoulder, he might have no part in it. They were close enough that as long as no more barbarians challenged them they would reach the praetors in a matter of days.

By now Galenus would have made his report. Varro regretted not being present for it. Not because he wanted to tell Cato the tribune had let himself be surprised from the rear. That would come out eventually. Instead, he hoped to see Cato chastise the tribune for not following exact orders. The consul had no tolerance for any deviation from his directives even when they were favorable to his own cause. Galenus was a man who needed a good bawling out by his superior and Varro had missed seeing it.

He also found himself with a moment of discretionary time, something more valuable than gold in this army. Galenus would not notice if he were missing for another hour. So rather than follow the main path to report to his tribune, he instead followed a different path to find the tents of the Second Legion hastati.

Curio's shouting echoed down the row as Varro approached. He found his diminutive friend red-faced and glaring up at a young hastatus standing at rigid attention.

"Do you have any other jokes to share?" he screamed. "Because they are so funny I might want you to stand out here all night and tell us more."

"No, sir, I have no more jokes." The soldier's face was white, and Varro noted no one else stood with him but were all piled into their tents. The cooking fire still burned and the pot simmered over it.

Curio stepped back from the soldier and scanned him head to toe with a look of total revulsion.

"Clean this up," he said, pointing to the fire. "And since you have so much energy today, go see the tessarius and he'll put you to work tonight."

Curio waved the soldier off after he saluted. The tessarius would have watch schedules already created, but if given more help he would give a favored soldier a break and work in Curio's man.

Curio turned back to where Falco was watching from his section, with folded arms and a crooked smile. But he had seen Varro's approach and nodded toward him.

They met behind the tent rows, as had been their custom since their first days together in the army. There was no privacy here, just more rows of tents. But these were for other centurions and optiones to manage and the soldiers knew enough to ignore an officer unless they wanted more work.

"What did your man do?" Varro asked as they gathered together. Both Curio and Falco were still dressed in their mail shirts and the sweat matting their hair reminded him of how much work he had been avoiding.

"More comments about my height. Nothing new," Curio said, then gestured to the sling. "So, did you break your arm taking notes?"

Falco leaned back in laughter. "Sounds like something I'd say. My, you're a fine centurion, Curio! So what happened, Varro?"

"Didn't you hear? We got ambushed from the rear. Slingers. I took a stone to the shoulder." He rubbed it. "Hurts enough, but it won't slow me down. The doctor said I'll be in this sling for a few weeks."

Falco and Curio exchanged glances. "We didn't realize. But they couldn't have been much of a threat."

"It only takes one sling stone to smash a man's brains out. If they had patience to draw closer, then the entire command group would've mixed their brains up in a pile. Fortunately, the slingers were mostly young boys with a few drunks among them. We broke them up without trouble."

"But not before you got hit," Curio said. "Sorry for teasing you like that."

Varro waved it off. "It won't be long before the tribune sends me back to the line. I'm not sure he's happy with me as an adjutant."

"Galenus is not happy with anyone," Falco said with a sniff. "The bastard was born unhappy."

Varro looked around, then leaned in closer. "I have some news."

Both Falco and Curio stepped forward, their smiles turned to concern.

"Yesterday, I overheard the consul's conversation with the paymasters. A large amount of silver has gone missing. The same amount we got from Centurion Longinus."

3

Varro's words hung between him and his friends as they huddled together. Behind them centurions shouted at their men, who returned sharp acknowledgments. The scent of evening cooking fires filled the air with sweet wood odors. But the space in the huddle had turned sour. Curio blinked at the news, and Falco rubbed his face with a growl.

"That smiling bastard," he said. "So Longinus stole the silver."

"I don't think so," Varro said. "When I spoke to him, he seemed to sincerely have no idea about it."

"But that was weeks ago," Curio said. "They're just discovering it now?"

Roughly a month ago, Varro had hatched a plan to acquire old helmets and broken gear to create dummy soldiers he hoped would fool the army besieging Rome's Ilegertes allies. He had arranged it with the First Spear, Centurion Longinus, and as far as Varro knew no other was aware of the plan. When he received the gear, a chest of silver denarii arrived with it.

Varro looked between his two friends. "Well, it wasn't the entire treasury."

"But pretty near to it," Falco said. "Someone is asleep at his guard post if that's where Longinus got the silver from."

"We don't know Longinus stole anything. I don't even think he is part of our organization." Varro patted the pugio at his hip with the silver inlaid owl head. It identified him as a Servus Capax member, who ostensibly worked behind the scenes to further Rome's goals. But yet, Varro had done little besides normal soldiering and a brief sojourn in Numidia.

Both Curio and Falco moved to touch their pugiones as if confirming they still possessed them.

"Then who else?" Falco stood back and looked over his shoulder. "It wasn't the old man who delivered the gear to us? What was his name?"

Varro thought about it. "He never gave us his name. He had a gap between his teeth, I remember that."

"Well, there it is," Curio said. "He's the only other one."

Falco hissed. "I'm surprised they let an old dog like that hold a spear in the battle line. He was a fucking cart driver at best."

"But who else could've helped us?" Varro scratched his head. "He said he had been with Longinus for many campaigns. But maybe he is one of us after all."

"Never accept a gift from a stranger," Falco said, shaking his head. "One of the few wise things my father ever said when he was sober. When he was drunk, he was also full of sayings, but none made any sense."

"I can't think of who else could've hidden that silver in the cart." Varro folded his arms. "I'll go find him. He's in Centurion Longinus's century. So he can't be hard to find."

"Do you remember what he looks like? I don't." Falco rubbed his chin and tilted his head. "And what are you going to say to him if you find him?"

"For one, I want to see if he carries the same sign we do. Then I want to ask about the silver."

"Can you be more careful this time?" Curio asked. "Last time, you told Longinus about it. If he finds out about the missing silver, he will connect your story to it."

Varro thought back to that moment, and Curio's admonition stung. He had been too rash and revealed too much. Now it might land them in serious trouble.

"I'll be cautious," Varro said, lowering his head. "And you two can help as well. Think about everything that happened since then."

"What did the consul say to the paymasters?" Falco asked. "Is he suspicious of us?"

"I was just outside his tent and couldn't linger. Of course, he was livid and worried that he'd have a revolt on his hands if he couldn't pay the men. The paymasters must find the silver or else repay him with their lives."

"And you're just telling us this now?" Falco folded his arms.

"This has been my first chance. And it was not even two days ago that I overheard the consul. He has said nothing to me yet. But we need to get that silver back or else we're all doomed along with the paymasters. Probably their guards, too. There are too many lives at risk and it's all on us."

"Fuck," Falco said, staring at the ground. "All our money is in that bank Consul Flamininus recommended. Otherwise, we could just cover it ourselves."

"I guess if we each paid in a third," Curio said. "But it's not fair that we lose our money. We got that for saving Rome and is far more money than what was stolen."

"Consul Cato could cover the loss out of his vast riches," Varro said. "But we are the ones who took the silver and then gave it to the Ilegertes. We can't ask for it back."

Curio raised his index finger. "Actually, I never said the silver was for them. And it was buried under Diorix's hall when it burned down. When we return north, maybe we can retrieve it."

"You can be sure Albus already dug that out," Varro said. "We should've insisted right then that it was Rome's property."

"Well, we were pretty much fucking dead at the time," Falco said. "I was just glad to get out of there. I wasn't thinking about Rome's property."

Varro ran both hands through his hair and tried to think who could've given them the silver and to what purpose.

"I have been ignoring this problem for too long. I should've jumped the moment Longinus denied giving us any silver, but just hoped the answer would reveal itself one day."

"All right, no sense crying about it," Falco said. "See if you can find out something from Longinus's man. Curio and I will think on it and look into anything that seems suspicious."

"In the meantime," Varro said. "Just go about your normal routine. We're almost to the mine where the praetors are waiting. There will be a battle, and after that, we'll have to see what happens."

Curio shook his head. "Pay is due in two weeks. Even if we find the right man, what will that gain us? Just another fool to be flogged to death alongside us. We've got to recover the silver from Albus and worry about who gave it to us later."

Varro knew it was the truth, and by now they were hundreds of miles distant from even being able to speak to Albus or King Bilistages. He might have been able to persuade them to surrender the silver, since for a kingdom it was not a large sum. However, all Iberian barbarians had a fierce pride. They would be insulted to return what they had assumed was theirs, as it was Cato's representatives who gave them the silver. While Bilistages and Albus had both been grateful after defeating Diorix, Varro remembered how fickle their moods could be. Demanding the silver's return would strain their alliance, which many of their people still questioned. They would complain to Cato, and then Varro and the rest would still be in trouble.

He rapped his knuckles against his skull in frustration.

"I really thought the silver came from some sort of Servus Capax treasury." He drew a deep breath and reevaluated his plan. "I'm still going to speak to Longinus's man and learn what I can. But Curio is right. We need to replace the lost silver somehow, without Consul Cato learning of our part in any of this, and do it in two weeks. We'll need the paymasters on our side, too. But I fear what they'll do if we tell them the truth. This is all our responsibility to fix."

Falco growled in frustration. "Sure, we'll just search the purses of every barbarian we kill and take their denarii. We'll just need to kill about three thousand men on our own. Seems quite reasonable."

"Look, I don't have all the answers," Varro said. "We'll figure out something."

"In two weeks?" Falco's heavy brows drew together. "We're better off just hiding from the paymasters and let them take the blame."

Varro stared at Falco, who tilted his head back as if in challenge.

"I cannot let innocent men die for my thoughtlessness. They're not just paymasters. They're our brothers in the legion. They are the sons of good Roman citizens. They're victims who will have their skin flogged off because of us. And not just them. Their guards and anyone on their staff will face the same. Could you really stand in the crowd and watch them die?"

Blinking, Falco turned aside. "Well, it was their job to protect the treasury. We didn't ask for the silver. It's not our fault."

"That's true," Curio said. "If it was stolen, then they should've stopped it."

"We're at the root of it all," Varro said, his voice rising so that all three of them looked around. As daylight ebbed away, men were more concerned with packing up camp for the night before a long day of marching tomorrow. Varro continued more evenly.

"None of this would have happened if we did not go back to camp looking for help. Someone from Servus Capax had to be spying on us, and slipped us the silver to help bribe the Ilegertes or whoever else."

"Then why not come forward now?" Falco asked. "Why are they still in hiding?"

"I don't know." Varro tamped down on the fiery anger forming in his belly. "Maybe this is all some sort of test, or they acted in haste and now are just as scared as we are. That's why I want to see Longinus's man. Maybe he can explain what his plans were to cover the theft."

Curio rubbed his neck. "This feels less like something to help us, and more like a setup."

Varro's hands went cold, and Falco leaned back. Curio continued to shake his head, then blinked his eyes when he noticed the others staring at him.

"What? Do you really think it was the work of an enemy?"

"It's feeling like it," Falco said, folding his arms again. "It's feeling like an icy blade in the back."

Varro held up both hands. "Enough. We've been here too long. Tribune Galenus thinks I'm at the hospital still, but I need to report back to him. Just act normally. I'll get to that old triarius of Longinus's and let you know what I find out. You two see if you can learn what the paymasters are doing to recover their loss. We'll take it from there."

"They paymasters are keeping it quiet," Falco said. "Can you imagine the men if they learn they won't be paid?"

"And it'd be the infantry that misses out," Curio said. "The cavalry would certainly be paid."

"If we do this right, everyone will be paid."

Varro left them sneering at his last comment, Falco grumbling the loudest about another impossible problem to solve.

Throbbing in his shoulder matched the throbbing in his head, though one was for a wound and the other for his worries. He hardly saw the path ahead of him when he walked back to report to Tribune Galenus. The tribune looked over his injured arm and sniffed before making some comment about acting with better sense next time and to get some rest before tomorrow's march.

He wanted to explain to Galenus that had he not acted there would likely be more dead amongst the command staff. But he saluted and left his commander for one last errand that night.

Arriving at the prisoner pen, which was hastily constructed of leftover camp spikes, he waved over the two guards standing at the pen entrance.

"There's a boy in there who I am claiming as a slave. But his shoulder was badly injured, and he'll be no use to me if that wound goes bad. I'm taking him to get stitched up. I'll have him back within the hour."

The captives all huddled together in the pen, looking like dirty sheep awaiting the slaughter. If his boy was in there, he blended into the crowd. Several of them noticed the conversation and Varro's gestures, and they leaned forward as if to hear more.

The two guards looked uneasily at each other.

"Sir, we're not allowed to release prisoners."

"I'm allowing it." Varro opened the pen gate while the two guards hesitated. "Give my name to anyone who has a complaint."

Even with his arm in a sling, Varro remained an imposing sight. His long and hard years of service gave him a confident swagger, and his scars spoke to his combat experience. The guards weren't fresh-faced recruits, but from their youth Varro knew this was their first campaign.

So he fished out his slave from among the sullen crowd, still unsure why he wanted to do this. He hadn't yet got approval through the tribune. But the slave would serve the entire command group and not just him. So he doubted anyone would protest.

The boy's shoulder was thick with crusted blood and he held his arm as if it would fall off otherwise. His dark eyes had nothing but hatred for Varro as he led him out of the pen.

At the hospital, the doctor from earlier seemed aggravated but was otherwise accommodating. He did not speak, but grabbed the boy and got to work while Varro watched. Some of the injured also watched as if hoping to see the boy scream.

Yet he did not cry out when the stitching began, but an orderly held him down nonetheless. Varro admired the boy's willpower. It was a fast process, but he knew each stitch felt like a lifetime. The doctor dismissed him with a frown.

"He'll be fine. The cut is deep but clean. If he can keep dirt out of it, then he won't be infected."

"I owe you a favor," Varro said.

But the doctor's frown only deepened. "Be off with you, Centurion. Rest that arm and be well. That's payment enough for me."

So Varro led him back across the camp as the last light of the day slipped to the horizon. Men scurried to complete their duties, ignoring him and his young charge.

"I'll fetch you once I've received approval," he said, knowing the boy wouldn't understand. But he felt obligated to explain himself. "You'll be my responsibility though you'll serve the entire command group. You're not going to like it, but it's better than some fates. Aulus will teach you Latin, and then one day you can thank me properly."

They reached the prisoner pen and the boy halted, looking to Varro pale-faced and wide-eyed. He asked stuttering questions in his native language, pointing at the pen and the two guards who seemed relieved at his return. But he did not need to understand the language to know what was asked.

"You're going back for a short time. I'll get you tomorrow. Just sleep tonight." He then dragged the boy by his good arm to the guards. "Back as I promised. He's the property of Tribune Galenus's command staff now. So make sure nothing happens to him tonight. I'll be back for him before we march tomorrow."

His return to the command tents was a long and weary march. It had been a trying day, with a battle and injury to drain his strength and the burden of his mistakes to make his feet that much harder to lift. That the silver might be part of a scheme against them had never occurred to him. But now that Curio voiced it, nothing seemed more likely. Had he stepped in a trap? But whose trap, and why them? The thought of it hurt more than his shoulder.

"What a day," he mumbled to himself as the sky turned orange and the tents fell into shadow.

But outside his tent was a messenger he recognized, and his hands went cold.

The young soldier stood at attention as he approached.

"Centurion Varro, Consul Cato commands your attendance at his headquarters immediately. Please follow me, sir."

4

The dark interior of Consul Cato's command tent carried the faint notes of cabbage in the air mixed with the sour scent of lamp oil. The clay lamp on his empty desk threw wavering yellow light across his craggy face. He wore a plain white tunic bereft of any insignia of rank. His hair was so closely cropped he might be mistaken for being bald. As usual, he wore a deep scowl as Varro stood at attention in the center of the meeting space at the fore of the command tent.

His heart pounded in his chest as he waited for Cato to speak. He had expected Falco and Curio to arrive, but yet he stood alone. His eyes focused on the dark rear of the tent, beyond the plain canvas partitions where Cato made his simple bed. Of all the consuls Varro had served with, Cato was the most austere and plain of them. This endeared him to the common man under his command. There was nothing the consul wouldn't order a soldier to do that he wouldn't do himself, from leading a charge to cleaning a latrine.

But as Varro stood, feeling a sweat breaking out at the back of his neck, he couldn't admire these traits in his consul. His head swam with images of the chest of denarii that he had so unthinkingly accepted.

"All right, Centurion, at ease." Cato shifted on his chair and swept a hand across his desk as if clearing away dust only he could see.

"Thank you, sir." Varro studied the consul for any sign that he might be happy. Although he had recently raised Cato's esteem for himself and the others, Varro still expected Cato to take joy in reprimanding them, or worse. Yet he wore his usual scowl as he continued to wipe away nonexistent dust from the edge of his desk.

"You were injured today. What did the doctors say?"

"It's nothing, sir." A sudden pain shot through his shoulder as if to defy him, and he winced. "A sling stone struck me in the shoulder. The bone was bruised, that's all. I will be in this sling for a week."

While the doctor had instructed him to rest it at least two weeks, he wouldn't wait so long. He was stronger than the doctors knew.

Cato nodded solemnly. "That was fortunate. I've seen too many good men fall to slingers. It would've been a bitter end to have your brains dashed out by some barbarian farmer with a rock."

"Fortuna was with me today."

"Every day, it seems," Cato said, at last forming his crafty smile. Varro felt his throat close in anticipation. But then the consul returned to idly dusting his desk. "You've got a terrible scar over your eye. Where did you get that? If you told me, I've forgotten."

"At Cynoscephalae, sir. A Macedonian pike almost took my head off."

Cato bent his mouth and nodded in appreciation.

"You're a fine soldier, Centurion Varro. That battle was Flamininus's glorious moment. One he delayed reaching for so long."

Cato looked up and smiled again. "It is another reason I take exception to that man. How many lives did he spend dithering about Greece while waiting for his moment of maximum glory? You nearly sacrificed your life for his whims, or your eye at the least."

Varro's face warmed and he tilted his head at the consul.

"Sir, I don't remember wasting time. We chased King Philip across the breadth of that land, but he wouldn't bring the fight. We only got to grips with him that day because he wasn't aware of our position."

Cato waved his hand as if trying to extinguish a candle. "That's not the delay I'm speaking of. He could've negotiated an end of the war, but waited to confirm his proconsulship. Then he wouldn't offer any terms that King Philip could accept, just so he could continue the war and be the one to crush the heir to Alexander the Great's legacy. How many of your friends died while he did that?"

"Sir? I was an infantryman for all of that war. Consul Flamininus did not share his plans with me. Many good men die in war. It is the way of things. I do not blame my consuls if a friend falls in battle, not unless he led us foolishly. But I have not yet served under any consul who led me poorly."

Cato's laugh was short and rough. "Now, are you complimenting me, centurion?"

"Just offering my opinion, sir."

Cato stopped wiping his desk and let both his thick-veined hands settle on his lap.

"Flamininus is your benefactor, is he not? He has promoted you rapidly, I think." Here he paused and raised his palm. "But not undeservedly. He also promoted your friends. His recommendations for all three of you are quite high, which means much coming from Rome's new favorite senator. You must feel a great deal of loyalty to him. Isn't that so, Centurion Varro?"

Varro blinked. His icy hands twitched, as if wanting to grab a weapon or shield. Cato raised his brow and the heavy creases on his face filled with black shadows that quivered with the fluttering of his clay lamp.

"I owe him much, sir. But I am loyal to Rome first."

Cato's eyes narrowed then drifted down to the pugio at Varro's hip. He stared hard at it for a moment, then inclined his head.

"I do not doubt your loyalty to Rome. Your record speaks for itself."

Varro knew the words were exactly what Cato wanted to hear, and it helped that they were also the absolute truth. If this had been a sword fight, then Cato had rebounded off his shield without landing a blow. The consul continued, his voice now shifting to a more commanding note.

"I summoned you because I wanted to hear your report of the day's events. Tribune Galenus returned with several wounded and more captives than I wanted to handle on the march. Describe the battle, Centurion Varro."

"Sir, didn't Tribune Galenus report earlier?"

Cato offered a wintry smile. "Do not mistake our little banter as permission to treat with me so freely. I have asked you a question. If you answer it with a question a second time, I'll have my guards drag you by your heels to the flogging post. Now, in your own words, describe the battle to me. How did you come upon the enemy and what was their response? What did the tribune do? I want all the details as you understand them."

Varro's shoulder again shuddered with a sudden pinch of hot pain. He overplayed the wince, buying even just an extra moment to think.

For he understood the consul might have rebounded off his shield earlier, but now he had slipped under Varro's guard and had a blade pointed at his ribs.

He did not know what Galenus had reported. Varro knew the

tribune had disobeyed orders and engaged the enemy. He was only to have done so if the barbarians had left no other choice. Yet Galenus was hungry for glory and there was no better way to it than victory in battle. Much as Cato just described Flamininus, he realized. In any case, the skirmish had ended well, but the slinger ambush stained the triumph. If Varro had not acted as he did, the Iberians might have forced a heavy price for victory with a dead tribune in trade for a few hundred skirmishers.

So did Galenus lie to Cato and claim they had been ambushed from the start? It seemed likely, but Varro did not know the details of the lie the tribune had used to cover himself. Varro was Cato's view into the truth, since he had intercepted him before Galenus could feed him a revised version of the battle. But he had met the tribune earlier and he had seemed unconcerned. Had he told the truth or just assumed Cato believed his account?

These fears flashed through his mind in a rushed blur. Just as in an actual battle, he did not have long to consider. He must either strike back or recoil in defense, not knowing which maneuver would save or destroy him.

If he lied to Cato, his thin respect would be shattered and life would become harder when the eventual truth surfaced. Not to mention, he would be merciless if he ever discovered Varro at the bottom of the missing silver. If he failed to protect Galenus, during his next battle he might find himself accidentally pushed from the saddle while Galenus watched his loyal men accidentally drop their swords on his neck a dozen times.

"Centurion Varro, you were not struck in the head. Surely you can recall what happened only half a day ago."

He cleared his throat, straightened his back, and spoke the truth. To do otherwise would invite many complications. Galenus might become angry enough to be vengeful, but he had said nothing to Varro about covering his account.

Cato listened with his index finger resting alongside his nose.

He asked questions and probed some of Varro's statements. The entire time he did not betray his thoughts, and his creased, shadow-lined face remained inscrutable. Varro described everything in as much detail as he could, including his fight with the slinger. Perhaps he was carried away in his recounting, but he even revealed taking the captive to the doctor.

"With your permission along with Tribune Galenus's, I would claim that boy as a slave for the command group."

Cato shrugged. "Slavery is their fate. If you think the boy will serve well, then so be it. Be wary of him, though. There is no shortage of weapons for a slave to steal in a military camp. He has a good reason to see you dead."

"Perhaps, but he will not be mistreated. There is something unusual about that boy, sir. I think he will respect me as both his master and for defeating him in combat. If I am wrong, I will sell him off."

Stirring his hand in the air to keep Varro on pace, Cato leaned back in his chair. He concluded his account at his summons to the command tent. When finished, the silence felt overwhelming. Cato seemed lost in thought and rubbed his chin before speaking.

"Thank you for the report and your honesty. Galenus is a challenging man, and ambitious. I can admire both attributes in the right person. But not in him. Therefore, I wanted you close to him, Centurion Varro. However much we may disagree about certain things, I trust you to answer my questions honestly."

"Thank you, sir." Varro hoped the quiver in his voice was not audible to Cato. He seemed to pause overlong before speaking again, but it might have been Varro's own fears of being asked about the silver.

"You understand I expect strict adherence to orders. I do not speak whatever thoughts come to my mind. If I have issued a command, it is because I have weighed it and woven it into a wider plan. For that plan to succeed, you must do what I have commanded."

"Of course, sir."

It seemed Cato was about to dismiss him when he cocked his head and his voice took on a sly tone.

"I wonder if you would be so forthcoming if I asked you about Flamininus."

"Sir?" Varro's pulse quickened and the darkness in the tent seemed to close around him.

"Ah, so you'll pretend as if there isn't anything to ask about Rome's latest hero. He's just like Scipio only with less clout. Though I'm sure it won't be long before he claws his way to the top of the Senate, forcing his Greek ways on everyone as he does."

Varro bit his lip and Cato smirked. His best defense now was silence. Yet Cato continued to press him.

"You're a very interesting man, Centurion Varro. And if I am not mistaken, which I'm not, you are also a very rich man. You, Falco, and Curio are all rich men. All Flamininus's men."

"How would you know that, sir? The census has me on the register as a citizen, second class." Varro tried to keep his voice even. "Why would you think me any higher?"

"You bought a new horse with no trouble."

"I borrowed the money, sir."

Cato closed his eyes and nodded. "And you replace your armor and weapons without strain."

"I would die without them, sir."

Now Cato leaned forward with a wicked smile.

"And you have a huge deposit in a bank in Rome. You, Falco, and Curio. All rich men, far richer than any other soldier or even tribune that served with Flamininus in Macedonia."

"Are you investigating me, sir? I am not required to detail the condition of my estate to you." Varro hoped he sounded hard and in control, for his heart raced and threatened to leave him breathless.

"There is no such requirement, Centurion Varro. But I have my own ways of finding things out. Also, there is that matter of honesty and of loyalty. You three served six years with distinction and bravery. Your commendations and grass crowns prove it. That brings you honor and glory, but not a huge bank deposit."

Cato leaned back in his chair with a look of smug satisfaction, then folded his arms and lifted his chin.

"What did you do for Flamininus? What crime are you hiding for him?"

"Crime? Sir, I've only known Senator Flamininus to act with all the integrity and honor expected of a Roman consul."

Cato coughed a dry laugh. "You are lying to me, Centurion Varro. This is your greatest weakness, and you must improve if you are going to be the one guarding Flamininus's great secrets. All three of you were given enormous sums of silver and then taken into this secret group, Servus Capax. And before anyone could ask who you are or why you were given such an award you were whisked away to Numidia, all three of you. And not just to the capitol, but out into the desert mountains where you might have hidden for years beyond anyone's reach."

"That's not what happened, sir."

"Isn't it? It's exactly what happened. No one receives such rewards for mere good service. You were paid to be quiet then shipped out of sight in hopes you would be forgotten. Flamininus obviously has some future use for you. Otherwise, he should've killed you three to bury his crime, whatever it was."

Varro was rigid with fear. Cato knew much, but not everything. Flamininus had almost lost Macedonia's war indemnity along with a royal hostage. That might be a shame, but it was not a crime, especially since all was recovered. They had been paid out of the indemnity extracted from Boeotia, something the Senate had not expected. But he would not betray Flamininus to Cato, who was clearly his rival.

Anything he said could become a weapon in Cato's hands. So he came to attention and waited for direct orders to answer. The consul held his smug smile while he studied Varro's face.

"So now I know where your real loyalty lies. But you should think carefully before accepting a huge sum of silver."

Varro flinched and whatever else showed on his face seemed to draw Cato's interest. He leaned forward, licking his thin lips.

"Do you regret it now, Centurion Varro? I can't blame you. A farmer like you offered a fortune large enough to make a patrician's eyes water. How could you resist? Half of Flamininus's story must be where he got so much to award you. From the Macedonians, I suppose. But for what? I will soon find out."

Varro swallowed down his denial. He stared into the blackness at the rear of the tent. As Cato paused, outside he heard distant orders shouted as the camp prepared for sleep.

"There is still time to change sides, Centurion Varro. Once you are of no more use to Flamininus, you will die to protect his secret. All the silver he gave you, I'm certain it is a mere loan. When the three of you are gone, he'll sweep it all into his own treasury."

Sweat trickled down Varro's back and pooled under his arms. But he said nothing and did not meet Cato's bright eyes.

"Show your loyalty to Rome, Centurion Varro. Do not hold the criminal acts of a single man higher than the good of the people. Side with the righteous. Set aside that pugio you carry so proudly. Protect yourself, at the least. Or one day the good Senator Flamininus will summon you to a meeting which you will not leave alive. I promise you that is your ultimate fate."

"Sir, I have done nothing wrong. I have always served Rome and her people."

Cato hung his head and sighed. He sat back and folded his arms once more.

"I did not expect you to admit anything. Think about what I have told you. It could save your life and the lives of your friends. Tomorrow we will have a long march to meet the praetors. Rest your injured shoulder tonight. Dismissed."

It consumed all of Varro's willpower to salute then walk out of the command tent. The guards flanking the entrance acknowledged him with shallow nods. He returned the same and stepped confidently toward his tent while his legs felt like sodden reeds unable to hold him upright.

Only when he had crossed the parade ground did he realize Falco and Curio would likely be subjected to the same questioning. He had to warn them and be sure they said nothing foolish.

But his feet stuck in place.

What if they had already spoken with Cato? What if one of them accepted Cato's offer? Then that person would be a danger to the others.

A lump formed in Varro's throat. This was bad. The consul had him wondering if his best friends might betray him to an uncertain end. He wasn't even aware of there being anything like a side to be on before tonight. It was all for the good of Rome.

Or so he believed.

So rather than delay any longer, he rubbed his aching shoulder and slipped into his tent.

And he found Tribune Galenus waiting inside.

5

Varro shared a tent with the other members of the command group, while Tribune Galenus had his own tent next to theirs where he slept alone in great comfort. Galenus seemed more like an apparition to Varro, seeing him surrounded by his own gear and the gear of his tentmates. The armor stands and weapon racks, the bedrolls and packs, all seemed out of place with Galenus sitting at the center with a low-burning lamp on the square table Varro shared with the others. The flame reflected in the unfinished broth sitting at the bottom of a wood bowl.

"They're all on watch tonight," Galenus said, his eyes bright with uncharacteristic good humor. "You should've seen their faces when I gave the order. They will not soon forget this night, and tomorrow they will remember the lack of sleep the common soldier has to endure all the time. I think it is important the men in my command group do not become soft."

Hung between the cool outside and the sweaty warmth of the interior, Varro wasn't sure if the heat on his face came from his nerves or his bifurcated state. He stepped inside and let the flaps close behind him.

"Forgive my surprise, sir."

Galenus waved his hand and shook his head. "How is your shoulder feeling now? No different I suppose, but a private meeting with the consul makes any existing pain worse."

Varro looked at the sling. "I get shooting pains, sir. I was just wondering if I should wear it while I slept."

"Ah, sleep," Galenus said. "It is in short supply tonight, and unfortunately right before a long march. Then there will be the battle for the mines. I understand the local rebels have brought in ten thousand Celtiberian mercenaries to bolster their ranks. It should be quite a fight."

"Celtiberians, sir? They are a long way from home." Varro stepped cautiously closer to the tribune. Galenus sat relaxed, with legs crossed and a serene smile. That he looked so disarming was cause for alarm.

"The promise of silver lures greedy men from afar."

Any more allusions to silver, Varro decided, and he would certainly go mad. But he instead offered a weak laugh and gestured to another empty stool.

"Sir, I did not expect you here. May I sit?"

With a grand sweep, Galenus indicated the stool. He continued to smile as Varro drew it to the table.

"You want to discuss my report to the consul, sir?"

Galenus gave a satisfied smile. "I already know what you discussed."

Varro's eyes widened. "You do, sir?"

"Of course, it's the biggest secret in the legions. Obviously, it cannot be shared widely, especially when we will face yet another rebel army that outnumbers us."

Blinking, Varro tilted his head.

"What is this secret, sir?"

Matching Varro's confused expression, Galenus also tilted his head. "The stolen pay, of course. Surely, that is what he spoke to you about. He told me as much during our meeting earlier when you were in the hospital. You, Falco, and Curio are going to help the investigation."

"We are?" Varro leaned back, touching the base of his throat. But he recovered himself and instead scratched his chin. "Well, of course we are. The consul has assigned us special duty."

"Yes," Galenus said suspiciously. "And he has assigned me to lead it. It's unseemly that something so important is managed at a lower level. Now, I understand you have already begun investigating. So, I've arranged this private meeting tonight so you can catch me up. I would have summoned the others, but if the culprits are watching, they might connect them to us. It is best if they believe only you and I are looking into the theft."

"Very wise, sir." But Varro's mind was swimming. Cato had merely alluded to the theft. He had also connected Varro to it. His stomach lurched at the implications, but he continued to smile at Galenus.

"Very well," he said, shifting to his characteristic imperious tone. "Tell me what you have discovered and what your plan is going forward."

"The plan, sir?"

"The plan, Centurion. Surely, you must have a plan. Several centuries will not be paid if the silver cannot be recovered. While I doubt we will see open the revolt that Consul Cato expects, we cannot expect men to risk their lives for no pay at all. The pay schedule is in two weeks, just as we will be connecting to this new barbarian army. So what is your plan to ensure the men will be paid?"

"Sir, I cannot guarantee anything. I told the consul as much."

He indulged the lie fully. "The truth is, we do not have a firm lead. I'm not sure what the consul told you. But I told him the denarii just seemed to vanish out of the paymaster's funds."

Galenus cupped his chin in thought. "I told him much the same. What do you think of the paymasters themselves? Could they have done it?"

"Anyone could have," Varro said. "The paymasters have their jobs because of their reputation for honesty. I cannot imagine they were involved, even if the silver was last in their hands. It would always be so, since they receive and distribute the pay."

"What bothers me most," Galenus said, still cupping his chin as he stared at the dirt floor, "is why steal so little? Why not steal all the pay chests? It can't be much harder."

"It was a theft of opportunity, sir. Probably one or two men saw a chance to grab what they could."

"Yes, of course!" Galenus snatched at the air as if he had just plucked the idea into his hands. "Half the legions are recruits and out of so many, some must think themselves smarter than the rest of us. Ah, but the fools will die horribly for their crime."

"Just so, sir." Varro realized he had a chance to misdirect the tribune while he was carried away with this new thought. "They would have had to hide their stolen treasure. Unless they deserted the legions, they will want to come back for it when no one is watching them. When did the consul say the theft happened?"

Galenus looked up and narrowed his eyes. "I don't think he said when he thought it happened. We recently discovered the shortage as the paymasters started their reconciliation process before distribution."

"We haven't been on campaign long, sir. Therefore, the theft was from the legion's original distribution. It could've been stolen any time between our arrival and now. But my suspicion is it happened back during our first battle at Emporiae, or close to it. There was enough confusion then to steal it, and they could bury the silver close to the shore where they could retrieve it later."

"So it must be!"

Now Galenus stood to his feet in excitement. He elaborated on Varro's ideas and spent the next hour constructing his theories while Varro tried to fish out what the consul knew about the missing silver.

It was exhausting mental work at the end of the bitterest day Varro could remember in many long years. Galenus was not cut out for investigation, but he was correct in that someone at his rank should be appointed to lead it. That he happened to be Varro's commander seemed an unlikely coincidence, particularly given Cato's actual conversation with him.

At the end of a long night of hypotheses, Varro teased out more information from Galenus while disguising his intentions. It seemed no one knew when the theft occurred and they believed only a few thieves were involved. The paymasters themselves were being held accountable, but were instructed to not conduct their own investigations.

Other than this, it seemed Cato did not know more. Also, he did not seem willing to cover the loss out of the riches gained campaigning against the rebels. Cato called it the property of Rome and the Legions, and was not to be touched in any circumstance. While the tribune agreed it would be wiser to pay the men out of this fund, he also pointed out Cato's mind could not be changed on this point. The effort it took Varro to appear helpful and curious while his heart raced left him wilted by the end of the night.

Galenus had also exhausted himself once the lamp ran down. He had returned to the stool after pacing the small area of tent, and now leaned on the small table as if he had been running all night.

"Get me a list of anyone who has been reported missing since our first landing, and speak to the tessarius about all the guard duty shifts. I will question every man who stood watch."

Varro realized the men Falco had bribed to gain access to the camp would likely crumble when subjected to an official interrogation. If they acted suspicious, Galenus might even use torture to get more out of them.

"That is a lot of men, sir. We don't have enough time, plus once it becomes known that you are interrogating suspects the word will spread and our thieves might vanish."

"Well, then we'll know who they are."

"And be no closer to finding the silver." Varro leaned closer and Galenus's eyes widened in anticipation. "We should only interrogate a select handful of men, starting with the tessarius himself. Who better to arrange for the silver to be moved without detection?"

Galenus snapped his fingers. "We should interrogate the tessarius first. Start with the organizer of the watch. Who better to smuggle stolen silver out of camp?"

Varro smiled at the echo of his words now become the tribune's own.

"An excellent idea, sir."

They broke up after that, and Varro lay on his bedroll, his shoulder burning with pain, and struggled to claim what shreds of sleep that he could.

The night passed with strange dreams of marching into a swamp with Falco. He realized it was the cold marsh where they had once captured King Philip, only now the king was not there. The two of them stumbled in darkness and Varro fell into the slimy water then sank up to his neck. No matter how he struggled and clawed at the muddy earth, he could not pull out of it and instead felt himself sinking. Falco searched nearby, calling out but never finding him.

Varro awakened to Aulus the interpreter shaking him by his free arm.

"Centurion Varro, is your shoulder hurting you?"

"What?" He looked up at the Iberian, his faded blue tattoos folded into the creases of his face. "Ah, I was dreaming."

He checked his shoulder and adjusted the sling. The pain was now only a dull throb and he would've dismissed it had a lance of bright agony not shot through it when he sat up.

"Well, you were groaning," Aulus said. "Anyway, time to awaken, sir. The sun is about to rise."

Now his fellows in the command group filled the tent. They were still stealing more sleep or rubbing their eyes.

"Looks like no one had any sleep," Aulus said, now moving to his own bedroll. "I don't know why Tribune Galenus decided now was the time to enforce discipline. Got a long march ahead today."

Varro nodded and yawned, then rubbed his neck. The image of a dark marsh still clung to him and he shook his head to chase it off.

"Say, Aulus, I will claim a slave for the command group this morning."

"Good, we need another, since the other one died. Maybe we'll get our meat in time for supper now."

"He's the slinger from the last battle. The boy I took down. I want you to teach him proper Latin. Could you do that?"

Aulus strapped his harness around his waist, then adjusted his gray tunic. "A slave just needs to understand orders. We don't need to hear anything he has to say."

"He's young and strong. He'll be more use to us if he can speak and understand complex orders, not just orders to fetch our rations or load our pack mules. Look, I will slip you a few obols every week to make up for your time."

Now Aulus paused, raising his brow and the tattoos floating above them.

47

"That will add up fast. How about three denarii at the end of each month that I teach him?"

"Thank you, Aulus."

The Iberian smiled and shook his head. "Sir, you sure don't mind spending your money, do you? Just to be clear, I can't guarantee how much he'll learn. But you still have to pay me even if he turns out to be stupid. He's a Turdentani, after all."

"I don't expect him to be as smart as you." Varro now stood and shared a chuckle with Aulus. It was a relaxing moment ruined when he remembered all that had happened yesterday.

The morning air was bracing even in the summer, but as the sun crawled up the eastern horizon to stain the sky white, he knew before long he would be sweating. The march ahead covered rugged terrain that would test even a veteran such as himself. For the moment, the camp was at peace but centurions would shortly begin shouting orders and the vast camp would rise as one. The entire stretch of it would be torn up and abandoned, leaving a temporary scar on the earth. In a week's time it would be as if no one had ever passed here.

The tribune was suspiciously tardy from the early morning activities. Varro supposed it was a perk of his rank and used the time to finish an infantryman's breakfast of bread dipped in wine. The rest of the command group sat down to cook, also a perk of their positions.

Varro used the morning to claim the boy from the prisoners, who would likely be sold as slaves to the praetors and their associates to work in the mines. A new set of guards did not question him too closely, being satisfied the slave was headed to Tribune Galenus's care. While Varro had not cleared this with the tribune, after last night and Consul Cato's approval, he did not feel it strictly necessary. As Aulus had pointed out, they should have two slaves, but one had died in his sleep weeks ago. Both were decrepit old men unsuited for camp life, giving Varro even more assurance his choice would be approved.

The boy's shoulder bandage had only the faintest line of brown to show where blood still seeped through his stitches. But he seemed otherwise healthy. The other slaves watched with a mixture of pitying and jealous stares as Varro led him away.

"You're going to need a good Roman name," he said as he escorted the boy back across the camp. "Do you have a name?"

The boy looked up at him with a frown. If he understood, he did not answer.

"I'll give you one then. We'll call you Servius. You'll learn it fast enough. So, Servius, you're in for a hard life. But nothing as hard as life in the mines. Slave miners don't live out a year, or so I'm told. You'll thank me for this one day."

Varro deposited the boy into Aulus's care, finding him and the rest of the command group now disassembling their tent.

Aulus rubbed his hands in anticipation, then pulled back in surprise. "His shoulder's a wreck like yours. What good is he?"

"Find something for him to do that won't tear the stitches. Treat him well enough that he recovers, and we'll enjoy his labor for the rest of the campaign."

The sun had now launched into the sky to infuse pink and orange into the thin clouds. Flies hovered around his head, the constant scourge of even a temporary camp, and one landed on his injured shoulder. He nearly swatted it before realizing he would hurt himself before the fly.

"Just like my life," he muttered to himself.

Tribune Galenus had left his tent to receive orders from Consul Cato for the upcoming march. Longinus, being the First Spear, would join the tribunes. So Varro judged it as the best time to visit his century.

The command group protested his leaving before helping pack their gear, but he waved at them without turning back.

Dodging between rows of deflating tents and common soldiers rolling up their tents, his mind turned over all he had learned since yesterday. He was lost in his thoughts, sometimes walking into groups of soldiers who stared at him with surprised irritation. Were he not a centurion they'd have cursed him for a fool. But he instead muttered apologies and continued on.

His heart battled with two different priorities. The pressure of the stolen silver and keeping Tribune Galenus from discovering his part in it was immediate. So he would speak with that old triarius and learn what he could. Less urgently but more painfully was the doubt Cato had seeded in Varro's heart.

With the benefit of a night's rest, however fitful and brief, much of what he said made sense. Flamininus never outwardly asked for silence. Indeed, he had seemed grateful and relieved at the time. He had asked them to cover up their entire debacle with a tale of rebelling Macedonians, which was true, and to just omit the embarrassing details in their accounts. He then awarded them a talent of silver each, plus one to distribute among the survivors of his century at the time. It never seemed Flamininus had any intention other than to reward them.

But just as Varro had unthinkingly taken silver from an unknown source, so had he accepted Flamininus's reward with no consideration of what accepting such wealth meant. Intended or not, it bound Varro and ensured he would betray nothing damaging about his benefactor. Indeed, last night he had not shared details with Cato surrounding Flamininus's bungling of the Macedonian war indemnity and nearly losing a royal hostage. Now that Varro was older and more experienced, he realized that Flamininus's political rivals could make much out of that unhappy event. The entire truth of it would not matter. Cato and others opposed to Flamininus would distort the truth until their rival was ruined.

And he, Falco, and Curio all knew the details of the truth.

"He wouldn't kill us." He spoke to himself as he arrived at the First Legion tents and the line of triarii breaking up camp.

Maybe Flamininus's outlook had changed since that time, now seeing himself as a hero to both Greeks and Romans. Varro remembered the glory of all Rome celebrating his return. Of course, such greatness would also attract enemies who wanted to destroy him. They would turn over every stone in Rome to find anything to bring Flamininus low. Now it seemed suspicious that he and the others were all immediately sent as far away as Flamininus could arrange.

Perhaps Consul Cato was not just toying with Varro. Perhaps he was right.

"He wouldn't kill us." He repeated it more like a prayer than a fact, but caught himself as he arrived at the line of triarii.

He sought the optio, who had passing familiarity with him from prior visits with Longinus. They exchanged greetings, and Varro explained his injured shoulder. He tried to make it seem like a casual visit and pretended he forgot Longinus would be occupied.

But he guided his questions carefully, describing the old triarius he sought.

"I had promised him a story he wanted to hear. But we've been so busy I've not gotten back to him in weeks. I figured since I was nearby I could give him and his friends a tale to laugh about on the march. Do you think I could see him?"

"Who was it again?" The optio, an older man like all the triarii, scratched under his helmet and scanned his men loading up their mules. "A gap in his front teeth? That's every third man in the legion. You didn't get his name?"

Varro summoned as much description of the old triarius as he could recall. It was like assembling the pieces of a shattered bust back into a recognizable face, but he eventually got the optio to understand who he wanted.

"You're looking for Proclus. Yes, he was with Longinus on many campaigns. I know now."

"I won't take much of his time," Varro said, now looking over the triarii alongside the optio. "It's just hard to get over here these days. So I hope to meet him now."

"Ah, well, you should've told him the story back when you had the chance. Proclus is dead."

6

The march was as arduous as Varro expected. The long marching column snaked up into the mountain pass. From his position with Tribune Galenus in the center of the column, he could see the glittering yellow of bronze helmets resting by their straps on the chests of thousands of soldiers in both directions. Against the dusty greens of shrubs and stout trees, it made the column seem like a golden snake.

Varro walked his horse up into the narrow pass. He had learned this from his time in Numidia where he constantly moved his horses from the plains up into his mountainous hideout. It was easier for the animal to navigate the treacherous footing, and he had less risk of falling. Conversely, if the Iberians ambushed the column, he would struggle to mount his horse in the confines of the path. From what he could see, most of the cavalry rode their mounts but moved no faster for it.

Galenus remained mounted and stared ahead as if he were directing all the legions. Varro wondered what the man thought of himself, for it seemed he imagined leading like a consul. Being a military tribune was a high enough honor, reserved only for the patrician class. So it struck Varro as strange that he should imagine himself at an even higher rank. Yet he also supposed there was no end to human ambition. Varro wouldn't want the responsibility of a tribune and all the politics that come with it. But then, he was unusual when it came to ambition. He was learning he would rather fight than talk, despite his youthfully idealistic vows of nonviolence.

"Ah, Papa, the legions changed me as you feared. It changed everything."

He had muttered to himself, but it still drew attention from Galenus on his horse.

"What's that, Centurion? You are feeling foolish for going on foot rather than letting your horse do the work?"

The comment drew sycophantic laughter from those riding with the tribune. Even Varro found it more expedient to accept the criticism rather than instruct the tribune on how he felt a horse should be treated.

"Just so, sir. I suppose I am infantry down to my bones."

Yet he led his horse, Thunderbolt, as he had named him, and it seemed appreciation glimmered in the animal's dark eyes. Or so he believed. Riding uphill in rocky terrain was hard enough with both hands free. With his arm in a sling, he found it easier to lead the horse.

They now climbed higher and it afforded Varro a better look at where Falco and Curio both led their centuries. At a glance, he could not locate them amid the hundreds of dark and haggard faces pulling up between boulders and scuttling over ledges. Instead, he looked even farther behind to where the baggage train followed. He hoped to spot Servius among them and hoped his wounded shoulder did not cause him to fall out. For whatever reason, he had invested himself in that boy's recovery. It was just an instinct, but he had learned to trust instinct over his years in the legion.

If only he had developed better instincts earlier on, he might not be marching with the additional weight of doubts about Flamininus and his friends today.

The column marched relentlessly through the pass as Cato led with energy that defied his aging body. He called for no rest periods while traversing the pass. If the barbarians planned an ambush, here was the perfect spot. So he kept scouts searching the flanks and ranging ahead, and the column only slowed when mules and horses decided they did not appreciate the consul's urgency.

Varro spoke little to anyone, even though no one enforced silence on this march. Be it old habits or just exhaustion, he could not do more than look to the ground underfoot and guide Thunderbolt behind him.

Yet the march ended, even if it seemed it might stretch on for a lifetime. The massive column of two full legions took all day to filter out of the pass, but by late afternoon the survey team had located an acceptable campsite. Everyone had an assignment in digging ditches and laying spikes, or else clearing paths to form the symmetrical blocks of the camp. Flags were laid out to show where Cato and headquarters would be established. Even fully exhausted, the power of routine kept Varro upright and working.

While building camp and erecting tents, he found a moment to speak with Galenus in private. "I need to speak with the others about our conversation last night."

Galenus returned a nod, then squinted all around as if some cloaked figure might leap out of thin air and attack them. It was a bit too dramatic for Varro, and it seemed as if the tribune imagined they were at the heart of some world-spanning conspiracy. The man had quite an active imagination for his role in society.

"Be discreet then report back with anything new. I want to interrogate the tessarius soon and it would be useful if we had something definite to work with."

After picketing Thunderbolt, he scurried across the unfinished camp. There were no idlers when it came to establishing a marching camp. The easiest job might be to stand guard around the perimeter while the camp went up. But since the consul did not expect a significant attack as the rebel army was still distant, the camp was packed with men at work. Slaves led mules from the baggage claim across paths not yet cleared. Men hammered on tent poles as Varro raced between them. Officers flashed their vine canes at anyone they felt lagged.

He found Falco doing just that when he called out for him. His tall and strong friend shifted from a maniacal grin to a smile. He was checking their tent row and apparently found progress lacking.

"Centurion Falco, a private word, please."

Varro kept it formal so that the men nearby might think he was on official business. Yet he knew from experience that a soldier was pleased to avoid an officer's scrutiny no matter the reason. So he waited while Falco approached, pointing out with his cane some detail to the men he passed. They both stepped away from the row but had no privacy other than to keep their distance from others.

"How's the shoulder?"

Varro rubbed it. "Not even a day has passed and I want to throw this sling into a ditch."

"Well, you've no worries. Every day is light duty for you now, Adjutant Varro."

"I don't think that's an official rank." Varro now stepped closer, lowering his voice but trying to mask his expression from the swirl of people surrounding them. "Listen, I've got news about our problem."

"So don't I," Falco said, matching his stiff demeanor. "Curio said the paymasters aren't doing anything as far as he can tell. He has a friend on their staff."

"Curio has a friend everywhere," Varro said, shaking his head. "Where is he?"

Falco's heavy brows bunched together, and he turned to the east. "Supervising the ditch and stakes. Should we get him?"

"Let's not bring too much attention to ourselves. I knew about the paymasters. Tribune Galenus told me."

"What?" Falco's thick brows now shot up, creasing his sweat-beaded forehead.

"Things became far more complicated since we last spoke."

Varro described his night in reverse, starting with Tribune Galenus's surprise visit and ending with his summons to Consul Cato. He described both interactions in great detail, pausing whenever anyone came too close. Fortunately, their ranks protected them from reprimands for idleness, unless a tribune should find them. But it did not prevent scowls from some passing by.

When Varro finished, Falco's mobile brows had settled back into a flat line. His sober stare reached into the distance, as if considering all he had just heard.

"What a fucking mess."

A laugh escaped Varro and drew a frown from Falco.

"Sorry, you are just so eloquent. But that about sums it all up, doesn't it?"

"It does. Do you think Cato is right about Flamininus? Did we step in the shit there, too?"

"I can't deny it makes sense when you think about it."

"Well, except we're not out of the way now, are we?"

"Far Iberia isn't out of the way? Just listen to the name, Falco. We're on the frontier where we could die without question."

Falco wiped his face. "I mean, it seems Cato hates Flamininus and here we are with his enemy. He even wrote a flattering summary of our careers. I mean, why would he do that? He's doing a poor job keeping us from his enemies."

"True," Varro shrugged. "But maybe he did not have a choice. Maybe Cato learned about us, then demanded we serve so that he can find out whatever he believes we're hiding from him."

"Then what the fuck are we going to do? Do we trust Cato or Flamininus?"

"We don't trust either, not for the moment. In any case, we've not heard or seen anything out of Flamininus. He even told me that I wouldn't always be reporting to him. But it makes me wonder if Servus Capax is part of a faction within the Senate. Cato doesn't seem to support it."

"Well, didn't you get us wrapped up in this shit because of a pugio your mother got from your great-grandfather?"

"That's true, but that doesn't mean Servus Capax is not part of a faction. By Jupiter's balls, Falco, we've picked a side in a war where we don't even know all the other sides."

"We don't know shit about anything," Falco said, looking over his shoulder again. "And it's not even our biggest problem right now. Now we've got Tribune Galenus snooping about, and you say Cato mentioned nothing about him to you?"

"He didn't. And Galenus is distracted with the tessarius right now. But here's another bit of news. This morning, before we set out, I visited Longinus's century to find our man and learned he's dead."

Falco's eyes widened and Varro warned him against appearing too shocked.

"He was killed at Emporiae. The optio said when the flank collapsed and it seemed they were going to be overrun, their century moved up to plug the gaps. Our man, Proclus was his name, got run through his liver."

Spitting on the ground against bad luck, Falco sneered. "I wonder if he was run through the front or the back."

"I wondered the same. So you also think whoever stole this silver wanted to silence him?"

"I don't know what to think." Falco rubbed his face. "Why steal silver at such risk and give it away, then kill the man who delivered it to us?"

"Maybe whoever stole the silver didn't really want us to have it," Varro said. "They were just using the opportunity to smuggle it out of camp, and might have planned to ambush us later to recover it."

Falco's eyes brightened at the idea. "Then something happened before they could."

"Emporiae happened," Varro said. "Maybe they died just like old Proclus, or were wounded, or just missed their chance to recover it before we spent it."

"Then we're dealing with some stupid thieves. But it doesn't solve the bigger problem, Varro. If you've convinced everyone the silver is hidden somewhere, then how are we going to produce it again? Who'll believe us? It won't even be in the same chest."

"One step at a time," Varro said. "First, we need to find someone to blame. Since Proclus is dead, he'll do. Longinus will raise a stink about it, and he will connect us to the silver thanks to my big mouth. So we've got to convince Galenus to make the accusation and ensure he has proof. Forget trying to find the actual thieves. If they had any sense, they would just let us stumble around until time runs out. Unless they come forward, we're never going to find them in time."

"Well, that sounds easier than doing a proper investigation," Falco said, crossing his arms. "But I'll let you figure out how that will work."

"Give me time to think. Galenus is listening to me, so I can feed him whatever story we want to tell. He's eager for glory, and if we offer him a chance to be a hero, he won't care much for the details."

"And the silver?"

"We could just say the silver is lost. Let Cato dip into all the riches he's captured from the barbarians to make up the difference. We just need to shift suspicion away from us. Poor Proclus's name will be ruined, and that might affect his family in Rome if he has any."

"This is becoming dark work, Varro. I'm not sure I like it."

"You'll like it more than being flogged to death."

"Shit," Falco again spit. "It all seemed so good at the time. And it did save us, too. But those denarii were cursed from the start."

"We're not done with our problems." Varro sighed and pinched the bridge of his nose. "King Bilistages and Albus have to remain silent about the silver. Thank the gods they have said nothing of it yet. But in time they might. We will have to create an excuse to visit them and then beg for their cooperation."

"Fuck, they'll have us by the stones then." Falco squeezed his fist to demonstrate the crushing grip the Ilegertes would have on them. "Do you think they would hold it over us?"

Varro shrugged. "They might be our friends, but they're politicians first. They know we have access to the consul. Who knows what they might ask of us in return for their cooperation?"

Falco let out a long groan and looked at the sky. Varro fell to silence and realized he had been overlong in plotting where the entire camp could see them.

"I need to get back before the rest of the command group complains. I can use this wounded shoulder as an excuse for avoiding work, but only for so long."

Falco waved him off. "None of you do any actual work, anyway. Not sure what they would complain about."

Varro laughed, but a sudden thought caused him to pause. While he did not want to indulge his fears, and he tried to shove them away, Falco noticed with a frown.

"What else?"

"Never mind," he said. But when he did not turn away, he

voiced his concern. "If Cato spoke to you in private and made you the same offer he did to me, you'd tell me about it, right?"

Falco cocked his head as if the question made no sense. Varro's stomach fluttered so much that he did not allow his friend to answer before pressing him.

"I need to know we're in this together. You're not now on the other side, are you?"

"What other side?" Falco's heavy brows drew together. "What the fuck are you asking me, Lily? If I'd jump in bed with Cato and cut your neck in the dark for him? Are you mad? We've been friends since birth."

"Well, I remember you beating me up and wishing that I could cut out your liver and feed it to wild dogs."

"Just boys being boys." Falco leaned away with his palm extended. "Besides, I toughened you up into the man you are today. But for the love of Jupiter, Varro, I'm glad you spoke up before I had to beat your face again. Of course, I'd say something and of course I'm not working for any side." He drew out the word as if it were something foreign to his speech. "I'm on our side alone. Fuck Consul Cato. Flamininus has been good to us. He's made us rich, and he's promoted us. Maybe he hopes we won't lift the cover off his pot of shit and let Rome know how much he almost ruined everything. But Philip's brat could do that to him anyway, and he's right at the heart of Rome. Why would Flamininus worry about us? Cato just wants us to hate each other. He has no friends and hates to see others who do. That's what I think, Lily, since you asked."

Varro raised his good hand to calm Falco. "Thank you, I believe you. But I don't think it's so simple. Philip's son has more to hide than Flamininus. If his father ever learns he wanted to overthrow him, he'd end up dead or imprisoned for life."

Falco clapped Varro's uninjured shoulder. "Just get to work

blaming Placus for everything. We need to get back to the relaxing work of fighting barbarians."

They both laughed, but Varro's was shorter lived. Falco crossed his arms and glared at him.

"What about Curio? Do you think he might accept the consul's offer?"

"Never," Falco said, turning his head aside. "The man is as good as they come. He's one of us, Lily. You know what he has been through. Did you forget Sparta already?"

"Not at all. Forget it. Consul Cato just got me wondering. He's a bastard that way."

"He is." But now Falco's laughter ebbed away faster, and it was his turn to look distracted. After Varro prodded his hesitation, he again folded his arms tight to his chest. "Well, Curio has gone missing a few times recently. I've wondered where he has been, and his optio is trying diplomatically to ask me the same."

"Isn't he trying to find out about the silver?"

Yet Falco shook his head. "It was before you told us about it. Ah, forget it. He's always up to something, that sneaky bastard."

They shared a laugh. Then, as they were about to conclude their meeting, Curio's century came trudging into their row and began setting up their tents. They waited for Curio to show, but only his optio supervised the soldiers. Curio himself was elsewhere.

Varro and Falco watched in tense silence.

"The tribune must have pulled him into something else," Varro offered.

Falco nodded but did not reply, his lips pressed into a thin line.

When Curio did not appear, they both shrugged, then Varro left Falco to wait for Curio's return. And while he reviewed all the reasons Curio might have left his century in his optio's command, Varro's doubts seeped back and the pain in his shoulder increased along with it.

7

The two praetors' meager force welcomed Cato's column with expressions of genuine relief. Varro felt like a conquering hero as he rode Thunderbolt into the camp as part of Tribune Galenus's command group. All around, the praetors' soldiers crowded their counterparts in the legions, offering welcome and praise in equal parts. Varro could not help but smile and wave out at the crowds, but Galenus clicked his tongue at him.

"We're not on a victory parade," he said. "All of you, look ahead and behave like soldiers."

Consul Cato had already gone to meet the two praetors while his column assembled into the camp amid the mountains. From horseback, Varro watched over the tops of gleaming helmets as Cato dismounted amid the cavalry that had the honor to escort him. His position now only showed as a gap in the ranks of men and horses making way for him.

Galenus's reception was less grand. Young soldiers of the praetors showed him and the command group where they would encamp along with their lines of regular soldiers. They had laid everything out, simplifying the logistics of gathering a legion of tired soldiers. Unfortunately, Varro noted that despite the preparations it still smelled rank like all other legion camps. He enjoyed the fresh mountain air of the pass and now suffered worse for it. Also, flies settled on them the moment they halted.

"Another day in the legion," he muttered.

He threw down his pack onto the rocky ground and shifted his wicker shield awkwardly over the same arm. He still wore the sling, which would remain with him for days yet. As much as he wanted to rid himself of it, he suspected the doctor had correctly assessed his recovery period. Most of the time he did not notice the pain until he had to twist it as he did now. His grimaces drew sneers from his fellows.

"You're not fooling us." The tubicen, Gaius, dropped his pack across from Varro's. "Are you planning to vanish again when we have to stake out our tent?"

"Not for something that simple," Varro said, shifting his pack aside with his foot. "I'll vanish when the tribune comes with another watch assignment."

Gaius laughed. The Iberian interpreter, Aulus, joined them. "Shit, we'll all vanish with you then."

"How is Servius coming in his lessons?" Varro asked. "You've had him for two days now. Is he ready to recite the classics to me?"

"He's ready to run away," Aulus said. "The boy is a lost cause, sir. He just talks about revenge and getting back to his father. I shut that down, of course. We're going to kill all his cousins before long, and I told him so."

"It has only been two days," Varro said. "Give him time to adjust to his new life. It must be hard for him."

Aulus fell quiet, and Varro sensed he might have touched on something sensitive. Perhaps Aulus had been threatened with slavery to Rome at some point. But Gaius continued laughing as he sorted through his pack.

"I bet if you taught him how to say 'Fuck off, Centurion Varro,' then he'd learn a lot faster."

Now Aulus laughed and Varro as well. They waited for the baggage train to catch up, where Servius and the other slave would lead the mules carrying their shared gear. They picketed their horses, then slaves from the host force delivered water for them. It was all routine boredom until he saw Curio emerge out of the crisscrossing groups of soldiers.

He halted away from most others and waved Varro closer.

The rest of the command group either were busy with their horses or else plotting where they would stake the tent when the slaves arrived with their mules. So Varro first walked to Thunderbolt and patted his side. The horse's muzzle was deep in a water bucket, but his tail swished as if to send him off. But the horse had screened him from the others, and he could pull away to meet Curio.

"Falco told me about the plan," he said as soon as Varro joined him. He looked around, trying to appear as if he were not nervous.

"You look nervous," Varro said. "Just talk to me centurion to centurion and no one will disturb us."

Curio's youthful face reddened. "You're right. All this sneaking around has got me feeling like I'm caught up in some shadow war. Anyway, I think your idea is good. But I've found out something."

"Have you told it to Falco?"

"Not yet." Curio again looked over his shoulder as if someone might sneak up on him. "I didn't know when you and I could get together again. This seemed the best time before we go into action."

Varro drew closer, and he had a sudden fear of being too close to Curio. It was a stupid thought, and he knew it. But somehow he was allowing Cato's doubts to take hold of him. For his part, Curio leaned in as well and appeared to notice nothing of Varro's apprehension.

"Tribune Galenus visited the treasurers around the time we returned to the camp. I can't be sure of the exact day, but it was just before we returned."

"How do you know that?"

"I have a friend on the paymaster's staff. Galenus was there asking about the salary distribution. My friend couldn't hear everything discussed, but he was in with the paymaster centurion."

Varro rubbed his chin. "That means nothing. He could've had a routine question."

"Or he could've been there to get a better look at the conditions around the treasury." Curio continued to look around.

"You're making me nervous," Varro said. "Stop acting like we're committing a crime. So, you think Galenus himself might be involved?"

"I don't know," Curio said. "It was the only unusual thing my friend noted around that time."

"But that would mean Galenus was planning to help us before we arrived. That is impossible."

Curio was again about to look over his shoulder, then stopped.

"Or more likely he planned to steal it just for himself, as you described to Falco. We've seen tribunes stealing from the legion before, haven't we?"

"I suppose. But no matter why he stole it, he should be just as eager as we are to blame Placus. I don't think he was involved, but I guess we cannot rule it out yet."

"That's the information I have," Curio said. "I don't know if it means anything. In the meantime, I'll think of what we can do to make Placus look guilty. I've got to go. Falco says I've been out of sight too often and my optio is asking questions."

"Has Consul Cato summoned you privately?"

Curio focused his wandering eyes on Varro. "No, and Falco asked me the same thing. What's wrong? Did he summon you?"

"He did. And he wanted me to give up Servus Capax and join with him."

"What?" Curio again started looking around. "What does that mean?"

"Falco will explain it to you," Varro said. "Just let us know if Cato tries to make a deal with you. I think he wants to turn us against each other."

Now Curio broke into a huge smile. "Well, he'll have an easier time climbing Mount Olympus to steal a kiss from Venus, won't he?"

The image Curio's comment summoned made Varro laugh. "That he would! Keep up the good work. We'll get out of this mess before long."

With a clap to Varro's good shoulder, Curio faded back into the humming churn of soldiers trying to find their places in camp.

No one in the command group had noticed his absence. The mules had arrived with their gear just as he returned, further distracting others from him. He did his best to set down tent poles and help with his good arm.

All the while, the newly enslaved Servius did as Aulus instructed him, using Roman commands first and following up with his native language. It seemed a painful means to learn to speak, but he did not know a better way. He had discovered an affinity for languages while in Numidia, and knew how difficult it was to acquire new ways of speech. It was not as simple as plugging foreign words into a Latin structure. He hoped Servius's young mind was a flexible as his body. He ignored Varro, who was happy to oblige for now.

Halfway through pitching their own tent, Tribune Galenus called on Varro and two others to work on his. But the tribune soon pulled Varro away from the rest, to where soldiers hammered stakes for the headquarters tent.

"Have you anything to report?"

Varro knew what he asked, and so he licked his lips and made what he hoped was an intriguing pause. "I've heard that someone in the First Legion acquired a cart late at night during the time the silver might have been stolen."

Galenus's eyes brightened from their usual dullness.

"Well, that is unusual. But you haven't got a name? How do you know it was someone from the First Legion?"

"The man came from their side of the camp to fetch the cart. It proves nothing, but it's a start. My contact saw him leading a mule to it, but did not linger. He was just off watch and tired."

The tribune rubbed his chin and squinted in thought. "That's a good lead. We'll want to find out more about it. I've not called in the tessarius yet. But he'll have a record of who was on watch when your man saw the cart. We can question those on duty that night."

"Well, sir, if anybody had seen a cart pass, they would've reported it."

"Exactly," Galenus said. "And since no one did, then whoever let it pass is part of the crime, even if just from negligence. Good job, Centurion. We'll have our thieves soon enough."

Despite the tribune's bright smile, Varro wondered if his happiness was less for Varro's so-called good work or finding someone to blame for his own theft. But he had no time to consider what was an unlikely possibility. The tribune's demeanor already shifted.

"The praetors are hosting a dinner and debrief tonight for the consul and all his tribunes. As my adjutant, you will attend with me."

Varro offered thanks though he would rather avoid mingling with the senior officers, most of who were wealthy patrician or equestrian class citizens. He feared coming under their scrutiny, particularly since many had noted his close relationship to Cato. Would they see him as threatening for it, or as an ally to court? He hoped they would sneer at him as a clod overstepping his station in life and ignore him.

Galenus absently dismissed him to work on the tent, then wandered off to speak to another of his peers.

Evening arrived too soon for Varro to leave his fellows and update Curio and Falco. Tubicen Gaius and Aulus both seemed on one side or the other of him, as if they had a tacit agreement to watch him at all times. But they all knew Varro's obligation to join Galenus and let him go with good-natured quips about better food and wine and how he deserved neither.

He wore a simple but clean tunic, one of two that he owned, and carried no weapons or armor with him. His Servus Capax pugio remained behind, but he wished he could have displayed it on the chance someone recognized it. Yet given all Cato had said to him, perhaps it was better he remained undiscovered.

White awnings and long tables had been set up on a hill above the camp where the praetors and consul made their tents. Local slaves, all young and attractive boys and girls dressed in startling white tunics, delivered wine to every empty cup. At the front table both praetors and Consul Cato stood before their seats in amicable conversation, or so it seemed from the far end.

A slave, a handsome girl with eyes like black jewels, greeted them in perfect Latin. She asked the tribune's name, then led him to his seat with Varro following. He thought of Servius compared to this girl. She was older, but spoke without an accent. Then he realized she was probably born and raised as a slave, and his hopes for Servius achieving the same level faded.

"Take a moment to mingle," Galenus said without a trace of enthusiasm. If anyone seemed to enjoy this occasion less than Varro, it was Tribune Galenus. "Go meet some other adjutants. We'll be called to order shortly."

Varro acknowledged what sounded like an order rather than a suggestion. He realized the source of Galenus's dissatisfaction, since he did not disguise his contemptuous glares at the tribunes seated closer to the praetors and consul. These were the officers of the First Legion and cavalry. While they were no higher status than Galenus, it seemed he took exception to being seated so far from the glory. Indeed, he left Varro and put on a smile as he strode toward the front of the tables, clearly angling to meet the praetors.

Varro was left to bob along like a lone duck on a pond. After a few moments, he revised his feelings of being a lost duckling and now felt more like a piece of flotsam bumping along a rotted pier. Groups had formed and they kept their backs turned to repel intruders. Laughter and clinking silver filled the long space beneath the awning. Torches threw golden light on the golden leaders of Rome's mighty legions. He had only ever seen such grandeur in the hall of King Masinissa, yet he was easily impressed, as these were military men and not a gathering of senators.

"Centurion Varro!"

He turned to his name and found the stout Centurion Longinus pushing toward him. His dark stubble shaded a firm jaw and combined with the white scar over his eye it made him seem even fiercer. But he held a toothy smile for Varro as he caught up to him.

"You're injured," he said, pointing to the sling.

"It could've been worse," Varro said, heat coming to his cheeks. "I rather foolishly charged a line of slingers on my own. This is nothing compared to what I should've gotten for that stupidity."

Longinus gave a hearty laugh. "I can't disagree with that. Let the line take care of them. They have the shields for the job. So, I heard you were looking for one of my men."

"I was." Varro met his smile. He had prepared for this, knowing Longinus would learn of his visit as part of a standard protocol.

"The man you sent to deliver those helmets wanted to hear the story of what we used them for."

"He did?" Longinus tilted his head. "I already told him the story you told me."

"Ah, well, I didn't realize and wanted to let him know what he took a risk for. Too bad about Placus, though."

Longinus's frown only deepened. But then, with a loud rapping from the head table, they were called to take their seats.

"We'll have to speak again later," Longinus said. "Best of luck with your shoulder."

Settling beside Galenus, Varro noted how his leader seemed only more angered for his efforts. He was perennially dissatisfied with everything, and Varro now realized it stemmed from what appeared to be a notion that he should be at the front of everything glorious. Anything, no matter how trivial, that did not credit his glory aggravated him.

Varro doubted such a man would steal from the treasury, or even consider taking part in a secret group like Servus Capax. Therefore, Varro discredited Curio's news. It had been coincidence only. However, this realization about Galenus reinforced how much he would love to be the hero who finds the thieves and the silver. It made him open to manipulation. As long as he had so-called proof that couldn't be refuted, he would seize it without question.

While Longinus would protect the reputation of an old friend, Varro would have to ensure the old triarius took the blame. He would have to triple the bribes to the guards who had helped them that night. But he could pay them to identify Placus far more easily than replenishing the silver out of his purse. Then he would put himself in King Bilistages's and Albus's debts to gain their compliance. That might be the hardest part of his entire plan, since he was not at liberty to meet them on his own. The consul would have to replace the stolen silver out of what he claimed from the defeated Iberians, since no one would ever discover where Placus hid his stolen fortune. Varro smiled to himself, glad to have seen the way out that would ruin nothing other than one dead man's reputation.

All the while his mind turned on these ideas, both praetors and consul addressed the assembled group. The praetors were eager for help against a barbarian alliance that had doubled in size with ten thousand Celtiberian mercenaries. Cato spoke eloquently about the defense already prepared and they praised his counterparts for acting swiftly.

To Varro it was too much self-congratulation to have come so far to hear. He sipped the wine from a silver cup, admiring both the smoothness of it and the value of the container itself. Certainly, Iberia was full of iron and silver, and that wealth was on display tonight, as if to remind everyone what they were fighting to keep.

So the talk turned to a debate on tactics and intelligence reports. Both praetors were eager to get the barbarians to fight. But Cato nodded with an uncharacteristic and grandfatherly smile creasing his rugged face. When the praetors had concluded their talks, he stood and announced that his legions would prevail in any fight with the barbarians.

When the cheers from the tribunes and their staff, Varro among them, settled, Cato raised his smooth palm for silence.

"But we must also be practical. While we will be the victors in any fight, replacements for our losses are harder to endure than they are for our enemy, who can pull any farmer from his fields and hand him a spear at a moment's notice. Therefore, I have concluded that mere bribery can dispense with these Celtiberian mercenaries. The Turdentani pay them to fight, and so we shall pay them more to fight for us. I bring not only the strength of my legions but also the war chests we have filled since arriving here. Let us not spend Roman lives before we spend barbarian silver."

While everyone under the awnings erupted into cheers, perhaps not all sincere but all enthusiastic, Galenus's fists balled on the table and he turned to Varro with an icy glare.

"You had best find those thieves soon, Centurion Varro, since the consul has spent our fortune rather than replace the stolen pay. I will not tolerate failure in this. Find them and the silver before time runs out."

While applause echoed in Varro's ears, his heart sank into the pit of his stomach.

8

The night air in the mountain pass was crisp. Varro stood outside the tent and rubbed his bare arms and stared out over rows of similar tents stretched into this plateau amid the soaring rocks and boulders surrounding them. Even now only three thousand men, they still appeared more numerous in the confined space.

He looked to his tent once more, then to Galenus's. Both were silent shadows under the moonlight. The camp was completely dark, with only torches set by the entrances on each of the four sides. He had no time to waste and headed toward the east side of the camp where he had arranged to meet both Curio and Falco.

Keeping his profile low against other tents, he threaded the camp. Given his rank, he could order off anyone who caught him. With only two tribunes commanding this force, he had no fear of meeting anyone higher. Still, he wanted this meeting to remain secret.

The wide space between the spiked ditch and the tents offered them a place to meet where whispers wouldn't wake any light sleeping soldiers nearby. Varro headed for the corner where the camp was anchored to a wall of stone. The sentries would not bother to patrol this spot as no one but a mountain goat could reach the camp from here.

Falco was easier to locate in the shadow, if only for his height. Curio would be next to him, but he remained invisible until Varro joined them.

They nodded to each other, but Falco could not resist pulling at the shoulder of Varro's tunic.

"Enjoying life without the sling?"

"My shoulder gets a little sore without it," Varro said, suddenly aware of a dull ache at Falco's comment. "But I couldn't stand to wear it any longer. It has been more than a week, anyway."

"Can we move along?" Curio asked. He remained lost in shadow, with only the faintest light touching his head. "My optio seems to know whenever I'm away."

"I've convinced Galenus to accuse Placus," Varro said. "Good work with your boys, Falco. Their statements convinced him Placus smuggled out the chest. The tessarius verified they were on duty during that time. It all came together, and Galenus is relieved to have someone to blame."

"Perfect," Falco said. "I'll be glad to get this done. I still can't figure out who gave the denarii to us, but at least we can wait on that."

Varro grunted in agreement. "Curio, did you turn up anything on that?"

The small shadow shifted. "Nothing. Well, nothing, since you don't believe Galenus was part of it. My friends with the paymasters have nothing more for me, and they're now all back with the main force."

Falco chuckled. "They'll wish they thought harder once our boys get back with them after not being paid."

"Well, that's on the consul," Varro said. "He overpaid the

Celtiberians knowing he had to pay his own men first. Now he'll suffer for it."

Both Falco and Curio shook their heads.

It had been a whirlwind week for Varro. He accompanied Galenus as part of the emissaries sent to the bring the Celtiberians to Rome's side. They failed. However, Cato authorized a bribe for them to return to their homes. This succeeded, and with the major threat of the mercenaries resolved, Cato then left most of his legions with the praetors. They would complete the pacification of Far Iberia while Cato led three thousand men back north to mop up rebel tribes still holding out despite their defeat earlier in the year.

"Time for you to report," Falco said. "What's the plan for Albus?"

Varro again rubbed his shoulder, feeling a dull stab of pain.

"We will send a message to him asking for a private meeting. I'll draft up something as soon as we are within reach of Ilegertes territory again."

"Send a message?" Though Falco's face hid in shadow, his disgust showed in his voice. "As soon as it's known you're sending a message to the Ilegertes, your letter will end up on Cato's desk."

"Credit me more than that," Varro said. "I've been considering how to get the letter out without being caught. We need a man we can trust to deliver it. And, of course, we can't say much in the letter in case it does somehow get back to Cato."

Curio shifted again, his face now catching some of the moonlight to reveal a skeptical cast. "Where will we find that man? He'd have to know the land like a native."

"Exactly," Varro said. "I think we can trust Aulus."

"The interpreter in your command group?" Falco's arm rose to the back of his head. "Won't he be missed?"

"Not for him to send the message," Varro explained. "But to

find us a local willing to send it for us. We can pay to have it delivered."

"So much bribery," Falco's said. "We're going to be poor men when this is done. And yes, Varro, I'd rather be poor than executed. I see that look on your face."

"He's not Roman," Curio said. "Can we trust him?"

"I think we can," Varro said. "He has been teaching my slave Latin, and that boy has come a long way in just a week. It has given me cause to speak to Aulus more. Do you know he has served the legions since Scipio was here?"

"How old is he?" Curio asked. "I thought he was our age, but he must be forty at least."

Falco lowered his arm and folded both across his chest. "With all those face tattoos of his I can't even tell what he looks like, never mind his age."

"None of that is important," Varro said. "He can help us arrange the meeting. From there, it's up to us to convince Albus to remain quiet. We'll be in his debt, but it's not like we'll be here forever. I think this campaign won't last another season."

Both Falco and Curio grunted their agreement.

"So Galenus will speak to Cato once we reach our destination tomorrow." Varro looked over his shoulder, half expecting to find someone listening in on them. But the moonlit camp stretched out in placid silence. "Longinus might protest, but it will be his word against two witnesses and the tessarius's statement."

Falco sighed. "Longinus couldn't have stayed with the main force? Why take the First Spear on a mop up campaign?"

"The praetors have their own First Spear," Varro said. "And Longinus is a good soldier. We need the best since we have so few men. He'll want to defend his friend, but I'm sure he'll realize it's more practical just to stay quiet."

"I wouldn't count on that," Falco said, arms still folded. "We don't have that kind of luck."

"True," Curio said. "But I think he'll realize if he speaks up too much that he could fall under suspicion himself. After all, people will say he should've controlled his subordinates better."

So they concluded their plotting under moonlight. As Varro crossed back to his tent, he felt their solution was the best possible given the circumstances. Galenus had proved easily led, and not too interested in doing any of the investigative work. It led Varro to remember other times his actions were under scrutiny, like when Centurion Fidelis went after him for the accidental killing of then-Consul Galba's favorite slave. If it were Fidelis now rather than Galenus, they were certain to all be caught.

He slipped back into his tent, finding no one awake, and returned to his bedroll. Given all the marching through rugged terrain in addition to the stress of shaking off this investigation, he fell into a swift and blank sleep.

The next morning he was not as alert as the others, and he blamed the hard ground for a terrible night. Gaius, the tubicen, said he was too dainty for life on the march. But Varro shut down his laughter with a cold glare. His face was full of battle scars while Gaius had the soft features of an equestrian class soldier who suffered no dangers.

At breakfast, Servius delivered their meat for the day. He also watered the horses and did a dozen other menial tasks. Aulus shouted orders at him in their shared tongue.

"He'll never learn like that," Varro said.

"Sir, you asked me to teach him. So I am doing it the same way I learned. If you want to use another method, then you should find a better teacher than me."

Gaius howled with laughter. "That shut you down, didn't it?"

"Go blow your horn," Varro said. He then called Servius to him where he crouched by the cooking fire.

The Iberian boy's shoulder had healed nicely, though the stitches remained with a tinge of redness around them. His fine shoulder tattoo would be forever interrupted when the scar formed. He gave Varro a blank, tired look.

"Who am I?"

Servius's eyes flashed and he glanced at Aulus.

"Don't look at him, but look at me. Who am I?"

"Centurion Varro."

"Centurion Varro, sir." Varro offered a firm but soft-spoken correction. "What is your name?"

"I am Servius. Sir. I am a slave. My life belongs to Rome. I do as I am told."

Gaius clapped, then said through a mouthful of porridge, "Aulus, you're fucking amazing. You made the idiot talk and taught him his place."

"Go blow your horn."

Servius's words were clear and true, and it frightened Varro as much as it astonished him. Even Gaius's face hung slack.

Only Aulus laughed and collected the boy back to his duties.

"So, may I continue to instruct him, sir?"

Varro shook his head in disbelief. "Please do. That's better results than I ever hoped for."

Aulus gave a bland smile and guided Servius back toward the horses, while Gaius continued to stare after him slack-jawed.

"You deserved it," Varro said. "Let the boy alone this once."

"Only because you asked, Varro. Next time, I'll twist that arrogant head off his shoulders for speaking to me like that."

They were back on the march through the pass by early morning. Cato rode with his small contingent of cavalry just behind the vanguard. Galenus had drawn the rearguard position, which ate the most road dust while on the march and therefore was considered the least desirable position. Only the baggage train had it worse.

As a result, the tribune rode his horse out of the mountain pass with a look of sheer revulsion. Every word from him, no matter how mild, seemed a curse. Varro did not risk speaking to him further about the investigation. His mood would remain black until he felt something once more added to his glory.

Falco and Curio followed behind with their maniple of hastati, followed by principes and triarii, then finally a complement of velites. Again, Varro could not see them from stolen glances to the rear. But he knew they were watching and likely poking fun at him on his horse.

Now that they were filtering out of the pass, he had remounted. Thunderbolt had seemed appreciative of the lessened burden while climbing into the pass. Now he snorted and seemed to toss his head as if trying to complain. But Varro had learned how to speak to him so that he would relax and leaned forward to stroke his neck.

Yet Thunderbolt did not relax, and Varro noted the ears on Thunderbolt and the other horses pricked up.

"Something is wrong," he said, first to himself. But then he turned to the tribune. "Sir, the horses are hearing something unusual. We might be in a trap."

Galenus let out a suffering groan. "The scouts would've flushed out any danger, Centurion. And there are a hundred horses ahead of us that are not nervous."

Yet to Varro, Thunderbolt and the other horses seemed alert to something unusual. The rest of the command group leaned forward to check their horses as well, and this drew a sharp intake of breath from Galenus.

"Are you led by your horses or do you lead them? The scouting teams keep our flanks flushed out. We are leaving the pass now. The horses are probably just excited to get clear of this terrain, as I'm sure we all are. Centurion Varro, keep your fears to yourself."

He looked up to the tall sides of the pass. It was studded with defiant trees growing from the narrowest of ledges, or else large outcroppings and deep clefts could shelter scores of enemies. He knew from his own experience how easy it was to hide in the mountains.

"Sir, we're the rear guard. We have a duty to—"

"You have a duty to obey. I am ord—"

An earth-shaking grinding of stone on stone cut off Galenus's tirade. Varro and everyone else looked downslope to where Cato had emerged from the pass. Rocks collapsed from one side, throwing up a wake of brown haze as they washed directly into the center of the line.

The soldiers in the rockslide's path had no means of escape. The tumbling rocks, some bouncing up and slamming down as if launched from a catapult, crashed into them before they could shift away. Their bodies flew into the air while others vanished into dust clouds. It was as if a giant earthen foot had stomped on the center of a bronze snake.

Then thin, distant howls echoed across the pass. Looking up from the wreckage below, Varro saw the dark shapes of men emerge from hiding. They carried round shields and raised their heavy swords overhead.

Centurions shouted orders to form up their ranks. Galenus paused atop his horse while his mind absorbed the sudden change in fortunes. But then assumed command.

"They're on all sides of us, sir," Aulus shouted from behind Varro, who had turned to look farther back in their line. He saw the mules of the baggage train startle at the activity.

"And they're going for our baggage, sir."

Galenus had no time to set up a good defense. The Iberians had been following and now dictated the terms of battle. He looked ahead to where his counterpart rode. The rockslide had cut them off, leaving half the army temporarily stranded.

To his credit, he gave solid orders to form a box defense with an opening for reinforcements to join from the front after they recovered. But the Iberians moved faster than the soldiers could rank up.

They came screaming down the slope. Sling stones and javelins now arced down into the ranks. But these were individual casts versus units of men. The Roman ranks absorbed these on their massive shields, something Varro wished for now as he looped his lighter, wicker shield over his still-hurting arm. He drew his cavalry sword and took position beside Galenus as he tried to gain the center of his hoped-for formation.

But the first barbarians reached the line, coming to grips with hastati on the left flank. Varro spotted Falco leading his hastily assembled ranks forward to cut off their advance.

The triarii and velites moved to protect the baggage train, and Varro could not see behind.

The two sides slammed together, shield upon shield. The clash was always louder than it would seem either side could make. Wood thudded on wood. Bronze on bronze, and war cries and screams from both sides. Varro stood at the center with the tribune who shifted his horse back and forth as the command group drew around him. The signifier raised the legion standard while his runners drew their swords and prepared to defend their leader.

"Centurion Varro, command the west flank for me. I cannot see all around."

"Yes, sir!" He pulled his horse about, catching Aulus's eye as he did. The man seemed grimly determined, with taut lines on his tattooed face.

Then he came to the principes, men now not much older than himself. They were the prime fighting force and their centurions were brave and experienced. He saw they had not only formed a cohesive line, but were already driving it forward.

Men collapsed in the line, and those in the rear dragged their bodies out of the way. Varro noted the barbarians had no similar system, and as they fell, they became obstacles to those still standing.

Yet he noticed the left flank had gotten ahead of the line, and so he trotted his horse over to their rear.

"Keep the line!" he shouted. "Watch for overlapping."

Being a centurion, he had trained his lungs to produce a bellow that could match the roar a rockslide. Even so, combat was loud and chaotic. The optio in the rear heard the order and repeated it forward.

Yet the centurion at the front had already gone too far.

Iberians came charging up from hiding holes in the rear. They charged with spears lowered beside their round shields, screaming curses as they rushed.

The principe flank was caught from the side. The optio tried to pull men to meet the new threat, but Varro watched as they struggled to meet the enemy.

He had never been in this position before. Instinct told him to charge in and turn the enemy back. But his order was to command the entire line.

With a quick scan, he judged the principes held.

"Thunderbolt, to battle!"

He kicked the sides of his mount, and he lunged forward. The principes had now turned, but threatened from the fore they could not ward off the new attack.

A horse was not meant to stick in battle, but to charge alongside it and return for another strike. Varro had learned this while in Numidia. He wished for those riders now, each man guarding the other's flank as they swooped into battle.

He slashed at the first enemy he reached, who held up a shield and stabbed blindly with his spear. But Varro deftly guided Thunderbolt from that clumsy strike and lopped off the enemy's arm. The heavy cavalry blade carried devastating force from horseback, ruining bone as easily as it did armor.

Thunderbolt cried out as if in joy, and pushed along the edge of the Iberian line. Varro laughed at the terrified faces that shrank from him as he leaned to the side with his red sword flashing. The long blade skidded off a shield, then slashed through the mouth of the next man in line. He saw a yellow tooth spill out with the blood. Then he clipped the ear and neck of yet another enemy before charging out of reach.

He galloped a short distance, then turned Thunderbolt. The horse responded to the gestures of his heels and knees as expertly as the finest cavalry horse. He had a clear line for a second charge. Iberians lay scattered on the ground as the massive shields and feathered helmets of the principes loomed over them. The Iberian line was collapsing against the mountains, and if they did not flee, then they'd be trampled down.

But behind this, Varro saw the legion standard shaking over the heads of Tribune Galenus and the rest of the command group.

The barbarians had broken through the hastati right and now swarmed the tribune, eager to capture the standard and inflict not only death but humiliation on the Romans.

Galenus's horse reared, and the tribune struggled to hold on amid a thicket of spears aimed at him.

Varro kicked Thunderbolt's flanks and pointed him at the chaos unfolding in the center.

9

Shrieking horses, screaming men, and the clash of bronze filled Varro's ears as he charged Thunderbolt ahead. His own throaty war cry added to the madness. Iberians massed around the standard, wary of the fearsome signifier who slashed at them with defiant roars.

Reaching the line of principes, he called to the optio at their rear.

"Defend the standard!"

He had no time to say more as he charged past, leaving the optio to turn behind in confusion.

Galenus fell from his horse and vanished into the spears aiming at him from all directions. Varro cursed for reaching the rear of the press too late. At least Galenus's horse scattered the men, trying to reach him as it flailed its hooves in terror.

Thunderbolt battered aside the loose men at the rear. Varro hacked viciously at a red-haired barbarian, shearing a spearhead off with one stroke.

But the other barbarians aimed a dozen more spears at him. Thunderbolt now reared up as well, hooves kicking at the spearmen arrayed around him. This spoiled Varro's next strike, and its timing left him off balance.

Rather than try to stabilize himself, knowing he was already halfway out of the saddle, he leaped away from his mount. The Numidians had taught him to fall from a horse before learning to ride one. That training spared him now, for he leaped clear of his enemies and landed in a controlled roll.

His shoulder wound flared even though he protected it from the worst of the impact. Yet he leaped upright, then raised his shield and charged into the press. Behind the enemies trying to reach him, the tribune's shouts were clear but muffled. As the signifier fought off his foes, horses bucked around him. The command group had collapsed into a knot and was being whittled down.

Varro reached them, slamming his wicker shield into the back of an Iberian's head. Had he carried his scutum, he would have shattered the skull. Still, the man collapsed, and Thunderbolt slammed his hooves down on his spine, completing the kill.

He fought to his horse and tried to defend it from the spearmen still poking at him. But he was in just as much danger from Thunderbolt as the barbarians. So he dove into the knot of enemies. He missed the efficiency of his gladius. The long sword was unsuited for close quarters fighting on foot. So he threw it aside and drew his pugio.

The enemies grabbing for the standard were oblivious to anything else. One barbarian seemed to exhort everyone to this end. Varro could see Galenus scrambling to regain his feet amid so many trying to claim him.

Varro plunged his dagger into the naked ribs of an enemy. Hot blood poured over his fist as the Iberian stiffened and screamed. But Varro hauled him away to reveal an astonished Aulus beneath him. Blood slathered his tattooed face, but the whites of his eyes were even more brilliant for it.

Now the principes reached them, and the Iberians let out a collective groan. Varro focused ahead, but saw men fleeing as he pushed into them. Galenus lay facedown on the ground. Varro stepped over him and planted his foot between one of the fallen runners and a dead barbarian.

He sensed a brightening and realized that it was from the Iberians escaping this brawl. The signifier leaned on his pole, bloodied and limp, but slashed out at the last Iberian attempting to snatch it out of his grip. But signifiers were always the strongest and most durable fighters in any legion. He warded off the attempt, somehow holding himself and the standard upright.

Varro fell on a barbarian wresting a gold ring from Galenus's finger. His pugio stabbed up through the bottom of the man's neck, pinning his jaw to his skull. Varro twisted and tore the pugio free, ruining the barbarian's throat and sending him collapsing backward and gargling blood. In his last moment, he had tugged off the ring and it now rolled out of his hand into a red puddle.

"Centurion Varro," Galenus called, his voice weak. "What is the situation?"

Varro blinked, then craned his head up to scan around.

"The barbarians retreat on all sides, sir. Consul Cato is bringing up reinforcements. Congratulations, sir, you defeated them."

"I did," he said with a smile, staring blankly into the sky.

Varro's throat tightened. He had no love for Galenus, but he was a competent soldier even if he sometimes blundered. So he got to his knees beside his commander and cleared the bloody mud from his muscled breastplate. He knew what that blank stare and ashen complexion meant.

"It is a glorious victory, sir."

"I'm sure." Galenus's voice was weak and his eyes remained fixed in the sky's glare. Then his brows drew together. "Centurion, I think I'm injured."

A dark pool of blood spread beneath Galenus's body. From the front, he had only scratches and a few cuts to his cheeks. But Varro saw his breastplate stood up from his torso, as if something pushed from beneath it.

Aulus reached Varro's side, kneeling beside him. "Sir, are you hurt?"

"I believe so," he said. His eyes did not move to Aulus, and his voice had dropped so that the surrounding thunder of a dying battle overcame it.

"Help me turn him," Varro said. "He has something in his back."

"No, Centurion Varro, I am fine. Help me up."

With Aulus's aid, they turned Galenus onto his side. He let out a long groan as he rolled over.

A broken spear shaft had hammered through his back, just below his left shoulder blade. Dark blood flowed around the shaft, drizzling into the bloody muck beneath him.

"It's no use," Varro said. "The spear went through his chest."

Aulus shook his head. "No, we can help him still."

"No, we can't." Varro spoke so softly that he could hardly hear himself. He turned Galenus onto his back once more. "He's dead already."

The tribune's eyes stared blankly into the sky. For a man who had been perennially dissatisfied and who had died with such violence, he wore an incongruent expression of peace.

Varro picked Galenus's ring out of the thickening, bloody puddle and set it back on the tribune's hand. He would not want it lost or claimed by another.

Aulus had closed the tribune's eyes. "Sir, the barbarians have not fully retreated."

Roused from the poignant moment, Varro staged up to his feet, his shoulder protesting every motion now that he had cooled off. With Galenus dead, he was in command for the moment.

Several horses lay dead where the command group had stood. The principes had driven off the attackers and the clear-headed of their number also calmed the surviving horses, Thunderbolt among them. They also buoyed the signifier, holding him and the standard up and proclaiming victory.

There was not much for him to command as the centurions all knew their duty. They would not pursue without an express order, which Varro would not give. Cato led his men across the division the rockslide created, and now joined up with the rear. The Iberians were already vanishing into their mountain hide-out. He watched their dark shapes clamber up into the trees and boulders, turning to hurl a last curse at the Romans before escaping.

Varro's ears throbbed with the echoes of the receding battle. His shoulder ached as badly as the day he had first hurt it. His cavalry sword lay somewhere amid the destruction of the command group. He wicked blood from the pugio, but held it in hand as he studied the battlefield.

His temporary command ended with the arrival of Cato and his other tribune. He first looked to his own, congratulating the signifier on his heroic stand. A jagged cut bled beneath his left eye, but he returned a satisfied smile.

Gaius had survived his ordeal and was now laughing with the principes who had come to their rescue.

Varro narrowed his eyes at him. He was certain they had killed Gaius, but had he instead pretended to die to spare himself? His nostrils flared at the thought, and his blood-slick fist tightened on his pugio. But then he realized Gaius could have fallen or else been stunned. Anything could have happened in that madness. He let the rage flow out with a long exhalation and continued through the battle site.

So he found Thunderbolt now calmed by a soldier who had claimed to have grown up around horses and knew how to handle them. Varro thanked him and led Thunderbolt to where the other escaped horses and mules were already picketed.

"You fought bravely," he said, stroking the horse's neck. "I'll have to find a reward for you. But later. Take your rest now."

Thunderbolt snorted as if to tell Varro not to expect the same next time.

As Cato reorganized the column, Varro wandered through it. With his officer dead along with most of his companions, he felt as if he deserved a moment to wander. The baggage train had been hit the worst, and while the triarii had chased off the attackers, the damage was done. Varro recognized right away that this was the aim of the Iberian attack. Whoever commanded them wanted to raid their supplies. They had looted the provisions out of carts. Dead barbarians draped over them, their blood streaking the sides and dripping into the rocky ground. But the beds were emptied and what provisions were not carried off now lay scattered in the dirt.

He shook his head. The barbarians likely hoped this would hamstring the column. But now Cato would march to the nearest settlements and take everything he lost. The Iberians only hurt themselves this day.

His wandering took him to the hastati where both Falco and Curio reorganized their men according to Cato's orders. With Galenus and his command staff dead, orders took longer to reach their destinations. Varro realized the consul might hold him accountable for that, but the threat was over and speed was not as important. Cato would not pursue into the mountains.

"You're holding your shoulder," Falco shouted as he closed the distance.

Varro didn't even realize he favored the injury. "I fell from my horse."

Both Falco and Curio could not go far from their centuries, but they joined in the gap between them. The red-faced, sweating hastati appeared content to lean on their shields and gasp for breath while their centurions spoke.

"That was unexpected," Curio said. He bled from a superficial cut across his neck, a scratch that might have been decapitation in another circumstance.

Varro ran a line along his own neck. "Cut yourself during your morning shave, did you?"

Curio dabbed the blood clotting at the pit of his throat. "A spear got around my scutum. Not sure how that happened. There were a lot of smelly barbarians in that attack."

Falco chuckled at Curio's wound. "Not as many as it seemed. The small area made it seem worse."

"Galenus is dead," Varro announced. "And our provisions ransacked."

Both Falco and Curio exclaimed disbelief at once, turning to look toward the standard. Cato had already gathered there with his personal guards and the other tribune.

"I better get back before Cato accuses me of desertion."

Falco grabbed Varro's arm. "What happens now? Galenus never reported to the consul on that little problem."

He referred to the missing silver with a euphemism since they were in earshot of others. But Varro was too tired to be concerned with anyone listening.

"You still have your witness? They survived the battle?"

Falco nodded, glancing at his men. "Didn't lose a single man, just lost some combat effectives. They'll be back after they heal up."

"Then I'll make the report and have your witnesses' support."

Falco drew closer and whispered. "We paid them to speak to Galenus. They're going to want a lot more to do the same for the consul."

"We'll pay it. Whatever they want. I better go. Curio, it's a scratch on your neck, but take care of it. Don't let it become infected."

"Yes, sir," he said. "I'll go to the hospital as soon as we make camp. I'm sure they won't laugh me out of the tent."

Halfway to the consul, Varro thought of Servius in the baggage claim. By now, he must have escaped. He was a Turdentani, the same tribe that controlled this territory. It only made sense he would run, but Varro had to know. Chaos ruled the battlefield, and he might have been injured or killed.

He searched around the carts and mule lines. The triarii were still trying to establish order by shouting at slaves and hauling reluctant mules into line. Most of the slaves did not run, since they were taken from Rome or else not Turdentani. Apparently, they might be considered too Roman by their so-called kinsmen and end up remaining slaves with new masters who wouldn't offer a chance to buy their freedom one day.

He did not waste time on an exhaustive search before concluding Servius was gone. He found the command group's mule still laden with gear. But the group's old slave lay with his brains spilled out from a cleft in his head. He seemed like a dark and withered root laying on his side. Flies were already dancing on the ejected contents of his skull. The mule stood patiently by his side. Varro could not read mules like horses. Yet he felt this one stood guard beside a fallen companion, both being slaves to the same masters.

He called Servius's name and as expected the boy did not answer. He smiled, wondering if they might once more meet in battle. If they did, then Varro would give him no quarter. But in the meantime, he hoped the boy would grow up and raise a fine family that could live at peace with Rome. It was naïve to think so, he knew, but it was a far more pleasant thought than what might be Servius's reality of a lifetime of struggle and warfare.

He rejoined Cato, whose creased face was drawn into taut and deep lines.

"What is the report from the baggage train?"

Varro raised his brows, surprised that Cato thought him gathering a report.

"Sir, it seems the Turdentani aimed to raid our supplies. They stole or ruined most of the provisions."

Cato closed his eyes and shook his head. He then heard Varro's account of what happened in the center, and why Tribune Galenus had fallen. As he made his statements, he looked at Tubicen Gaius who seemed to hold his head low either in respect for the dead tribune at their feet or out of shame.

In the end, Cato commended him for bravery and for bolstering the principe's left flank. Their optio gave his account of how Varro's charge single-handedly flipped the momentum back to their side.

The consul left it for Varro to join with everyone else in clearing a path for the baggage train to exit the pass. Of course, the baggage itself had to be reordered and salvaged. This fell to the velites and hastati, while Varro supervised the principes in standing guard during this effort. The Iberians could regroup for another attack. But none came.

By the end of the day, the column at last exited the mountain pass. They marched far enough to find a suitable campsite. No matter how tired the men were, they established the camp with a ditch and stakes. Since they were in hostile territory, the cavalry stood guard as the infantry labored.

The final count of the dead came to ninety-two men on Rome's side, mostly from those caught by the rockslide. The actual battle had been a shock attack followed by a shoving match that ended with the Turdentani withdrawing. Estimates of their dead were less accurate, but numbered less than one hundred.

As Varro completed a walk of the camp perimeter, something

Galenus would've done, he felt ready to collapse. If he felt this way, he imagined the rest of the soldiers felt the same. Yet they had not only dug a camp but also deep graves. It occurred to him that for all Galenus's station in life, he now slept in the earth alongside the common infantryman. His gold ring went to Cato for him to return it to Galenus's family in Rome. Other than this distinction, Varro thought, death was a great equalizer of men.

The command tent was quiet, with only Gaius, Aulus, and the signifier, Lars, who now had a bandage wrapped over the cut under his eye. Varro nodded to each, but lingered over Gaius. If he had more strength, he would question him on what happened.

Instead, he rolled out of his bed and whispered to Aulus.

"Servius is gone. I'll pay you for your time, but you've lost your job."

"Keep the pay, sir. You saved my life today."

Varro shook his head and smiled. "You'd have done the same for me. I'll pay you all the same. You earned it. Servius learned a lot in a week."

Here Aulus turned his face aside. "Truth is, sir, he knew a fair deal of Latin already. I had to just polish it up."

Varro pursed his lips. "Really? I suppose that's not completely unexpected. I guess he wanted to hide what he knew, maybe to use it against us one day. Well, he's free again and I doubt we'll hear more from him. Let me get that coin for you while I'm still thinking of it."

Aulus kept his head lowered, but both Gaius and Lars stared blankly as Varro extended the denarius. Aulus gazed at it a moment before snatching it as if he expected it to be pulled away.

"Thank you, sir. It's generous of you. And more than what I hear we'll be paid this month."

Varro, who had been shoving his purse back into his pack, now stopped halfway. "What does that mean?"

Aulus looked to the others as if needing permission to speak, though they still only looked on in silence. He kept his tattooed face down as he spoke.

"I hear the consul gave all our spoils away to bribe the Celtiberians, and that we won't be paid. There's not enough denarii to cover everyone."

Gaius now sat up straight on his bedroll. "We're overdue our pay to make this march. We should've been paid with the others before we set out. Now we'll get nothing, all of us."

Signifier Lars rolled over and put his back to them, as if he had no concerns about his pay.

"Where did you hear this?" Varro asked. "Is this rumor widespread?"

Both men looked to Lars, and Aulus pointed at him.

"He heard Tribune Galenus arguing with the consul before we set out. They were trying to find coins to pay us, and Galenus seemed to think there wasn't anything left in the treasury. Isn't that so, Lars?"

The valiant signifier remained facing away on his side. But his deep voice was clear. "That's what I heard the tribune say, that there was no coin to pay the men and that the consul would have to find a way. I didn't hear what else they said. But you should know the details, Centurion Varro."

"And why is that?" He drew his hand out of the pack and leaned forward.

Lars twisted so that his unwounded eye met Varro's.

"Your good friend was with the consul—Centurion Curio."

10

Falco snorted, then turned to spit in the grass. His heavy brows had drawn into a single black line, and the muscles of his jaws twitched as he stared out over the expanse of camp. Dawn had just broken and the camp was coming to life. Varro let his old friend have a moment to consider the news about Curio and Cato.

"I don't believe it," he said at last. "Curio wouldn't lie to us."

Varro sighed and followed Falco's gaze. He seemed to look across the camp to the shadows of the mountains arrayed behind it. They both stood on the outskirts of camp, where the guards on watch noticed them but dared not approach.

"I spent all night wrestling with the same thoughts," he said, putting his hand on Falco's burn-scarred shoulder. "But Lars was certain Curio was inside the command tent with both Galenus and Cato."

"And what was Lars doing? Why did he overhear all this?"

"Because he had drawn guard duty for the consul's tent that day. I can verify that myself, since I remember him complaining about it before he left."

Falco let a long breath escape and rubbed both of his rugged hands over his face.

"We've been through too much together for him to turn against us." He shifted his hands over his head, clasping both in place as he gave Varro a pleading look. "I cannot think why he would hide this from us."

"I wondered the same," Varro said. "But I also have to wonder what Lars gains by lying about it?"

"So maybe Curio was there for a different reason. It was just before we marched out, right when you returned from giving everything away to the Celtiberians. I can't keep track of where Curio is all the time. He's a centurion now, with his own duties. So maybe it was just some routine thing he wouldn't bother to mention."

"Are you listening to yourself, Falco? Talk about the stolen silver is not routine. Curio should've said something to us, even if it was just to explain why he was in a private meeting with the consul."

Falco held up both hands. "All right, that's true. Let's just confront him. If he wants to work for Cato, then it's not wrong, is it? Flamininus didn't have us take a vow of secrecy. So Cato is going to get some dirt on how he screwed up. Is that so bad? If he's so determined, then he'll find out eventually."

But Varro started shaking his head from the start of Falco's excuses.

"Cato wants us to abandon Servus Capax and join him. Look, we can debate what will happen all day. We don't know. But we do know that if Cato has turned Curio to his side, then we need to be careful what we say and do around him and we'll have to report that to Flamininus."

"I'm going to be sick," Falco held his stomach and frowned. "We've saved each other's lives so many times. We were hung from the walls of Sparta together. He couldn't have forgotten that."

"He hasn't." Varro softened his voice and patted Falco's shoulder. "But maybe he wants out of Servus Capax. Look, I got both of you involved without knowing what you were doing. I'm certain now that they also deceived me into joining without a clear idea of what I joined. It's not unreasonable to think Curio might find Cato's offer attractive. If he's going to get out, then he'll need a powerful patron to make it possible. This could be his chance."

"It should be all of our chances," Falco said, now pulling out from Varro's hand. "It should be the three of us deciding together."

Varro gave a bitter smile. "Nothing in our lives has ever been for us to decide. That is for the gods and senators."

"So what do we do now?" Falco put his hands on his hips and turned to the camp. "We have little time before we both need to get back."

"We'll confront Curio," Varro said. "But we'll do it together."

Falco nodded. "And now that Galenus is dead, you're good to accuse Placus?"

"I'll do it today. Better to settle this matter before we reach Emporiae. Centurion Longinus might jump in to defend his old friend, but we have your witnesses. Maybe Galenus had notes or something to support me as well. In the meantime, I've asked the others to keep what they heard from Lars a secret. They're all smart enough to know if they let the rumor out, then we'd have big trouble."

"Well, Cato still needs to come up with the silver to make payroll," Falco said, then shook his head. "But that should be no trouble. He'll just raise a tax on the Iberians to make up for it."

Varro's stomach tightened at that logical conclusion. He chose not to worry Falco with his concern, but if Cato tried to collect taxes from the Ilegertes, that made it far more likely they would speak about the silver. So Varro knew he had to work fast to reach King Bilistages and Albus.

They returned across the camp as men emerged from their

tents to the light of a cloudless morning. He and Falco parted in the center, and Varro plodded back to the command tent. Now that Galenus was dead, Cato would likely disband his command group with Varro being shifted back to Cato or else given a role suitable for his rank. Lars and Gaius would go back to the ranks, and Aulus would join another command group, as interpreters were too valuable to feed into an infantry line.

So he arrived at their tent expecting to break it down for the last time. Yet it surprised him to be intercepted by one of the consul's runners who summoned him to the morning staff meeting.

Aulus had emerged from the tent while hauling the cooking pot. He gave Varro a wry smile. "You have a knack for getting out of work, sir. Lars and Gaius will be jealous."

There were other names left unmentioned now that those runners and staff had fallen beside their tribune. But Varro chuckled nonetheless.

"If you had to deal with Consul Cato, then you'd think twice about that comment."

The consul's tent glowed with morning light diffused through the roof. It cast soft shadows over Cato's craggy face. He sat at his desk behind stacks of wax tablets provided him by his officers. Varro knew they were strength reports and inventories taken after yesterday's clash, and Cato would read each one in detail.

Having arrived last, he found the other tribune already present. This was Tribune Manius, a tall and aristocratic man whose head seemed forever titled upward as if listening to the words of the gods. He had his adjutant, a wiry man going prematurely bald who smiled at Varro's arrival. First Spear Centurion Longinus stood beside Cato's desk. It struck Varro as an odd place, as if he were attending Cato who frowned in thought. But Longinus gave Varro a bright smile. He had not yet shaved, as his beard was darker and heavier than usual. There was no blade that could defeat that heavy growth, or so it seemed.

Cato pulled a wax tablet off his stack, scanned it, then tossed it back with a clack.

"We lost a fine tribune yesterday." His voice was dry and strained, taking Varro by surprise. Was Cato shaken by Galenus's loss?

"He was as good a friend to me as he was a soldier." Tribune Manius, whom Varro seldom interacted with, had a voice that sounded as if his mouth were full of rare delicacies. "It was a significant loss for Rome.'

"And an unnecessary one." Cato's gnarled hand slapped his desk and he frowned at Varro. "If it weren't for the principes' ineptitude, he might yet live. Centurion Varro would have saved him."

He blinked at the consul's unexpected praise. "He fought to the last, sir."

"And so you have already said." Cato again snatched a different wax tablet and seemed to stare right through it before slapping it back to the desk. "And we lost too many other good men to a barbarian ruse. Tribune Manius, can you explain how your scouts failed to identify the ambush?"

Manius looked around as if there were another with the same name who should answer. But neither his adjutant nor Longinus had anything for him. He then blubbered a long explanation that left Varro feeling like Manius might have been asleep on duty, for he seemed to have no clear idea what his scouts reported. All the while, Cato's frown deepened.

Varro was glad to see someone else suffer Cato's wrath. He did not hesitate to call Manius a fool and then explain all the ways he could have prevented the situation. It left Varro wondering why the consul would've selected this man to be one of two tribunes to lead his reduced army.

"You tarnished a fine record," Cato said. "You were one of the few men at Emporiae I could commend."

Manius's neck at last bent in humiliation. Both his adjutant and Longinus studied their feet. But Varro agreed with Cato, and so shared his disappointment.

"There must be reprisal for this." Cato reached for another wax slate, one set opposite of all the others. "These barbarians cannot claim the life of a leader like Galenus without suffering consequences. We must deal with this entire mountain tribe. I want them eradicated down to their last child. No slaves. Only corpses."

Tribune Manius recouped his haughty grace and once more tilted his head back. "Yes, sir. I will ensure the complete destruction of this mountain tribe."

Yet Cato shook his round head, his frown deepening as he reviewed the wax slate.

"No, Tribune Manius, your skills are unsuited to mountain fighting. But there is one here who has a record of mountain warfare."

Cato smiled blithely at Varro, and the others all looked to him in surprise. Centurion Longinus, however, seemed more admiring than shocked.

"Sir?" Varro held his voice steady. "I operated from a mountain hideout. I did not lead large-scale battles in them."

"That's more experience than anyone else here." Cato waved the wax slate dismissively. "I've drawn up a force for you to lead into the mountains. Besides, you should have the honor of avenging your commanding officer."

Manius, who had lost his voice, now recovered. "Sir, Centurion Varro is a fine soldier, but he is not of the correct class to lead. The responsibility should be mine, sir, and if not, then First Spear Longinus should command. This command should not go to an adjutant."

Cato smiled, which Varro had learned indicated severe irritation.

"Thank you for your advice, Tribune. I will note the concern in my records. But we do not have the resources to be particular about class integrity. Centurion Varro will lead this task force, and will drive the barbarians out of their mountain homes and into the open where you can have the pleasure of destroying whatever remnants are flushed out."

Manius's expression flattened, but his face shaded red. Cato seemed to put him out of mind and turned to Varro.

"You'll have three days to flush them out. Maybe they will not leave whatever bolt hole they have created for themselves. I will leave it to your ingenuity to devise a means to kill all of them in place."

Varro swallowed hard and could only acknowledge his orders. Cato now extended the slate he held toward him.

"Here is the force I've devised for you. You'll have five hundred men. I cannot imagine threading more through the mountains. It is not a standard organization. You will need heavy infantry to break their fortifications and I've drawn men and officers from different centuries. I will have Tribune Manius and the cavalry arrayed to sweep up whoever escapes into the plains."

Accepting the cold slate from Cato, Varro scanned the neatly incised lettering while tilting the tablet to let shadow fill the grooves like ink.

Cato continued to speak while Varro reviewed the slate. "You will have the significant benefit of Centurion Longinus's experience. He will be your second in command for this operation. I'm certain he can advise on any leadership matters that arise."

Varro found one century and centurion on the slate that he expected. But another century and centurion were missing.

"Sir, Centurion Curio is part of the Tenth Maniple Hastati. I see you've assigned Centurion Falco, but not Centurion Curio?"

"I just said this is not a standard force organization."

"Sir, Centurion Curio has the same mountain fighting experience as me and Falco."

"Correct," Cato said. He leaned back in his chair and his irritated smile now shaded toward anger. "I would not send all my experienced men into the mountains. Centurion Curio would be just the man needed if I had to send a force to find you."

"A good idea, sir!" Tribune Manius glared at Varro, as if he had just committed a heinous breach of common sense. "Five hundred men is quite enough for one so inexperienced."

Now Varro glared back. He wanted to question the tribune's own history and compare the scars of experience. But he had learned better than to indulge those kinds of feelings.

While the tribune adopted a smug smile, his balding adjutant seemed to offer Varro encouragement with a quick wink.

Cato cleared his throat. "I will address the men this morning. Assemble them after this meeting concludes, Tribune. This is an important operation as a lesson to the barbarians. But more practically we cannot leave active hostiles in our rear. I expect a quick victory here, and then we will resume the march north to destroy the Bergistani revolt once and for all. I will call upon the Ilegertes for their aid in that. Centurion Varro, you and your friends will be glad for their company, I'm sure."

Despite a queasy wave overtaking him, Varro inclined his head and agreed. Cato then dismissed them with a promise for a later meeting to plan details. Yet Varro lingered at the tent flap after the others had left.

"Sir, may I have a private word with you about another matter?"

Cato had returned to his slates and looked up with a wrinkled nose. "There are many reports here, Centurion. Is this so urgent?"

When Varro nodded, Cato let go a long sigh and waved him

back inside. They faced each other in silence. Cato's brows lifted as if he did not know why they were meeting.

"Sir, Tribune Galenus was investigating the stolen silver. Did he report his findings to you?"

"Ah," Cato now turned back to the slate set on his desk. "Yes, he was looking into it for me. He claimed he had some idea of who did it, but needed conclusive proof. I assume he involved you as well?"

"He did, sir. And he had determined the culprit."

Given the severity of the crime, Cato merely cocked a brow at Varro's revelation.

"I assume from your eager tone he passed all of his findings to you before his untimely death."

"Yes, sir, I know who did it, and Tribune Galenus planned to inform you upon reaching our destination."

"Then you can make that report at the same time."

Varro blinked and rubbed his hands against his thighs. "Sir, why should this wait? If something happens in the mountains to me, then you will never find out."

Cato rubbed his face, letting his hands rest over his cheeks so that his bottom eyelids pulled down to reveal pink flesh.

"Because, Centurion, there is a process to follow. You will make an accusation that will require clear proof. Then the entire matter must be reviewed by Tribune Manius as well as me." Cato now paused, as if thinking. "You must deal with these barbarians first. That is my primary concern, and I want no other distractions. When you return, you can make your report to me. Depending on what you reveal, I will decide what action to take."

Clenching his teeth against the urge to blurt out Placus's name, Varro instead said nothing. If Cato wanted to wait, then it only gave him more time to improve his position. In fact, since Centurion Longinus would accompany him into the mountains, Varro

104

could judge what kind of resistance he might have to the accusation. So instead he saluted.

"Thank you, sir. I will be ready when you ask for the report."

He waited for dismissal, but Cato continued to study his wax slates. This drew out past absentmindedness, to where Varro had to prod him.

"May I be dismissed, sir?"

"Have you given more consideration to my recommendation?"

Thoughts of playing dumb crossed Varro's mind, but he knew better. "I have, sir. I am loyal to Rome, and have served dutifully all this time."

"Well, I'm not questioning your record." Cato set his wax tablet down. "But I am questioning what secrets you keep for Senator Flamininus. Why did he pay the three of you so much? Why did he ship you out of the way rather than let you return home? Better still, what is he planning for you that he did not have you killed off?"

"I don't know what you are saying, sir."

But Cato lowered his head and chuckled.

"That is willful blindness, Centurion. You describe your service as dutiful. But then you conceal the criminal acts of one man for a huge payment. Dutiful, but to Rome?"

"Senator Flamininus has committed no crime."

"Perhaps," Cato said with a deferential shrug. "But he has done something that would cause him great shame. Something he deems damaging enough to pay for your silence. You are playing a deadly game, Centurion Varro, one too far over your head. When Flamininus's shame comes to light, which one day it must, you will find the burden of your fortune quite heavy indeed. I will not help you then, even if I could. But today, I extend my hand to aid a fellow Sabine and admirable soldier. Do not fear what your friends would say. They follow you, and blindly at that. Give up your pugio and join me on the side of righteousness."

"Sir, I have much to prepare for. May I be dismissed?"

"So that is still your answer." Cato picked up the wax slate and scanned it with his finger. "I will not make this offer many more times. Think about your future and that of your friends. Step into the light or skulk in the dark. I know which choice I would make. Be careful as you walk the shadows, for you may veer off your path and fall into doom."

Cato looked up with a thin smile.

"Dismissed."

11

Varro called a halt to the column's progress into the mountain range. The hard turns, trees, and deep channels of rock interrupted his view of his force. An eagle soared above them moments after his order to rest repeated down the line. Men pointed up and a thin cheer rose at the good omen of the bird passing above them.

"Glad the consul selected such a chipper group." Falco set his pack down and wiped sweat from his forehead as he too followed the eagle's soaring path.

Varro had inherited Tribune Galenus's command group and added both Longinus and Falco to it, giving Falco's century over to a different centurion. While Cato had assigned the men, Varro was free to arrange them as he desired and so kept Falco with him.

"Only the youngest and strongest." Varro repeated Cato's description of them from their later planning meeting. "We'll see how they feel when we meet the enemy."

Longinus, who seemed boundlessly happy to join Varro on the mission, did not sit when everyone else found a place amid the rocks. Instead, he vanished down the line to inspect the condition of the men after a half-day climb.

Varro used the moment to sit beside Falco and lean in to whisper. They had no chance to speak in private since the morning assembly. So Varro filled him in on Cato's offer while Falco shook his head.

"If we told him the fucking truth, the bastard won't believe it." Falco scratched at the side of his head. "He thinks Flamininus killed someone, or worse."

"You know those senators only need half a truth to burn down a man's reputation. Anyway, I didn't get to meet with Curio. Did you speak to him?"

Falco's heavy brows stitched together. "You said we'd do it together. Plus, Lily, I've got my century to look after. Rowdy boys with more energy than sense."

"Sounds like us during our recruit days," Varro said, and both men shared a fleeting laugh. "There's something wrong with all of this. Cato didn't even care to know who stole the silver. Does that sound like him?"

Falco shook his head. "But he's a tricky bastard and you can't know what he's going to do next. He's built his whole life that way. Talk about walking in the light. Ha! With him it's more like walking through a forest of lies. One day he's going to walk right into a tree and knock himself out."

"You've become quite descriptive these days." Varro thumped his arm.

"Probably from all the reading I had to do when teaching Curio."

Mention of the name caused both of them to fall into silence. Varro wanted to hear Falco's thoughts, but now he seemed more interested in the tall peaks ahead of them.

"I don't think Curio went over to Cato," Varro said. "If he did, why would Cato press me for information? Wouldn't Curio have told him already?"

Falco remained looking at the peaks, and Varro sensed he had more to say. He again punched Falco's shoulder, more forcefully now. It made him draw back and clap his hand over it.

"Watch it or I'll remind you of your broken shoulder."

"It was never broken, just bruised. Now, what are you not telling me?"

"I didn't speak to Curio because you wanted to do that together. But I spoke to his optio. If Cato summoned him, then his optio never knew. That's not procedure, of course. So if what your signifier Lars said is true, then he was there secretly."

Both of them turned to Lars, who had pulled off his sandals to study his feet. The command group had become accustomed to riding everywhere. But horses would not help them in the mountains.

"He has no reason to lie," Varro said.

"I understand," Falco said. "But the optio also said that Curio left during sword drills right before we set out on this march. He just put the optio in charge and disappeared for no apparent reason, and didn't come back until well past the time he said he would be away. The optio was considering reporting this to Tribune Galenus."

Varro felt his shoulders hunching. "He didn't have any idea where Curio went? Did anything unusual happen in camp that day?"

"Ah, I guess you were still away at that time. Well, nothing special happened. Cato and the praetors told us how we'd divide up. Resupply arrived in time for us to draw more of what we needed, just rations, gear, and such. So, I don't know why any of that would've taken his attention. He just went off on his own secret business."

"But it doesn't mean he was with Cato." Varro tried to be hopeful, but Falco was already shaking his head.

"Well, where else would he be? He won't admit it. If we confront him, he's just going to say he has been investigating the silver like we asked."

"Something else is going on," Varro said. "I can feel it, but I can't see it. Now Curio is being kept away from us. Is it because he went over to Cato, or did he find something out?"

Falco tilted his head. "Maybe, but Curio gets excited when he does good work. If he had a discovery, then he'd tell us."

Varro had set his helmet aside and now ran his fingers over the tips of his black helmet feathers as he considered whether Curio went over to Cato and what that would mean for their future.

"Maybe we should go over," Falco said in a near whisper. "Just to be done with all this sneaking around. Cato might be right about Flamininus. Maybe he's going to sacrifice us one day for some other purpose, and we'll die like loyal little soldiers and take his secret with us."

"He has only ever invested in us," Varro said. "And never once asked us to keep any secrets other than membership in Servus Capax. Cato is just trying to create a scandal for a rival and using fear to weaken us."

Longinus came bounding back up the slope, his stubble-shaded jaw set firm. Both Falco and Varro knew to lean away and end their debate.

Scouts returned with their reports, and soon Varro had the column marching again. They had found caves and other hidden areas that showed signs of recent use. So they would pursue deeper into the range and inspect these locations for clues to where the Iberians hid.

The attack came without warning.

Varro had been directing the column following the guidance of his scouts, unaware that they were straining to reach a trap.

As they passed a high wall of craggy gray stone topped with stunted trees, rocks rolled out from between them and plummeted into the drawn-out column.

They fell with minimal noise, and if Varro had not been looking back as often as he had looked ahead he might never have seen them falling. Most rocks shot straight down, but others struck the rock face and bounded wide to spare the men beneath.

The first volley of rocks crashed amid the ranks, sending men flying away from the impact. Screams followed, as did shouted commands to raise shields.

"Sir, about one hundred on those ridges." Centurion Longinus pointed to the scores of Iberians that had waited in hiding for them. They emerged now, hefting stone between them to hurl over the ledge while others raised javelins or spun slings overhead.

"So much for warrior pride and all that shit." Falco raised his scutum shield.

Varro did as well, glad to once more carry an infantryman's kit into battle. But he was no soldier; he was the commander. Tubicen Gaius looked to him for the orders to sound on his bronze horn. Lars planted the standard. Aulus stood beside Falco and Longinus, all sheltering from the initial volley of sling stones, dropped rocks, and javelins.

"Shields up," he said, an order he would give as a centurion but not as a commander. Gaius stared blankly at him. "All centuries, testudo formation, march forward on my pace."

"We've got to sweep them off that ledge," Longinus shouted from under his shield. "The boys at the front have that task, sir."

Gaius sounded the order. The brief moments it took to decide had already permitted another volley of dropped rocks to crash among the men. But now heavy shields stacked together over the soldiers, forming a protective shell that denied all but the heaviest rocks from penetrating. The stones thudded on curved wood, making more noise than damage. This advantage justified Cato's confidence in sending a reduced force to flush out the Iberians.

Varro's shield shuddered from stones cracking against it. His freshly healed shoulder ached, as if echoing the pain from the last time he stood before slingers. But now he tramped up the uneven ground, more fearful of twisting his ankle in a rush to reach the enemy before they could do more damage.

The Iberians held all the advantages. Varro realized they had selected this section of the path because it would lead to the clustering of his men. He had been stringing out the column to minimize this vulnerability, but the natives' knowledge of the terrain defeated him.

The centurions behind Varro bellowed for their men to keep steady and hold their shields up. Their voices echoed behind the shields of their testudo formations. Varro and his command group sheltered together, but hardly formed the defensive wall of regular troops.

"We're coming to the top," Longinus said.

"Then they won't stay to greet us," Varro said. "They're going to pull back. We need to cut them in half before they escape. I want prisoners."

"Let me lead a century into their rear, sir." Longinus deferred to Varro as if he were a tribune, but his rank was higher. Varro agreed.

At last, gaining the ledge, Varro's shield no longer shuddered with the impact of sling shot. He peeked from behind his shield, and as he feared, the Iberians were rushing to escape.

"Charge!" Varro shouted.

"Sir, what?" Tubicen Gaius stood with his horn hovering over his mouth. Varro and Longinus raced forward, with Falco and Aulus joining.

As Varro bounded ahead, he heard the notes for a general charge sound behind. The lead centurions would know what to do, he thought, and the Iberian escape had to be stemmed or they would encounter them again in another ambush.

He was the first to mount the ledge, with Longinus cursing him from behind.

"Let me take the risks, sir!"

But Varro was already lumbering forward with his scutum up. He drew his gladius with a sharp rasp and gave a throaty battle cry.

The Iberians had scant room to retreat, but Varro saw at least a dozen climbing higher into the rocks and pines. He was uncertain if they planned to regroup, but Varro intended to let them go. Instead, as the first of his soldiers reached the ledge, he shouted direct commands.

"First century, with Longinus. The rest with me!"

The men swarmed the ledge even as the Iberians took advantage to sling more stones at the exposed climbers. But the men in the rear covered the climbers with their shields, making it far harder to do actual damage. Still, amid the clatter and crash of stone, Varro heard the cries of the injured.

About fifty of the Iberians remained trapped on their ledge. Desire to inflict greater casualties on the Romans had led them to prolong what should've been a hit-and-run attack. Now Varro brought up the front of his column to finish them.

But for the moment, he was a lone commander with his small group of staff and the first of the hastati to join him. He would make a fine captive.

The barbarians closest to him now drew their short swords, much the same as the one Varro held, and charged with their own vicious battle cries.

For a fleeting instant, Varro worried he had exposed himself. But the confines of the ledge along with the trees and boulders that clogged it denied the Iberians any advantage in numbers.

The first attacker leaped upon Varro's shield, using his whole body in a gambit to overwhelm Varro. He did stagger back, and the enemy jabbed his blade around the edge of the shield. But the strike got tangled in his mail shirt, merely pricking the skin of his upper arm.

Varro used his shield to hurl him against a tree, slamming him once more with the iron boss to stun the Iberian. At the same time, Falco and the others pushed past him to fill the gap he left.

The Iberian slid down the trunk, blood flowing from his broken nose. Varro punched him again with his shield, then stabbed him through his neck before pressing into the ledge.

From behind, he heard the deep and commanding voice of Longinus as he led a rear guard to pick off any others escaping and to prevent them from rallying in Varro's rear.

He smiled as he wove between trees, seeking his enemies. This was not the kind of battle Roman soldiers normally fought. But they had prevailed and now pushed half of their ambushers into an inescapable corner.

Shoving from between a rock and a tree, he found Falco clashing with a bald-headed man. For an instant, his eyes played tricks on him, for the Iberian looked like Consul Cato. But blue tattoos covered his head, and while his face was as creased and folded as Cato's, he shared no other commonality.

Falco growled as the enemy wrestled against his shield. Being anchored to a large stone he could not be defeated, but neither could he strike with his sword. They shoved back and forth until Varro reached them.

He scraped the attacker away with his own shield, flattening him to the rocky ground. Falco shouted with glee as he sprung forward. "Let me kill the bastard!"

So Varro left him to take his revenge and continued to plow forward.

But even as he fought and soaked himself in the blood of his enemies, he realized he was remiss in his greater duty to the entire force. He was too deep in the fight, just like a common soldier. He had even abandoned his command group in the frenzy.

All around, snarling faces swirled in individual clashes. The ringing of metal was sharp in his ears and the coppery taste of blood spread on his tongue. Sweat ran into his eyes and stung them. Varro could not even determine who prevailed. He was too low to the ground to see beyond the nearest foe. To gain elevation would expose him and likely cost his life.

Another Iberian, one who seemed as if he had emerged from a pool of blood, leaped at him. Someone had badly gashed him on the head, and he blinked against the blood sheeting over his face. He seemed blinded, but his sword was as dangerous as any.

Varro slammed his shield down on the knee of the Iberian as he overstepped his strike. He then delivered a swift thrust to the Iberian's chest and ended his suffering, though he collapsed laughing at his own demise.

So it came to be a grinding death for these Iberians. Varro could not command, having committed himself to deep battle. His men seemed enthralled with the desire for revenge and the Iberians had no place to flee. In the end, only a handful threw down their swords and begged for their lives. Varro was there at the front, his face dripping with sweat-diluted gore, to call an end to the fighting.

He raised his sword and received the cheers of a victorious column of Romans. Pointing to the Iberians on their knees, he ordered them restrained. His men surged forward, kicking the barbarians flat while disarming them. At last able to look back, Varro saw a rock-strewn ledge flowing with blood. Bodies and parts of bodies were heaped everywhere. At his feet, he found a pile that looked like gray worms only to realize these were severed fingers.

Roman shields and helmets were strewn among the corpses

and it chilled him to think of the cost he might have paid to capture these few Iberians.

Centurions restored order out of chaos, pushing their men into semblances of formations. A third of the column was still beneath the ledge. Those around Varro cheered him for his bravery, and while he was grateful the men saw this as victory, he had not yet seen the full scope of the battle.

"That was murder," Falco said as he and Aulus pushed through to him. "They let themselves become trapped up here. Fools."

"I wonder," Varro said, peering past him to the trees that climbed up the mountain path. He then looked back at Falco. "I need a full casualty report, theirs and ours, as soon as you can produce one. Aulus, go with the captives and learn what you can. I'm going to see what Longinus did."

He pressed through his men who had all been ordered to stand under the surly scrutiny of their centurions. Along the way, he picked up both Tubicen Gaius and Signifier Lars, though he had no standard to carry into the mountains. That remained with the Second Legion and wouldn't be risked in the mountains.

The men at the rear indicated Longinus's path. It was easy enough to follow, marked as it was with twisted and shattered Iberian corpses. Just from reading the landscape, Varro knew Longinus had executed an ordered pursuit. But then he came to a sharp incline that sprouted from the path that was covered to the left by a mound of high boulders capped with milky green lichen.

He found the first legion halted on the other side of it. The optio in charge of them had taken a deep gash to his shoulder and he clamped a hand over the leaking blood as he reported to Varro.

"They turned on us here, sir, right at this blind corner. Stopped us cold and dropped trees in their path. Got men clearing them now, sir. But Centurion Longinus is missing. I think they captured him and a few of our own, sir."

12

Varro watched as soldiers hauled the last of the trees off the path. The trunks were not wide, but their branches entangled each other to form a lattice that hindered any attempt to climb over them. Additionally, rocks and debris had been thrown into the path to shore up the barrier. A centurion paced around the men, directing and just as often cursing them when they paused.

He looked skyward and found the sun had vanished into a gray haze. The air was already cool at this elevation and grew cooler as a breeze developed into a wind.

"Rain?" Falco said, standing beside him with arms folded. "The gods want to kick us between the legs now? I thought we were their favorites."

"What gods rule here?" Varro asked, staring blankly at the workers dragging a ragged black trunk to the side of the path. "Maybe not ours."

Falco sniffed. "Jupiter is best and first, and barbarian gods mean nothing in comparison."

The battle had not been as costly as Varro had expected. He

counted about twenty dead or severely wounded, mostly from the initial attack. Two had been thrown from the ledge and the rest fell in battle. The Iberians had sacrificed more than double that number of casualties and all of them were dead. Aulus was still interrogating the captives back where they surrendered. The rest of the column moved up and prepared to advance after the barrier was cleared.

"We'll evacuate the wounded," Varro said. "Do you want to lead them back?"

Falco cupped his chin as if in deep thought. "But then I'd miss my chance to die with you in an overly complex hostage rescue scheme. I couldn't let that opportunity go. Assign that task to some other unlucky bastard."

"If they took any hostages. We won't know more until we can progress up the path and see for ourselves."

Varro imagined Longinus's head on a spear set on the perimeter of the barbarians' mountain hideout. He squeezed his eyes shut to banish the thought.

Falco lowered his voice. "Well, it might mean one less complication when we return to Consul Cato."

Varro recoiled at the suggestion. "Are you serious? He is the First Spear, the best of us. We must make every effort to bring him back unharmed."

"Hold on. I wasn't suggesting we do nothing. But it would make things easier if he wasn't around to complicate our story."

"Don't say it again." Varro adopted his commander voice, one that he hoped sounded as stern and resolute as the fine officers he imitated. Falco lowered his head and said nothing more.

Aulus now emerged from down the path, his stride bouncy and his shoulders back. The entire line of men waiting on the roadblock seemed to study his approach, concern written on their faces. News of First Spear Longinus's disappearance had dampened the spirits of the erstwhile victors.

Aulus wiped his tattooed face after saluting. He was covered with sweat and Varro noted a bead of fresh blood dangled from his nose. It was not his own.

"They weren't talkative, sir." He grimaced as he spoke. "But the men you assigned to help me certainly knew how to loosen them up."

"Are the captives still alive?" Varro looked down the slope, but of course the captives were far to the rear and out of sight.

"Some survived. They had to see how serious we were before they spoke. They are a branch of the Turdentani that claims these mountains for their home. It's a sacred place and they are defending it against our trespassing."

"An interesting detail," Varro said. "But unhelpful to our task. Did you learn where they are hiding? How many people, defenses, leaders?"

Aulus again wiped at his nose, and the spot of blood smeared.

"There are about a thousand of them in total. All but the young and old would defend against us. They have built their homes in a hidden vale high between the peaks. They won't reveal the location, sir. Before we took more expedient means to learn it from them, I thought to report to you."

Varro nodded and stroked his chin. Longinus's capture had hardened his heart to what he must do next.

"Thank you for doing so. Do you think they will keep Longinus and the others alive?"

Aulus looked skyward as well, squinting against the glare.

"That depends on their leader, sir. The people might be eager for revenge and kill them outright. Or they could be used as a sacrifice to the gods. That is the most likely possibility. If they recognize Centurion Longinus's rank, they might try to negotiate. But they understand Rome too well. They know we've decided to destroy them, and any truce would be temporary."

"So we've backed them into a corner," Varro said. "And they

have no means to escape. Therefore, they will fight like mad bulls."

Falco had been listening to the report, and now growled in frustration.

"I liked this plan better when we were just going to chase them off the mountain and let the main legion smash them. Now we've got to kill a thousand barbarians. Fuck, my blade won't keep its edge through all that."

"They will surrender rather than die to a man," Aulus said. "They are Turdentani, and so they are full of bluster but cowards at heart. That has always been so with these people."

Varro tilted his head with a grin. "I am certain you are not of their tribe."

"Ausetani, sir. You'd have far greater challenge if you faced my old tribe."

"May it never be so." Varro then made his own grimace. "We need to reach that vale without delay. I've no patience with their empty bravado. Centurion Falco, work with the centurions to find the best throwing arms in the ranks. Then gather enemy javelins and have them practice casting these at the remaining captives. Be precise rather than deadly. The drill can end once one is willing to lead us to the vale. If none are prepared to cooperate, then kill them except for their least willful man. We will continue to work on him until we learn what we need."

Falco stared at Varro as if meeting him for the first time. He held his friend's gaze until his heavy brows settled in acceptance.

"Yes, sir. I'm sure a few javelins through the knees will change their minds."

So it was that Varro had authorized torture, something his young mind could never have conceived. He knew he would wrestle with this decision for a long time. Being the commander, he owned responsibility for the choice no matter who cast the actual javelins. Yet such were the exigencies of war. Both the

Roman and Iberian sides were long past any chance of rational discussion. The only common language left for them was brutality.

The work teams had at last cleared the path. Varro inspected it while Falco organized the continued interrogation. The Iberians had known they were coming, likely watching them before they even left camp. They staged a fine trap and delay, their only mistake being an overreaching greed to kill. Even with a thousand of them waiting up in those peaks, not all of them were warriors. Yet they had spent a good number of them in this ambush. He scanned the road once more, wondering what other traps lay ahead.

The spectacle of the javelin throwing brightened the moods of his men, and Varro sensed it increased their respect for him. He accepted this with grace, though it knotted his stomach to think of how he earned this regard.

A half-dozen men now hefted the thin Iberian javelins. They tied four men to trees across a short opening. As many of the Romans as could pile into the area called out bets, their centurions even joining in. Falco served as the overseer and arranged his picked men in a line. He then signaled the first to make his cast.

One Iberian with a flowing iron-gray beard and protruding gut shouted in defiance. The other three joined him. Varro considered how Albus had once tortured his enemies in private, so that they could not take heart from each other. Varro would test that theory now.

Of course, the caster targeted the defiant man. The javelin whistled through the air and the crowd of soldiers hushed. Then the shaft plunged deep into the meat of the Iberian's thigh. Cheers and groans went up in equal measure. The Iberian struggled against his bonds, his face turning purple from biting back his scream. This again caused some to cheer and others to moan. It seemed soldiers would bet on anything, from where the javelin would hit, to whether the victim would cry out, and probably a dozen more things Varro was not creative enough to think of.

Aulus and the rest of the command group remained with him. Given his own stony silence, they kept their wagering to whispers. Only Aulus watched silently with a grin of satisfaction. It seemed he hated these people, for every cast that drew blood widened his smile.

All the men Falco had selected had cast once in turn, and four of the six casts had landed true. A missed cast planted in the tree just below one man's crotch, causing him to shout and drawing raucous jeers from the crowd. Another round began, and now one Iberian died when a javelin slammed through his neck. Unfortunately for him, he did not die right away, but gurgled blood and struggled while the casting continued.

Varro's lips pressed so tightly he thought they might split. He feigned indifference to their suffering, but he prayed for one of them to surrender. A second man now slumped against the rope holding him up, probably dying from the blood flowing out of his punctured thigh.

Aulus laughed. "Centurion Falco selected the best throwing arms, sir. They're so accurate."

The next caster jumped the javelin in his hand as he took aim, then stepped into his throw, sending the white streak arcing across the clearing to plunge into the prodigious gut of the long bearded-barbarian. It pierced his side, a terrible flesh wound but not deadly. He already suffered a javelin through his thigh and a near-miss to his face. This cast broke him and he began to sob and babble.

"There's our man," Aulus said. "He'll talk."

The sobbing drew cheers from the crowd, regardless of how they had bet. Falco looked questioningly from across the opening, and Varro gestured to untie the broken Iberian.

However, the last survivor now shouted in rage and fought against his bonds. A javelin had stuck in his hip, but he still kicked and roared at his traitorous kinsman.

Falco's shouted orders echoed clearly across the opening. "Kill the one on the right, then cut down the fat one."

Three of the casters hurled their javelins and all of them landed in a cluster through the protesting Iberian's chest. He arched his back and let out a howl that vanished under a wave of cheers from the crowd, then slumped forward to hang from the tree trunk.

Aulus clicked his tongue as the last Iberian dropped to the ground when soldiers cut his rope. "It's always the brazen ones that surrender first."

"Is it?" Varro felt weak but knew better than to show it. Instead, he would let the tortured corpses hang from the trees. He joined Falco, then shouted toward the crowd. "The entertainment is over. Stand ready to march!"

Centurions snapped back into character, one moment laughing and betting with their fellows then the next moment whipping vine canes at the legs of stragglers and shouting commands.

"Harsh, but effective," Falco said as he watched the fat barbarian flop between the two men dragging him forward. "And a show for the boys. If this all goes well, you're going to be a fucking hero when we return."

With Aulus, Gaius, and others around him, he gave a weak smile rather than express disgust at his decision. But it had worked. As he waited for the prisoner to reach him, he considered this might have saved the lives of his men. Otherwise, they could become lost or ambushed again. The barbarians might kill Longinus while they searched for this vale. So he set aside his feelings and now studied the haggard and tear-streaked face looking up at him from between two men.

He was an older man with a flowing iron-gray beard sitting over a protruding belly. Apparently, life was easy in these mountains, Varro thought. Two javelins quivered in the man's flesh and bright blood flowed from his leg. He was dying. If he had only held on a little longer, he might have defied his captors.

Varro set his hand on the javelin in the man's side, causing him to groan.

"I will have my doctors heal you if you cooperate. I will also spare your family if I can. Lie to me, and my doctors will still heal you. Then I will kill you slowly."

He waited for Aulus to translate. He did not have any doctors on his staff, only two medical orderlies to help with triage. But he needed to give the barbarian hope, or else all of this was a waste.

The fat Iberian's eyes lit up and he babbled, but Aulus shouted him into silence.

"Sir, he will guide us. He wants your promise to spare his family. He has three daughters, two sons, and a wife. He also has two chickens and a goat that he wants to keep. In exchange, he will show us the back way into the village."

Falco grunted. "How can we trust him?"

"How can we?" Varro echoed the same question. "He might well lead us off a cliff. But he begged for his life, and therefore he must value it. So we hold that against his honesty. It's the best we can do."

The Iberian spoke again, and one soldier holding him was about to strike when Varro held up his hand. He then looked at Aulus for translation.

"He said they have our supplies and our slaves. These were taken by their chief and hidden. He can help us find them."

Varro gave a thin smile, thinking of young Servius and his single day of freedom. Aulus apparently had the same thought.

"You'll get your slave back, sir. But if I may make a suggestion, you're better off just selling him for a profit. He's a headstrong boy."

"That's for later," Varro said. "This Iberian is going to bleed to death before he can show us the way. Let's get all we can from him now. I'll leave that to you, Aulus. Since he will cooperate, do not torture him further. In fact, I will have a medical orderly up here to see what he can do to keep the fat one alive. Learn all the details you can. How far away we are, defensive capabilities, any other tricks they have prepared for us. In the meantime, I will lead a force to scout ahead."

The scouting mission was more to keep his men active and focused than to gain information. He led about half his column up the trail and determined that the Iberians had vacated the area. The sky continued to threaten rain, and a heavy gray sheet of clouds diffused the sun into an irritating glare.

Upon their return, Aulus had a full report from the Iberian, who seemed he would live at least a while longer. Varro was not interested in his survival. If he could fulfill his terms to the captive, he would, but not risk his men.

"He doesn't know what they'll do with the prisoners," Aulus said after they resumed the march. "Nothing good, that's for sure. Since they expect us to pursue, they might keep our men as hostages and negotiate an exchange."

The prisoner had one javelin removed from his side and was bandaged. His leg was also bandaged and the javelin shaft cut down as close to his thigh as possible. Varro knew that pulling it out might doom the Iberian to a swift bleed-out. So they had given him a makeshift crutch and forced him to hobble along with the command group. Scouts went ahead according to his instructions, and Varro waited on their reports before advancing.

It made for slow progress, and while some might accuse him of being cautious, he would not lead five hundred men into a trap again.

By nightfall they had not reached the vale despite the Iberian's promises they were close to it. Varro warned if he was tricking them, he had men who could remove his skin starting from his toes while keeping him alive the entire time. He had seen this gruesome work in the torture chamber of the Spartan King Nabis. While he did not actually have anyone like that in his force, the prisoner didn't know.

"He swears he is true," Aulus said. "And that we are just moving too slow."

Falco looked up as they trod the rough paths into the peaks. "No rain yet, but those clouds won't even allow us starlight for a night march. This ground is too treacherous to continue when it's hidden in shadow."

"Centurion Longinus and the others cannot wait." Varro peered up as well, feeling a tiny point of cold touch his cheek, proof of rain that refused to fall.

"Maybe they are not waiting," Falco said ominously.

"We will assume that they are. Therefore, if we attack before we free the captives, then they will die either out of spite or when we refuse to negotiate terms for their release."

Falco and the rest of the command group turned to stare at him. Varro shook his head.

"Consul Cato's orders were explicit. We must destroy the barbarians to a man, flushing them out only if we must. Unless they are foolish enough to hand over their prisoners first, we will not negotiate. We will destroy them. Do not forget Tribune Galenus and our brothers who died because of their cunning tricks. We are here to deliver Rome's vengeance. One man can live to tell the story to all he meets, and that is our fat captive here. The rest are counting the hours until their deaths."

He meant what he said. While Galenus had been an ass, he had served Rome and died as a soldier defending his standard. He deserved to be avenged. These Turdentani barbarians should have realized that if they bit Rome in the tail then all its force would turn on them and show no mercy.

Falco at last cleared his throat.

"Excuse me, sir. But is this where you involve us all in your overly complicated hostage rescue plan?"

Varro smiled.

"You know me too well, Centurion Falco. I've had plenty of time to think of one. I suppose now is the time to share it."

13

The mountaintop settlement was not as far as Varro had thought. In the night's blackness, it seemed like a military stockade with wooden walls surrounding sturdy wooden structures. They anchored these stockade walls to steep rock outcroppings. A ring of hazy orange light pulsed from the torches that were set at intervals along the wall sections. The Iberians were on alert.

He crept forward, mindful of his steps. His sandaled feet ground against the loose rock-strewn path as he moved ahead. He could feel the presence of the others behind him as he observed the path. It was narrow and twisted, little more than a goat path that led from the rear of the settlement. His eyes darted side to side, taking in every detail—flickers of torchlight through the stockade wall or shadows passing across its top. The Iberians guarded the path even if no one was supposed to know this approach.

He crouched behind a cluster of pillar-like stones covered in etched runes long ago filled in with a spattering of lichen and moss. The air had a crisp, cool bite to it as the threat of rain remained. He kept low to the ground, hugging the shadows that pooled around him.

Turning back, he saw the clump of darker shadows formed of the three other men he selected for this operation. He had included Aulus since he might need an interpreter. Falco had chaffed at remaining with the main force.

"But you need me," he had said. "How many times have we done this sort of thing? I won't make a mess of it like these others will."

"I need someone I can trust to lead the main attack," Varro countered. "As well as someone who understands what I'm doing beyond the walls. Really, do you want to come with me and have Lars or Aulus lead the attack?"

That thought convinced Falco. Varro then selected two others, plus Aulus, who did not seem keen on the plan. But when he asked the centurions to secure volunteers for a rescue operation, he did not expect nearly half the force to step up. Apparently, Longinus was a much beloved man.

Seeing that the area was safe, he motioned the others forward. Aulus was the first to pile in beside him. The other two raced over, bent low as they carried a short ladder between them, and crashed in next to him. They did not carry shields, wear helmets, or have any other defensive gear beyond their chest plates. Nothing else was suited to their operation. Varro was the best armored in his mail shirt, but he had to leave his heavy shield behind as well. His accomplices' eyes shined with anticipation.

Varro huddled his team, drawing their heads close enough to feel the warmth of their flushed faces and smell their sour breath.

"You two are the ladder team." He spread his index and little fingers to point out his two volunteers. "Guard it with your life, and use the whistle signal if you're discovered. Aulus, you and I will extract the captives and lead them back here. With good fortune, we'll be over the wall and gone before the Iberians know it. Falco is ready to bring up a covering attack if we need it. A simple plan, boys, but the enemy will flip it on its head. Be ready to adjust."

Aulus's smile was barely discernible in the shadow. "Sir, how come Centurion Falco said your plan would be overly complicated?"

"He's remembering our days as recruits." Varro indulged himself in a smile of his own, then put his finger over his mouth. "No more talking. We're going in now."

The two men with the short ladder now picked it off the rocky ground, then swept out toward the darkest part of the stockade wall. Varro had his men construct ladders based on his captive's estimation of its height. As his two men set their ladder against the wall, he saw they were just short of the top, but long enough to allow a man to slide over the wall.

He set his foot on the first rung and felt it sag under his weight. They had worked all evening collecting wood and crafting the ladders. In total, he might have a dozen available for action. But as he pulled up, he wondered if they would support more than one man at a time.

The springy wood creaked and bounced, but as he was the heaviest of them in his chain shirt, he knew it would hold for the others. He reached the top and hauled up to it. He wished Curio was here, for he was an expert in stealthy movement. The sharpened tops were too blunt to be a genuine threat, as his mail protected his torso. But the points still pressed him as he lay straddled on the top. He looked below.

Guards had spread out in the cleared areas by the wall, carrying torches aloft and spears in their other hands. Fortunately, they did not hug the wall and looked to the settlement interior in postures of boredom. Varro looked across the settlement finding a mixture of wood and textile structures jumbled together in no pattern. The center area is where the chief made his home, but they would hold prisoners away from him. With the time he had, Varro picked a brightly lit patch just south of the chief's home. Why else would that area be lit if not to illuminate important captives and hamper any escape?

Slipping over the side, he dangled a moment then dropped. He fell only a short distance, but it still filled him with terror. When he thumped into the dirt on both feet, his mind flashed with visions of falling from a vast height. His experiences in Sparta would likely haunt him forever, as it had taken all his courage to drop the short length. Still, his feet hurt and his hobnailed sandals didn't cushion the impact.

Aulus mounted the wall next, and following him would come one of the ladder team. That man would stand guard by their planned exit point, while the other would bring the ladder over then lie flat on the wall to be ready to help captives who might be too injured to make it unassisted.

Still encased in darkness, Varro raced for the dark corner of the nearest building. The Iberians had demonstrated sense in keeping the area by the wall uncluttered. It made hiding there much harder. Yet they also failed to patrol it adequately and so allowed Varro and Aulus their chance.

Both men fell in at the corner and huddled together. Varro spoke in the barest whisper.

"You saw that lit zone? They probably hold Longinus there. We'll need a clear path there and back." He then leaned out to indicate the first of the guards in their way. "I'll drop him, and you clear the body behind me. We'll meet at the opposite side by that corner."

Aulus leaned out to study what Varro had indicated. He crouched low like a cat ready to pounce, then gave a sharp nod when he understood.

"Stay with me, and we should both be fine."

"You've done this before, haven't you, sir?"

"More times than I've wanted to."

Varro drew his pugio, preferring it for this close work. Stepping out of the false safety of the shadow, he swept toward the guard who shifted his weight restlessly from side to side. He was thin but broad shouldered, his light-brown hair worn in a braid down his back.

Clamping his hand over the Iberian's mouth, Varro drove his pugio blade deep into the Iberian's kidney. He bucked in shock and pain, and his wet breath bathed Varro's hand as he cried out. But Varro cut side to side and twisted as he withdrew the blade. The barbarian collapsed and Varro released his mouth to instead grab the torch. He guided the dying Iberian to the ground and settled the torch beside him.

Varro then raced for the next point to ensure it was a safe zone while he heard Aulus scrambling behind him to drag the body out of sight, while stamping out the torch. Varro's shadow vanished in front of him when Aulus put out that torch. He landed against the next wall, breathless and shaking. No matter how many times he had to operate in enemy territory, he would never become accustomed to it. It was far easier to march forward with shields up and companions on either side. Even in his heavy armor, he felt completely exposed in this village.

A heavy stench of manure and rot emanated from the darkness where they had landed. Aulus dragged the corpse into the corner of the building's foundation. Varro now looked down along a path of dark lanes broken up with faint patches of yellow light. It seemed like a maze to him, and if he had to run back in haste, he feared becoming lost.

"Sir?"

Aulus prodded him, noting another guard was now on the move. From his vantage, Varro could not see over buildings in the way but did note the orange haze of a torch glow drawing near.

The wind also gusted against them, blowing up suddenly and slicing cold into Varro's exposed legs.

So he ducked into the alley with Aulus following behind. The wind continued to gust as he threaded the paths. At each opening, he checked for activity before moving on. Yet Fortuna was with him again, as either no one stood watch or else they faced away.

Halfway to his goal, Varro heard the light plinking of rain on the roofs. The wind now remained steady, with gusts like invisible fists punching against his left side.

As he neared the bright area he had identified from the wall, rain began to fall. It evolved into a steady downpour and slanted with the wind. He did not appreciate any new variables in his plan, particularly something as capricious as weather. Aulus kept close to him, his feet keeping time with Varro's, so their movements were nearly synchronous. He paused before reaching the end of this maze and gave Aulus an appreciative nod.

"Maybe you've done this before?"

It was a foolish chance to make any sound so close to the enemy, and he realized perhaps he had grown too relaxed about these sorts of operations. Thankfully, Aulus responded only by inclining his head.

He now crouched and peered out at the lit zone. As expected, a bonfire defied both wind and rain and dominated the cleared area. It seemed like a place built to intimidate. Bodies hung from gibbets, gray forms that twisted with the wind. He saw their glistening white flesh in the unsteady light of the bonfire. The bodies had been lashed and stabbed, and it seemed for some, their livers had been removed through long cuts that now left flesh flapping in the wind.

Aulus groaned. "They ate their organs, sir. Some warriors believe it gives them power over their enemies."

"Animals." Varro gritted his teeth as he counted six men. He listed eight including Longinus gone missing after the ambush. "I don't see all our men."

He would have said more, but the wind gusted icy rain into his face. It proved once again to be the hand of the gods that had smothered his speech. For the same gust aggravated two men Varro had not seen standing to his left against the wall leading to his alley. His heart flipped when he heard them curse and turn aside from the blast of rain.

Aulus and he backed into the alley and crawled out of sight halfway down from the exit. In the faint light, Aulus's eyes caught a glint of the bonfire lighting the far end. Neither made any sound, as if both were trying to communicate without speech. It might have been possible if they were not ensconced in darkness. Varro was the first to whisper.

"They must have recognized Longinus's rank and plan to use him against us. So where would they hold him?"

"With their chief." Aulus did not hesitate. "He would be too valuable to keep elsewhere."

Varro rubbed the rain out of his face, then held his hand over his mouth as he stared back toward the bonfire. He couldn't help the men who had already died. But two more still lived, or so he hoped. If they were with the village chief, then they would be heavily guarded. Two men could not defeat them alone. He could only think of one solution.

"We'll have to signal for Falco to attack. It will draw out the chief and his guard, leaving Longinus and the other captive behind. We can then get them out from the back wall."

"Sir, I would wager all my pay that the chief would take Longinus to the walls with him. He'd want to use him to delay an attack."

Varro's hand once more returned to cover his mouth. Of course, Aulus was right, and drawing out the chief would only make saving Longinus more difficult and demoralize his own troops in the bargain. In the same instant, he realized these Turdentani barbarians had probably sent runners to fetch help. It would lead to a long siege, and Cato would have to send up all his men to destroy this stronghold. This would delay their advance to meet the larger Bergistani rebellion gathering in the north. Or it would force Cato to abandon this plan. Varro did not want to imagine the shame heaped on him for failure and the real possibility of demotion or dismissal.

"They plan on using Longinus to delay for reinforcements. They've sent runners already, I'm certain. We have to break them immediately. Time for a new plan. This village falls tonight."

Even in the darkness, Varro could see Aulus's eyes widen.

"Sir, what about Longinus?"

"I haven't forgotten him. Indeed, he will help secure this place. Falco is prepared with the men, though just for a feint. However, after Centurion Longinus is safe with us, we'll open the gates. Falco will know what to do."

"Those gates will be heavily guarded, sir."

"So go fetch the men watching the gate. I will visit the chief and get Longinus and the other man to meet you there. Provided they are both not too hurt, we will have six men on the inside to open the gate."

Aulus shook his head. "You can't go after the centurion alone."

"I'll work better that way. And if I am captured or killed, you can still escape to inform Falco that he is now in full command."

Aulus was about to further protest when Varro held up his hand for silence. He instead lowered his head.

"Centurion Falco was right after all."

"It's not too complicated. Be fast, because I'll have Centurion Longinus free in no time."

While Varro had projected perhaps too much confidence for Aulus to believe, he still thought his plan would succeed. Originally, he expected to shepherd eight injured men out of captivity.

Now, most were dead and he had only the centurion and one other. Even if they were wounded, they would be more capable of handling themselves. So he could use the opportunity to crack the shell around this village. Once the Iberians learned how he had infiltrated them, they would cut off any future chances. So, with the cover provided by the rain, he had his chance.

They separated without further discussion. Both wished the other luck, and Varro turned down the alley to where his dead companions hung. As expected, the two guards had moved off to seek shelter. Barbarians lacked discipline and did as they pleased. This was his understanding of how they thought, and he was not wrong. The rain hissed all around, now creating a haze along the ground as it fell. It scrubbed the corpses dangling from their gibbets, leaving their naked bodies cleaned of gore and white as a fish's underbelly. The dark slits in their sides were stark reminders of their hideous deaths and hardened Varro's resolve.

The path to the chief's hall offered no cover or hiding places. The bonfire light fell off before reaching it, but torches were lit at the front door, where two men stood guard. They pressed against the wall to avoid the sting of the cold rain. Varro tucked his head down as he strode out with calm confidence.

The enemy did not suspect someone had infiltrated them. He did not appear as a Roman, stripped down to a mail shirt that was common among the better warriors of these Iberians. Backlit from a bonfire and obscured with rain, no one would see his face and wonder at its unfamiliarity.

So he walked with confidence, hand on the gladius that looked like any other Iberian's. Only up close would they see the typical Roman harness that differed from their own simple belts. But the guards huddled against the wall, more worried about the rain in their faces than Varro's arrival.

His approach was so confident that even though the guards saw him, they remained still as if one of their own approached with a message. As he stepped up to the first guard, he had already drawn his pugio.

The blade slipped into the Iberian's ribs, cutting through his soaked tunic to plunge into his lungs. Varro pulled him close as if offering a companionable hug. The other guard, standing an arm's length away on the opposite side of the door, said something that sounded irritated but was still blind to the threat. Only when Varro wrenched the blade from his victim's ribs did the other guard realize the danger.

Varro rammed the pugio into the next guard's throat, turning the start of a shout into a strained and desperate gurgle. He forced the Iberian back against the wall and then to the ground. His blood ran in a rain-diluted sheet from the hole under his jaw and into the mud.

Wicking away the blood then wiping it clean on the shoulder of his first victim, he faced the door. It was sturdy with tight planks leaving no room to peer between. The fat iron nails in it had turned brown and bled rust in wide streaks. He tested it, finding it unbarred.

The chief's hall was not as large as the Ilegertes hall that Varro remembered. But it was of the same simple construction and likely of the same floor plan. Inside would be a larger room with a place for the chief to sit over his people. In the rear, he would have his chambers. Longinus probably slept in chains on the floor as this chief's "guest."

As he pushed the door open, he heard a distant horn sounding. It was not metallic like a Roman bucina, but full and sonorous like a ram's horn.

The Iberians had discovered Varro's intrusion behind their walls.

With a bitter smile, he shoved into the chief's hall.

14

The door burst open under Varro's foot, and he swept inside. For an instant, he was blind from the change in illumination. The hall was built of rich, dark wood. Bear and deer pelts hung from the walls and rafters. A low light spilled from a stone hearth to his left and a long table and benches dominated the center of the room. The strange odors of smoke and honey assailed him.

He stood poised for a strike, but the main room appeared empty. The long, low notes of the alarm horn sounded distant from inside the hall. Perhaps the guards he had killed to gain entrance would've alerted the occupants. Then something shifted in the gloom.

The shape was low to the ground and lifted wearily as if just awakened. It was a man stripped naked. The heavy clinking of chains accompanied his motions, and he craned his head toward the door where rain whipped in behind Varro.

Even in the darkness, he recognized Centurion Longinus. He was stout but muscular. Cuts crossed his chest and the hearth fire shined on a swollen and beaten face, but the white scar over his eye and the heavy stubble surrounding his firm jaw revealed his identity. Varro rushed inside, shoving past benches to reach him.

Longinus looked up in astonishment. Heavy iron cuffs held his hands together, and his feet were equally bound. He could not stand without aid. Varro set his hand over Longinus's mouth.

The First Spear regained his wits and nodded that he would be silent. So Varro pulled back, looking to the opened door where torchlight sparkled in the slashing rain beyond. As insistent as the alarm was, so far no one seemed to answer. But it had only started moments ago.

"Where is the other?"

Longinus's head dropped in defeat, and Varro realized he had found the only survivor among the captives. Perhaps these savages had eaten the livers of their enemies at the very tables he now crouched behind. They spared the First Spear as a hostage, but from his condition, it seemed these barbarians had little intention to keep him alive much longer.

Holding up his manacled wrists, he pointed with both hands toward the rear of the hall. He dared a low and hoarse whisper.

"The chief holds the keys. He's drunk and asleep."

Varro followed his pointing to see the faint outline of an opening at the rear of the hall. He grimaced, then pressed his pugio into Longinus's bound hands.

"We will take revenge tonight, friend."

"Strike with the fury of Mars, Varro." Longinus's whisper quivered with raw hatred. "They do not deserve life."

He stood and the door behind him now caught the wind and slammed against the wall again, as if an invisible intruder had broken in. Soon real men would enter and he had to escape before this happened. The horn was in the midst of a long, low note when it cut short. Varro didn't know whether it vanished behind the gusting wind or if Aulus had ended it.

In a half-dozen strides, hobnails clacking against the wood floor, he reached the chief's entrance and drew his gladius.

The snoring was as loud as the roaring wind outside. Water pattered steadily in one corner out of sight. Before him on a bed of logs matching the dark wood of the walls lay the chief and two women. He sprawled out under animal pelts, mouth open and arms draped across his women. Beside his bed was an oversized wooden chair with a gray wolf pelt tossed askew. Lying atop that was his bare short sword that reflected the weak light spilling in from the main hall.

With a snarl, Varro rushed forward to kill him. Even if he slept, he was a cannibal and a monster that was owed no honest death. Murder was not a word Varro could ascribe to this. This was justice.

He flung forward, feet slipping on something soft and heavy. He skidded as if on ice, pulling his inner thigh muscles as he crashed against the edge of the bed.

As often as the gods sheltered him, so did they taunt him.

The thud against the foot of the bed awakened the chief with a start. At the same moment, as Varro regained his footing, he heard shouts on the other side of the walls. The alarm had roused someone in this storm.

The Turdentani chief snapped up, sloughing off the two women as if dropping two sacks of grain. The furs covering him slipped down to reveal a muscular chest covered in wiry hair that obscured intricate and strange tattoos. His long, dark hair hung in disheveled waves around his face and his beard had flecks of silver in it. Sunken, boar-like eyes stared at Varro, framed between the blackened soles of his feet.

Something iron hung from a leather strip gleamed at the center of his chest.

Though drunk, the chief's reactions were as fast and sharp as the best-trained soldiers Varro knew. As he struggled to disentangle himself from the animal skin rug he had slipped on, the chief leaped out of bed and then grabbed his short sword. The two women, now awakened, screamed in terror.

Varro raised his own sword in time to parry the chief's thrust. He was still against the bed, the pelt underfoot as slippery as spilled oil. The clash of blade on blade rang out in Varro's ears. Rather than try to meet this barbarian, Varro pushed up onto his bed. The Turdentani chief was a brutish, hulking shadow in the gloom. His blade glittered as he pulled back for another strike.

Something warm and soft slipped over his head and then yanked him back. The chief's stab failed to penetrate, its force blunted from both an animal pelt and Varro's mail.

The women had thrown their covers over him and now tried to hold him down. Mail notwithstanding, Varro knew he was at the chief's mercy. So he slashed out with his gladius and felt it bite flesh. A woman screamed in pain and the covers slipped away.

Varro slid off the bed to thud on the floor as the chief crashed atop his women in his blind rage. He could not see the details in the darkness, only the mass of the chief leaping upon his bed to stab into nothing while his two women recoiled with ear-piercing shrieks.

Not wasting his moment, Varro sprang to his feet and plunged the gladius at the chief. But he too was wrapped up in his animal pelts and the thrust turned aside on the fur.

Now the chief cursed and seized Varro's sword arm to thrust with his own. Varro heard mail snap and felt a burn under his arm, but he had avoided the worst of the strike. So rather than try to escape the barbarian, he pushed into him and used his enemy's momentum to slam him back onto the bed. Varro freed his sword arm with a grunt and dragged the point across the chief's face. He growled like a bear and pawed at his slashed face. In the next moment, Varro brought his gladius back into the side of his neck.

The women let out horrified screams as their chief and lover arched his back and slapped his huge hand over his neck. While Varro couldn't see the wound, he felt the hot blood arc up to splash over his face and shoulder.

He slid off the bed, dragging the heavy skins with him. One woman charged at him with something like a club held overhead. She was a hissing shadow that cursed him even when he plunged his sword through her stomach. Whatever she held was heavy and it tumbled out of her grip to thud on his shoulder. She followed it to the floor, landing atop Varro's feet.

The last woman cowered in the corner, holding her slashed arm and spitting defiance at him. He paused, his sword wavering. The wind rattled the walls and the thin shouts of the enemy sounded behind it. The woman continued to curse him, but backed away from his cocked blade.

No more thought. He plunged the gladius into her shadowed body and she curled up around it with a pitiful cry, no more the defiant she-wolf. Her pulse thrummed up the blade into Varro's hand. He pulled the sword free and left her groaning as she died. He then turned back to the bed and ran his hand along the slain chief's hairy chest. His fingers closed over the key hanging there, and he yanked it free. Before leaving, he snatched the bearskin from the floor.

Outside, he found Centurion Longinus on his feet. He had hobbled to the door and closed it as well as set the bar. Someone banged on it and shouted.

"Did you get the keys?"

Varro nodded and looked to the hearth. It had burned down to red coals with a thin ribbon of fire still dancing with the air current. Set against the stone of the hearth were the tools for its maintenance, bellows, iron poker, and spade.

"You have my pugio for now," he said as he crossed the hall. The banging outside now became kicks. "Wear this bear skin. It will serve as your armor."

Longinus stood still as Varro fit the key to release his manacles before squatting to do the same for his feet.

"You're bleeding," Longinus said. "Is it bad?"

"My shoulder still hurts worse. They cut you up, Centurion."

"Let me at these animals and I'll show you what cut up is. These are scratches."

The irons around Longinus's feet clicked open and he kicked free. The bearskin covered him, but he would have to hold it in place with one hand.

Men at the door shouted as they rammed. The planks buckled and the bar groaned; it would not hold long.

"There's no other way out?" Varro asked, and Longinus confirmed he had seen no other. "Open the door on my command, and we'll fight our way out. We then head to the gate and open it for Falco."

Longinus blinked at him, but he already turned back. He raced to the hearth, grabbed the ash-stained spade, and shoveled out the burning coals. When he rejoined Longinus, he gave a thin smile on his swollen face.

"Open."

Longinus lifted the bar and the door flew open.

Varro launched the burning coals at the enemies who piled into the entrance. Flaming embers blazed with the rush of air as they blasted across the enemy. They fell back screaming into the rain. The coals fizzled into the mud as Varro charged with the spade, wielding it like an ax.

Outside, four men had pulled the dead bodies from the door and had been trying to batter their way inside. Now they danced with hot coals smoking in their collars and in their hair.

Varro buried the spade into the neck of the nearest man, nearly decapitating him. Then he drew his gladius once more as Longinus rushed out behind him. Rather than use his bear skin as armor, he threw it over the head of an enemy.

But Varro did not see how that fight ended, for he was already upon the next man. He stabbed and dodged and kept his calm while his enemies panicked. It made for easy work, and when he turned back, Longinus was wiping the pugio on the cloak of the dead man.

"Thanks for lending it to me," he said, extending the dagger. "I'll use one of their swords."

The village had at last come to life and shadows raced around the intermittent light of torches and the bonfire. Voices shouted all around, but Varro could not distinguish how many and how near. The rain raised a blue haze across the ground and turned the earth into mud. The barbarians suffered the same debility and so ran in confusion when they found no obvious danger.

"To the gate," Varro said, pointing to the entrance. "Aulus and my men will be there. The barbarians still don't know what's happening."

So they dashed across the open field that spilled toward the front gate. Longinus huddled in his bearskin, and in the confusion, they did not draw attention from their enemies. The common tribesmen either raced around or else bolted themselves inside their homes.

Reaching the gate, Aulus was already there with the two others from the ladder team, which they seemed to have abandoned. A dozen dead bodies lay in the mud, javelins protruding from some of their backs.

"We put barbarian javelins to good use," Aulus said. "Help us get the bar off."

Longinus jumped to help them, but Varro saw the Turdentani coming to defend their gate. At least a score of warriors had assembled, and they now rushed forward through the sheeting rain.

Varro fished out the wooden whistle he used as a centurion for commanding his men in battle. It would produce a loud and shrill tone that could slice through any noise. It had to carry, for nothing was louder than the front line of a battle. He drew a deep breath, then sounded the whistle. He blasted over and over as the others lifted the gate bar aside. It was a massive timber like the ridge beam of a titan's hall. But now it splashed into the muddy ground and Longinus led the effort to haul open the gates.

Just as the Turdentani were within reach, Varro heard the shrill answer from Falco's own whistle. It was faint, even though he was just within reach of the main walls. These had no parapets or men to walk them. They were intended to keep out animals or brigands, but not to use as a fighting platform.

Through the wavering gloom of the rain, Varro saw the glistening bronze of Falco's lead ranks emerge. Their pounding feet were as thunder in the rain.

The Turdentani now rushed to close their gates, but Falco sounded the charge.

In the end, Varro stepped aside as nearly five hundred of Rome's finest men clamored to enter the Turdentani stronghold. He fought small skirmishes, spent from his efforts to save Longinus and open the gates. If an enemy fled, he let him.

It took all night, but Falco's men spread to every corner and brought bloody doom to all they encountered. By dawn, Varro was weary but back in command. The sun rose on carnage on a scale he had not seen since his battles in Greece. Yet he had to ensure no one lived, as this was Cato's command.

The rain had ended and the puddles that reflected the nascent sun were stained red. It left the buildings too soaked to set afire. Even the bonfire had died in the torrent. So Varro could not destroy the place, but he could make it so no other Turdentani would want to live there.

He reunited with his command group, and Longinus now wore a filthy tunic looted from the Turdentani.

"It stinks," he said as he observed the final mop-up of the settlement. "Looks like we've carried out our orders."

Varro nodded, trying not to look too hard at the women and children among the pile of corpses. He reminded himself that these would grow up to become cannibals just like their fathers had been.

Falco's eyes were ringed with heavy black circles. "I barely heard your whistle. That rain was fierce last night. I thought the boys were going to revolt. Fortunately, they didn't have any warm fires to retreat to."

"I think the gods sent that rain," Varro said. "Aulus, did you find Servius?"

He shook his head. "Unless you want me to go through the body pile, sir."

"No, he's probably dead. I'm sure he would've tried to fight and so met his end. What is our cost?"

Tubicen Gaius and Signifier Lars both looked at each other, then at Falco.

"I don't think we lost anyone." Falco frowned. "Some were hurt, of course. But we took this place with complete surprise. Most of them were trying to escape through the rear. There's a small gate back there, too."

"Was there?" Varro narrowed his eyes. "And our fat prisoner?"

"He found his wife, if you can believe it. I don't know about his children."

Before setting back down the mountain, he ordered the walls torn down and the Turdentani bodies piled up where they had hung the captive Romans. He then had their chief's head set on a pole so that he looked down on his dead tribesmen. He abandoned the last survivor, his wounded captive, to the remnants of his family. His wounds would likely kill him, but Varro had kept his promise.

The men were weary from lack of sleep, but no one wanted to

encamp so close to this carnage. So he marched them down the mountain paths, carrying the few wounded and the slain captives. By the end of the day, he led the column out of the mountains. As they stepped onto level ground and saw Cato's camp, they cheered. Varro allowed it, though he knew he should enforce discipline. Only Longinus seemed disturbed by the lapse.

"I understand they're tired," he said to Varro as they trudged at the column's front. "But they know better."

"There will be plenty of discipline back in camp, Centurion Longinus. It's not as if they are slowing down their pace."

The First Spear scowled and fell to silence. Then he sighed and patted Varro's aching shoulder.

"You took an incredible risk to save my life. I think they wanted to use me for bargaining leverage. But I know you wouldn't negotiate, and I also know this mountain tribe is a bloodthirsty lot. My dreams will be forever haunted after witnessing what they did to our men. They would have done the same to me, and maybe worse. If you had attacked before rescuing me, I would've died with my hands bound. I owe you my life. There is no one else in this army mad enough to do what you did."

"Mad," Varro said with a chuckle. "That's true. Listen, Centurion Longinus, soon I may need your understanding and support in something of great importance. I hope I can count on that?"

Longinus's swollen face was incapable of subtle expression, yet Varro still sensed doubt there.

"Of course you can count on me," he said. "You were willing to trade your life for mine. How could I betray that?"

Varro noticed Falco listening in as he followed behind. He then called a rest period for the column, as a long march remained ahead to reach camp. During this time, he maneuvered Falco away from the column now stretched out on the grass or sitting against gray boulders. Only Longinus remained on foot, and again walked the length of the column with his vine cane ready to excoriate anyone he judged out of regulation.

"If he ever made consul," Falco said as they both watched him striding down the line. "He'd be harder than Cato. He'd drive us into the ground."

"You heard what I said to him?"

Falco's heavy brows drew together, and he nodded.

"As hard as this mission was, it did clear my mind of all that sneaky bullshit we left in camp. I'd even forgotten about Curio. All I could think of was the next step forward and if I'd live through the next fight. Nothing more complicated."

"The same for me," Varro said, peering after Longinus. "Commanding even a small force like this took all my concentration. And I had to make some decisions that don't sit well with me. How could I think of anything else?"

Falco waved his hand as if trying to clear the air.

"It comes with the command. I thought you gave up that whole peace-thing years ago. There's no sense in it, especially serving in the legion."

"It's not a peace-thing." Varro's voice rose, and Aulus, who sat with the command group, glanced back. So he continued in a measured tone. "It was a vow to the gods. One I've broken so often I cannot imagine what black pit they will toss me in when I die."

"A vow you made as a boy. It doesn't count once you become a man."

"Do you just make up these rules when it suits you?"

Falco flashed a smile. "It's been working great so far."

Shaking his head, Varro stepped closer.

"Look, I still plan to accuse Placus for stealing the silver. Centurion Longinus will support me now even if he's mad at my choice."

"He should give support after all you did for him. I'd have not taken that chance, not for him anyway."

"That's not why I did it. But in any case, I'm not sure we'll need Longinus's support. Just like you said, this battle cleared my mind as well. Remember when we set out, I said something was wrong but I couldn't tell what it was? Well, this entire march down the mountain, I've thought about it with a clear mind. And now I know what it is."

Falco stood straighter and looked around as if someone might leap out from behind the dozens of boulders dotting the foothills. He then raised his eyebrows.

Varro licked his lips. He had been thinking all morning in a state of near-exhaustion. Maybe his conjectures were wrong, produced from a weary brain. But by now he had convinced himself he was right and could share his ideas with Falco.

"I know who gave us the silver. I don't know why, but I have my suspicions. And I think we're in far more danger than we ever realized."

15

Varro stood before Consul Cato's command tent, staring at two burly guards he had never seen before. He even wondered if these men were from the legion or local brutes fitted with Roman helmets and given Roman gear. Their impassive eyes met his, but they did not move. Instead, they held their spears at rigid attention.

As the sun set, the camp remained active. The reunion of weary men to their home units made for a minor celebration. The count of the dead and injured dampened this mood, but Varro still heard laughter and animated conversations echoing in the cool evening air. A heavy stench of cabbage emanated from within Cato's tent.

Having been summoned alone, and having not yet seen Curio, Varro knew his fears were about to be realized. His only consolation was that he had no legitimate way out of what he expected next. He had led the column back in triumph, been greeted by Tribune Manius and Consul Cato, and provided a debrief to them. By now he had gone so long without sleep that he no longer felt tired.

His hesitation drew a frown from one guard, who then pulled aside the tent flap to allow Varro entrance.

He ducked into a warmly lit space, where Consul Cato sat at his desk as if he had never moved since the last summons. He had stacked a pile of wax tablets to his right side to show he had reviewed these, while a smaller stack sat to his left. The consul looked up from his reading, the lamp on his desk casting a thick light over the folds and dips of his face. His expression of disgust at least flattened out when he addressed him.

"Centurion Varro, please enter and be at ease. We've important matters to discuss."

Varro stepped into the tent and the scent of boiled cabbage filled his nostrils. A plain bronze bowl sat beside the tablets with a wooden spoon sitting in the remains of a cloudy broth. Cato pushed it away as if someone would clear it, yet only he and Varro were in the tent.

"I must congratulate you again, Centurion. You handled the barbarians magnificently. Centurion Longinus made it clear that he is only alive through your heroic efforts. Truly, such daring is rare in the ranks."

"Thank you, sir."

His mouth was tacky and his stomach burned. Cato seemed genuine in his praise, making the next moments even more terrifying for him.

"Well, time for your report. You have brought the results of Tribune Galenus's investigation?"

"Yes, sir." Varro looked around. "But I thought Tribune Manius would be present?"

Cato waved the slate in his hand before setting it down.

"Once you share your findings, we can review them with him if necessary. Please, we have only limited time."

Varro cleared his throat and produced the wax tablet that

contained his summary of the investigation. He set it with a soft clack on Cato's desk, but the consul did not move to touch it.

"Sir, a triarius by the name of Placus under the command of First Spear, Centurion Longinus, was seen leaving the camp with a mule-drawn cart and crate that matches the shape and size used by the paymasters. He was gone several hours and returned with an empty cart. The tribune has the testimony and sworn statements of two witnesses. The tessarius has also made a statement as well. But, then again, sir, you should have all this as part of Tribune Galenus's belongings. Perhaps you have not reviewed his notes?"

"Perhaps I have not." Cato now collected the wax tablet and opened the wood cover. He tilted his head back and raised his brows to scan it, then clapped it down to his desk.

"So, you believe Placus acted alone? He went to the treasury and picked out his favorite box of denarii, then threw it on a stolen cart and left camp unnoticed for several hours. You give this Placus fellow a great deal of credit. He bypassed so many other guards, yet was somehow observed in detail by men who report to Centurion Falco. Quite a coincidence."

"These are Tribune Galenus's conclusions, sir. I'm certain you would find them written in his personal notes. Perhaps those will provide more details than he shared with me."

Cato gave a sharp smile. "Well, then I shall have a look. So, we should summon the First Spear and his man, Placus."

"Unfortunately, sir, Placus was killed in the fighting at Emporiae." Varro's stomach ached and his feet were like ice, but he persisted in his lie. "We do not know where Placus buried the silver. The tribune believed it must be near the coast, and he planned to retrieve it at a better time, perhaps even after the campaign was finished and the legions sent home."

"An elaborate scheme for one man," Cato said. "You are certain he had no other help? Perhaps Centurion Longinus himself? As First Spear, he has more liberties than all but a tribune."

"Centurion Longinus is above reproach, sir."

Cato's explosive laughter jarred Varro. So far, their exchange had been sedate. But the consul leaned back in his chair as he laughed and slapped his desk.

"No man is ever above reproach. There is always something hidden behind even the most sincere smile."

"That is a terrible way of thinking, if I may be bold, sir."

"Terrible?" Cato's mirth vanished and he leaned across the desk to fix one eye on Varro. "Or practical? I say your view of the world is naïve. Not something I would expect from a seasoned veteran such as you, and especially not from one who carries that pugio of yours. Such a childish understanding of people will one day cost you, Centurion Varro."

Varro remained at attention and bit back on his reply. He had fed Cato the story, and whatever happened next was beyond his control. At last, Cato's smile faded and he folded his hands atop the desk.

"Have you considered my offer any further?"

"Sir?"

Cato lowered his head with a bitter smile.

"You are a stubborn man, aren't you? You cannot see what is to your own advantage, but cling to what you wish to believe. Another useless way of thinking, Centurion. You should be more practical. Such as Centurion Curio."

The name nearly knocked Varro flat. But he had to remain calm.

"What about Curio, sir?"

Spreading his hands, Cato looked about as if Curio were hiding in the shadows. "Well, you must have noticed? Curio and I have come to an understanding about what is best for his future. After all, I urged him to become literate. I promoted him to his current rank. And while I have not bribed him with coin, I have shown him less tangible but far more powerful benefits of aligning himself to me. In every meaningful way, I have always been his benefactor. He now understands this and no longer resists the idea. He only needed to be away from your naïve thinking to come to the correct decision. He's practical, unlike you."

"Is he, sir?" Varro raised his brow. "Well, you have no need of me or Falco in this case. Curio will have exposed all those secrets that you have been seeking."

Cato tilted his head. "Yes, of course. But why would I not want you and Falco to join us? Really, you disappointment me with such short-term thinking. Look at your achievements, Centurion. A man does not set aside his best sword when he goes to war. Don't you see I have been developing you for greater things? I assigned you as a liaison to our Ilegertes allies, and you had outstanding success. I then placed you with Tribune Galenus to increase your strategic skills. Now I assigned you a command of five hundred men, and look at your victory. Yes, it was yours alone, Tribune Varro. I need no more convincing that you would serve as an excellent replacement for Galenus."

Varro stuttered his response. "Sir, I am not of the right class."

"Nonsense," Cato said, his face folding up so that it reminded Varro of a cabbage. "A military tribune can come from any class if the man has a record such as yours. The consul makes all final appointments. Tribune Galenus has fallen in battle. I can see you in his place."

"Sir, there are dozens of other qualified men in the cavalry."

"I need men who can execute my commands, not who fulfill social niceties. Tribune Varro, doesn't the title sound right? A relative of yours once served as a consul years ago in the war against Hannibal. Surely we can find some precedent in your family if we needed."

"I'm not sure of that relation, sir. No one in my family ever spoke of him. I don't know where he is or if he is even still alive."

Cato's eyes flashed and he smirked. "He was at Cannae, after all. Not Rome's or his finest moment. But do not put me off the discussion. I have made an offer to you. Will you continue to stand with Flamininus or will you pursue your own best interests and join me and Curio?"

Now was Varro's moment to test his theory.

"Sir, if you can confirm what Curio has revealed to you, then I might consider that offer."

"I will ask the questions." Cato's voice slipped into his commander's voice. "What is your choice? No more games."

"Sir, I believe you plan many more games." Varro's stomach fluttered and his breath was hot. But he as he spoke he gained confidence.

"Be careful how you speak to me," Cato warned. "I am your consul."

"Right now, we are just two men. You won't answer my simple question because Curio revealed nothing. That is because Curio has not joined with you. You're dividing and defeating us just as you would a larger enemy force."

Cato gave a wide smile.

"So you can suspect others of bad intentions. Good, I had thought you hopelessly idealistic." Cato leaned back and licked his lips. "But he has revealed Flamininus's shame to me, and why Flamininus paid so much to hide it."

"Then you have no reason to hide it from me. Tell me what Curio revealed. If he is truly with you, then perhaps I should reconsider my stance."

Cato stared hard at him, and to Varro he looked like a bear with its front paw in a trap. He collected his hands together and leaned forward, speaking in a low, snarling voice.

"Flamininus nearly lost the Macedonian war indemnity to some of his scheming tribunes. You three recovered it for him."

Varro stepped back as if staggered by a punch. His head felt wooly and his stomach churned.

Curio had gone over. He had revealed Flamininus's fumbling of the indemnity. It seemed impossible, but everything lined up now. Lars the Signifier had seen Curio meet with Cato in private. His optio had suspected he worked in secret, and these times did not line up with anything Varro had asked him to do. So now Varro had confirmation, something he could not believe even as Cato sat back and folded his arms in victory.

"Will you give up your pugio? Remember, Tribune Varro, I make my offers in the light and not the shadow."

"No you don't." Varro narrowed his eyes and his fists balled. "You twist the truth of things and use intimidation to get what you want. Sir, here's a question for you. What is your ruling in the case of Placus's theft?"

Cato's brow furrowed.

"I don't see how that is connected. I will decide after examining your witnesses."

"Sir, you are standing nowhere in the light. We both know who stole that silver, and now I know why."

Cato sat back, head titled to the side with a bemused smile. He blinked before speaking in a relaxed voice.

"You think I know who stole the silver?"

"Of course." Varro folded his arms and straightened his back. "You stole it. You are the only one who could have done so without raising any questions. You arranged it with Tribune Galenus. This entire investigation was a sham to create fear and panic between me, Falco, and Curio. You hoped it would make us easier to manipulate."

Cato's smile faded and he mirrored Varro's folded arms.

"There are simpler ways to create fear in a man."

"Maybe. But if we do not agree to join with you, then you will frame us for the theft. Giving us the silver served a dual purpose: to assuage the Ilegertes and act as leverage against us. You are the consul, after all. No one else could've slipped that chest onto the cart. You knew everything we were doing and set us up."

"So you are admitting to the theft?" Cato leaned forward, a wicked smile now spreading on his face. "Well, that changes everything."

"There was no theft," Varro said, his voice straining to remain calm. "Treasury funds are yours to dispense as you see fit. Nor is there any gap in the men's pay unless you choose to make it so. You have every means to replace what you claim was stolen."

Cato sat back, the lamplight creating dark shadows in the crags of his face. His eyes seemed to float in two puddles of ink. He did not speak, but remained staring with both arms folded across his chest. In response, Varro stood to attention.

"This is my last offer to join me and Curio. Remember you are here with me and Flamininus is far away. Now that I know his secret, he will no longer trust you. You will be friendless in this world, and, since you entrusted your riches to his handling, you will know nothing but bitter poverty. So choose carefully, Tribune Varro. One choice leads into darkness, and the other might one day see you sitting where I am now."

"Then both choices lead to darkness." Varro stood at attention, eyes fixed on the gloom of the private section of the command tent behind Cato.

"How poetic," Cato said, shaking his head. "Are you truly this foolish?"

"I have given my vow to Servus Capax. I will not break it." He shifted his eyes to meet Cato's, which now regarded him like a raptor about to swoop down on a rat. Varro gritted his teeth. "I joined Servus Capax of my own will and was offered rewards for loyal service to Rome. Not to any one person, not Flamininus, Galba, or anyone else."

Cato's eyes narrowed and his lips pressed until they turned white. But Varro would not hold back.

"It was an offer made freely and one accepted freely. But you, Consul Cato, twist the truth, scheme in secret, and lie. You offer a threat disguised as a choice. You would see friendships divided to keep control over your servants. But Servus Capax used strength in friendships to achieve a higher goal. What have you to offer me but more lies, more darkness, and the shame of breaking my vow to serve Rome and serve only one man? A man who deceives his allies, his soldiers, and himself.

"No, sir, I decline your offer. I decline it today and tomorrow. I decline it and accept whatever mockery of justice you intend to use in ruining me. Do dangle your enticements of rank before me. Do not think that I would sell my honor because you led my friends astray. I will not waver, no matter what you bring against me."

Cato now unfolded his arms and sat back as if wearied from a long march. For the moment, Varro was flush with righteousness and gloated over the slouching consul. But the moment was both vain and fleeting.

Cato let go a long sigh.

"You cannot fault me for not allowing you a last speech. Bolds words, Centurion Varro, delivered with authentic emotion. Words that would move the hearts of men. I wonder what we could have achieved together if I could have instructed you in oration. If you think strength of arms alone changes the world or saves the lives of men, then you are wrong. Words have both killed more and saved more than any one soldier fighting from the shadows. But I suppose we are past that now."

Varro again stood to attention, his body rigid and trembling with fury and fear coursing through him. His mind raced over what would come next. What would happen to Curio and Falco? Why had he not figured out Cato from the start? He could have done more to save all of them from this mess.

The consul made another remark that Varro was too distracted to hear. But then he straightened up at his desk, restoring the same confident and curmudgeonly appearance Varro knew so well.

"Well, you have admitted to stealing from the treasury. This is a grave offense, even if at the time you considered your actions necessary to serve Rome. A soldier's pay is also necessary, and now I will have to inform the men that you have stolen it. Of course, we'll have a trial when we reach the north again."

"A trial?" Varro raised his brows and sneered. "You're going to put on a show for the men?"

"I can't have them misguided into believing you are some sort of hero. You stole their pay and handed it to a marginally loyal ally. People like you and the other scum of Servus Capax cannot exist when exposed in the light. It is my duty to dispel the shadows, after all."

"So you will just accuse me at trial and everyone will accept? You call me naïve, yet you think the men who serve you are all stupid. Most will be wise enough to see what you are doing. And all that effort of yours to bond with the common soldier will have gone to waste."

Cato smiled and it made Varro pause. The smile was serene and confident, but also brimming with anticipation. The consul shifted on his chair so that his body pointed toward the gloomy private area behind him.

"Well, as it happens, I have a credible witness who is equally beloved of the men."

Now someone shuffled in the gloomy area sectioned off by long drapes. A figure seemed to rise from sitting then pulled the drape aside.

Varro looked into the swollen and bruised face of Centurion Longinus. He nodded to Consul Cato, then looked unflinchingly at Varro.

"Yes, sir. I will be your witness to Centurion Varro's theft and his admission of guilt. I saw him loading the cart at the treasury with the help of some others. There is no mistake, though. One of the thieves is this man right here."

Cato turned his smile back to Varro.

"You'll be held under guard until we reach the north," he said through the smile. "At which time Centurion Longinus will present his testimony at your trial. Until then, enjoy your days. The punishment for such a crime is of course the fustuarium—execution by clubbing."

16

Varro and Falco both spent the last three days marching along the rugged tracks north, passing the edges of deep forests or crawling over hilltops spotted with sparse vegetation. Being relieved of all his gear and weapons made the march easier on him. Falco was equally disarmed and marched on the other side of the lead rank where Cato kept them. Both had their hands bound at their laps. While Varro could not see his friend behind the horses of Cato's bodyguards, he knew he must have hung his head the same way Varro did.

Even if the march did not physically burden him, humiliation added a burden like no other he had ever felt. Behind him, three thousand sets of eyes stared at him and each stung like a scourge. While he had done nothing wrong and had not yet been formally charged, everyone knew he and Falco had suffered some disgrace.

When encamped on the march, Varro and Falco were held in separate locations with four guards each selected from the cavalry. They were provided regular meals which they did not need to cook. They did not take part in nightly camp constructions. As far as marches went, this was one of the easiest Varro could recall. But atop the humiliation, loneliness also bothered him. Cato had barred them from communication. If they made a sound, their guards would threaten them into silence. Though these lacked genuine conviction, as neither Varro nor Falco had been yet stripped of rank.

Varro had been among soldiers for years and he knew how to read their moods. He and Falco's imprisonment did not sit well with them, and their confusion and anger manifested in less laughter and more whispers.

The five hundred men who had accompanied him into the mountains had all been drawn from different centuries. Varro now understood that Cato had done so because he expected this moment, and did not want them to join in support of their new hero. Instead, they mixed into the three thousand and their support for Varro would dilute in such numbers.

For his part, Varro accepted his predicament but never failed to test his bonds in case he might escape. At every meal, the ropes were untied so that he could eat and drink. The cavalrymen who guarded him had been contemptuous or neutral, with only one exhibiting anything like respect. His fellows teased him for it, and he replied that "we don't know why they're being held yet."

So Cato had not stirred up the men with threats of delayed pay. A soldier who might die any day did not want to learn his drinking and gambling funds would be paid at some future point. Today and only today was the time for a pot of wine and a dice game. Tomorrow he could find himself with an enemy sword in his belly. So once Cato did make his false accusations, Varro and Falco would lose any of the already thin support they held.

Of course, Curio would not have to worry.

Varro could not believe it, but it seemed Curio had truly gone over to Cato. The consul had wisely kept him from either himself or Falco. He marched along with his men in the column's rear.

Now that they had come to their final camp, any chance meeting with Curio effectively ended.

On the first day of their march, Varro spent it denying Curio's betrayal. On the second day, he would've cut Curio's throat if he had the chance. Now, on the third day, he considered Curio's decision more rationally. Of course, he had not joined Servus Capax for any other reason than to be with his friends. But after listening to Cato's chilling predictions, he might have decided it was best to preserve his fortune and his life. Certainly, there was a voice in Varro's mind telling him he had chosen a fool's death by remaining true to his vow. But Falco had not given in, and he came to that decision separately from Varro. Cato had questioned him at some time after guards led away Varro from the consul's tent. His reasoning was harder to understand, but Varro guessed he had done so out of loyalty. He would know Varro wouldn't give in, and so made the same choice.

It had taken three days of fast marching to reach Cato's planned base of operations. Now that Cato settled his army, he ordered a pen constructed outside the camp to hold them. This was a further humiliation as setting men outside the camp symbolized disowning them. Everyone in the army now knew they were to be considered outcasts even before any sort of trial took place.

They would remain under guard until the time came for Cato and the treacherous Centurion Longinus to convince Tribune Manius of their guilt. Of course, Varro knew that the tribune was already convinced and would follow Cato's instructions to the letter. It was no doubt the reason the consul had selected him to come north.

So by nightfall, Varro met Falco as they were both herded into the pen. Four men stood guard around it, one on each side. They were triarii from Longinus's century and their long spears, heavy shields, and chain shirts ensured four were enough to handle two bound men. Now their legs were bound as well as their hands. Both of them sat on the cold grass as the sun set. Their four guards complained about drawing the duty and spoke loudly about how it would all be over by tomorrow.

Varro stared at Falco across from him. Dressed in a plain tunic with no military gear, he seemed more like the boy who had left the farm with Varro years ago. Only now he had a crazed and angry look in his eyes. Neither spoke until the sun set, as if darkness would somehow make their whispers inaudible to anyone else. So they shifted on the grass until resting back to back. Varro had a view of the camp and the torches being lit for the first watch of the night.

"Cato can't kill me," Falco said. "I'm already dead."

"Are you certain? Your back feels warm enough."

"I mean Curio. He fucking betrayed us."

Varro closed his eyes. "He saved himself, that's all. If we were all going down on a sinking ship, would you blame him if he jumped onto a raft?"

"Well, he's jumping onto a raft with room enough for the two of us. But then he's sailing off on his own. So I'd not only blame him, but if I could reach the raft, then I'd flip it over and watch him drown."

Varro chuckled and nudged Falco's back.

"I know. I've thought about it too. During this march, I have had time to think."

"Tell me you've thought of a way out of this mess. I'm too young and handsome to be beaten to death in a muddy field far from home. Wherever home is anymore."

"I don't have a plan. Run if one or both of us can get free. Maybe if we could get back to Rome somehow, then we could explain ourselves to Flamininus. He might protect us."

Falco snorted. "Not much of a plan. Besides, Flamininus will probably blame us. We'd get nothing from him."

"We'd at least get a fair trial." Varro tested the rope tied around his wrists once more, finding it as tight as the last check. "I always suspected Cato might want to be rid of us, but I never once thought he'd see us killed like this."

"What do you expect from someone like him? He thinks anyone not of his class is worthless. To him, killing us is like throwing out garbage to normal people. We're just shit on his floor to sweep away."

Varro considered those words, letting the silence return. Their guards paced and yawned, staring out at the night-shrouded hills. They seemed unconcerned with their whispering, so he continued.

"I've been thinking about Curio more today."

Falco growled at the name. "Well, don't ruin your last days alive thinking of a traitor. He should've been tied up with us tonight."

"But he's not," Varro said. "And maybe that is by design."

He paused, expecting a stream of curses from Falco. Instead, he shifted on the grass and then remained still. So Varro continued to share what he had been thinking.

"Cato only knew about the war indemnity. He did not know about Philip's son and how he nearly became a usurper. That is by far the bigger story and would have more use to Cato than just knowing Flamininus almost lost the silver. In fact, who cares about something that almost happened?"

"Wait, you've been saying all along that Cato just needs a half-truth to wreck Flamininus's reputation. Now you're saying no one will care about it?"

"No, I'm saying that Cato doesn't know the actual story, but just part of it. He probably found out about the indemnity long before we even showed up in Iberia. Think of all the men that helped us with recovering it."

Falco cleared his throat. "Most of them are dead."

"But many are alive and they were richly rewarded. So you know what most men would do with that wealth."

"They'd get drunk playing dice and tell anyone who'd listen exactly how they became so rich." Falco shoved harder against Varro's back. "And so Cato would've known about this already and Curio didn't tell him anything new."

"Exactly so. And none of the men knew the situation with Philip's son. So Cato thinks he has the full story."

"Or he suspects he doesn't have the full story."

Varro paused at Falco's idea and tilted his head.

"You're probably right. But our revealing the stolen indemnity is Cato's loyalty test. If we will reveal the truth to him, even though he knew it already, then he could be sure of our loyalty. He could work on his suspicions later when we were fully under his control. I think Curio figured that out and is using it against Cato."

He could feel Falco's head shaking as they remained pressed back to back.

"He isn't so devious. If he did as you've described, then it's an accident."

"You underestimate him. Remember how fast he learned to write? He lacks confidence in his own judgment, and for years he has been subordinate in rank. So he follows our commands and sets aside his own ideas. But he is clever and he knows everyone."

"We never cared about rank when it was just us."

"Even so, our ranks were different. You've seen how he has changed since his promotion." Varro leaned forward, heart suddenly racing. "He's on the outside. He can get us free. I'm sure of it."

"Then what?" Falco's voice was bitter. "Free to really make ourselves guilty of deserting?"

"What happens next depends on how Curio plans to free us. He's going to save us once more, just as he did with Diorix."

Falco chuckled. "My hero, Curio. I'm still giving him a beating for putting us through this."

They both fell quiet. For Varro, his mind raced over what Curio could be plotting. He held a new admiration for his friend, for he could not see what Curio planned. Why he hadn't shared it with either him or Falco confused things. He had operated alone and was often gone on secret business. So his plan had been long in the making, for Signifier Lars had spotted him in a private meeting with both Tribune Galenus and the consul. Whatever he plotted probably required extreme secrecy, so that he could not even dare reveal it to his closest friends.

At last, Falco broke the silence.

"Whatever Curio is planning, it better include revenge on that treacherous shit, Longinus."

"Now there's a name I never want to hear again." Varro tapped his forehead with his bound hands. "To think how much I trusted him. He was never on our side. I'm sure Cato ordered him to get friendly with us just so he could spy on what we were doing."

"I told you it would've been better to let the barbarians eat his liver. But you had to be a hero."

"How could I have known at the time?" Varro pressed his eyes closed against the horrible memory of Centurion Longinus in Cato's tent. He had risked everything to save the centurion, and he did not even so much as flinch in his accusation. He was Cato's pet to his very heart and did not deserve the esteemed rank he held.

Falco let out a long sigh.

"And he ran to Cato the instant we showed up asking for help. What a shit. But how did Cato know we would show up and have the silver ready for us?"

Varro cocked his head. "He had a day to prepare it. It couldn't have been hard. He's the consul and can do whatever he wants. I'm sure he requisitioned the funds that morning and Longinus just sent it along to us."

The sound of Falco cursing and thumping his heels into the grass caught the attention of a guard. "What's that? Keep still over there!"

But something bothered Varro. While they both fell silent as the guards glared at them by the light of their torches, Varro considered Falco's question.

"Hold on, Falco. I think you've hit on something."

"Really? Usually I only hit things like your hard head."

Varro ignored the jibe, his mind swimming with rival ideas that fought for his attention.

"If Cato had requisitioned the money, then the paymasters would not be reporting it as missing."

"Right," Falco said in his most patronizing voice. "So he stole it, just."

"Even for a consul, stealing a full pay chest with no time to plan for it was a tremendous risk. If he wanted to set us up for a crime, he could've come up with anything. He could've even proclaimed us deserters when we left the Ilegertes fort. So why this specific crime? Why blame us for stolen pay?"

"That's right!" Falco leaned away, his voice rising with his excitement. "Everyone in the army would be enraged and would want to see us dead for it. It guaranteed no one would look deeper."

"Well, there is that," Varro said, tempering his friend's enthusiasm. "But it still does not answer why he undertook such a large risk on what must have been just a fortunate opportunity. I believe more is at play here."

"Would the great Centurion Varro then care to share his vast thoughts with lesser people like me?"

"I have to share it with someone, don't I?" He shoved back against Falco. "Think about it. He wants us to be guilty of stealing from the treasury. Why? Because that is his crime. Consul Cato is skimming off the treasury. It's why he had the chest ready when we showed up. He'd already stolen it. But then he saw an opportunity. He realized we would use it to keep the Ilegertes happy, whom he had just betrayed. Then he could later accuse us of stealing the silver to give it to what he called barely loyal allies."

"Consul Cato is stealing from the treasury?" Falco slouched against his back. "For what purpose? He is taking a fortune from the Iberian tribes. Can't he just be happy with those riches? Some people never have enough."

"I don't believe it is for himself." Varro summoned the memory of his first sight of the denarii, all clean and shining coins. "Sure, he takes spoils from the defeated tribes and takes what he needs from the land. But don't you remember when we first arrived in Iberia how he refused the merchants that followed our fleet?"

Falco now twisted around to face him.

"Sorry if I wasn't keeping updated with the most boring possible news. I was too busy learning how to be a soldier again."

"We talked about it in passing. You just don't remember. Anyway, Cato made a big deal of sending them away. He said, 'The war pays for itself.' You must remember that because it was the end of every joke for weeks."

"I remember him saying that, but what's the connection?"

"He did not want to pay the merchants in coin. Consul Cato claims he's on the side of Rome and we walk in the dark. It's all great poetry, but the key truth is there are factions at war with each other in the Senate." Varro raised both of his bound hands to emphasize his words. "Cato is diverting Roman coins to his faction. He can take wealth in iron and silver, slaves, and captured livestock. He can take barbarian coins, half of which are Carthaginian. But whoever he works for needs real Roman coins for whatever dirty work they're up to back home."

"Gods, Varro, that makes sense. But it doesn't do much for us." He held up his own bound hands. "We're still set up to be beaten to death at dawn. Even if we escape, we've no proof Cato has done anything wrong."

"Curio has proof," Varro said flatly. "He's close to uncovering something. Remember, he has friends working with the paymasters. Something must have broken loose there. Someone spoke to him or he pried up something."

"The paymasters are in on this, aren't they?" Falco said. "But then, why would they make such a public stink?"

"Because only one of them was in on it," Varro said. "And he must have died at Emporiae, since right after that battle the missing silver came to light. It was Cato's bad luck, though he had Galenus and Longinus threaten and misdirect the paymasters who remained. By now Cato has probably bent another of them to his side."

"So Curio knows the dirt?" Falco said, a smile growing. "And if we can all escape, then that's how we clear our names or prevent Cato from accusing us in the first place. Curio, you little bastard! Why didn't he tell us?"

"I don't know. But he's playing a deadly game. Cato is going to figure him out. I only hope he lives long enough to get all of us away and reveal what he discovered."

"Silence in there!"

One of the triarii guards now leaned over the rough wooden fence of their pen. He glowered at them then shook his head. "You're chattering like two boys at a festival. You know tomorrow you're both dead?"

"We're owed a trial," Falco said.

All the guards laughed and the one speaking to them slapped his forehead.

"You two aren't recruits. No one gets penned outside of camp if they're not guilty."

"You bastards should be in here," Falco shouted. "You don't

even know who you're serving. Longinus is scum, not even worth the mud between my toes."

"Watch what you say." The guard lowered his torch to better light them. "Or you might have an accident before your trial."

Falco and the guard continued to threaten each other, bringing the other three to the fence to join in. But something had caught Varro's eye.

Dark shapes rose from the ground and swept toward the triarii who had gathered themselves into a neat group.

While Falco shouted down his guards, who enjoyed riling him to even greater anger, Varro caught the gleam of metal.

And then the shadows sprang like specters of vengeance upon the guards.

17

Chapter-17

Black shapes enveloped the triarii guards, wrapping their hands over each one, then dragging him from the pen fence. Their torches shed burning flakes as they tumbled to the ground, momentarily illuminating the horrified faces of their bearers. As they vanished into darkness, Varro heard men struggling and something heavy thudding against flesh. The shouts of the guards were muffled as they wrestled against their attackers. Falco and the remaining guard both stopped in the middle of their cursing to stare in shock. Only Varro had expected the moment.

He leaped up onto his bound feet. Knowing he could not aid the fight, he could at least foul the last guard's attempt to draw his dagger. With a grunt, he launched himself shoulder-first into the guard.

The old triarius howled with surprise and staggered back. Varro slid down and crashed to the fence, bounced off it, then flopped to the ground. Dull pain rocked his shoulder where he had suffered a sling stone wound. But more terrifying was lying on his side with arms and legs bound while his enraged enemy cursed above him. He tensed, expecting a spear to lance into his exposed ribs.

Instead, he heard the crack of something heavy then a shout cut short before a thump into the grass. In the dark night, he heard others struggling. The dark shapes hovered over their victims and he heard rope being measured out through someone's hands. The shadowy attackers worked quickly, flipping over the guards and tying their arms back. Then the figures delivered vicious beatings to the prone guards before stopping to catch their breaths.

For a single moment, the night returned to pristine silence with not even a cricket to disturb it. Then Falco broke into it.

"By all the gods, Curio! You timed that well."

Varro squirmed onto his other side and now looked at the dark lump of a guard with a leather sack over his head and arms tied at his back. Someone bent to pick up his dropped torch before it went out.

"It's not Curio, sir."

Sitting upright again, Varro stared into the glare of torches as his rescuers opened the crude pen. He could only see shadows, but he recognized the voice.

"Aulus? What are you doing here?"

"I thought it should be obvious, sir. We're here to rescue you. Otherwise, you'll be dead tomorrow."

Aulus crouched beside him, holding the torch away. Varro felt its heat on the side of his face. One other went to Falco, who had shifted from rage to bewilderment at his change in fortune.

"But where's Curio?" He held his hands up for his rescuer to cut the bonds.

Varro did the same and asked the same of Aulus, who shook his head.

"I wouldn't know, sir. It took all my effort and attention to plan your escape. Since Curio has left the service, I don't see any reason to consider him further. Sorry, sir, I know you were friends, but he made his choice."

Aulus set the torch into the ground, then used both hands to slice through Varro's bindings.

"What are you talking about? What do you mean he left the service?"

"Servus Capax, sir. He's Cato's pet now, isn't he? I was warned Cato would be trouble for you, and so he has been. Worse than I expected."

The rope bonds on his wrists snapped free, but Varro hardly felt the release and the tingle of blood flowing back into his hands.

"You are with Servus Capax?"

Aulus now shifted down to Varro's ankles, but he looked up with a sly smile.

"You are quite smart, sir. But you cannot see what is right in front of you. I suppose you look at me and just see one more barbarian who thinks he's Roman. We have lived and fought side by side for months now. But you've never looked at me, have you?"

"I don't know what you're saying." Varro at last rubbed his stiff hands together as Aulus began cutting the rope binding his ankles. "I look at you every day."

"You see what you expect to see. But I've identified myself as Servus Capax from the moment I met you. You just didn't recognize it." He cut through the looser bindings on his feet and the rope popped away. He then reached for the torch and brought its light closer to his face. "Look again, sir."

While it was now nighttime, the golden light of the torch spread across Aulus's face. It was framed in wild, intertwined blue tattoos common to all the warriors in Iberia. He knew these markings meant certain things to others of their kind. To Varro, the tattoos had served only to obscure his face and to give him a fearsome countenance even at rest.

But now he saw it. On his left cheek at the bottom corner of his eye and melding into the swirling designs that reached back into his hairline was a stylized owl head.

It was a match to the Servus Capax mark on Varro's pugio.

A smile distorted the owl as Aulus nodded.

"You see it now, sir. You carry the sign on your pugiones, a bad idea in my opinion. But I wear the sign always."

"Why didn't you say something when I didn't recognize it?"

"My orders were not to join you, but to aid you if needed. So here I am. This is a time for my aid if there ever was."

The man assisting Falco to his feet hissed. "Can you save the explanations for later? I don't know what all this Servus Capax business means. But we've got to get out of here now."

"Tubicen Gaius?" Varro now gathered his legs under himself and stood. "I thought you were a coward."

"What?" Gaius frowned and shook his head. "Sir, you'll have to explain that one to me. I'm taking a massive risk to aid you."

The other rescuer applied gags to the hooded and unconscious guards. He had also arranged their torches around the pen, forcing them into the ground so that at least from camp it might appear they still kept watch. When he tied the last gag, he stood up and wiped his forehead before stepping into the light of a torch.

"You're here because we were both promised rewards. Promotions and pay, everything Aulus's friends can arrange for us. Don't treat Centurion Varro like a fool."

"Lars?" Varro could not believe the survivors of his command group had come to his rescue. Falco stood with his eyes wide and mouth agape.

"Yes, sir," Lars said as he again bent to check the binding on one guard. "Aulus explained it to us. You all work undercover for the Senate. Consul Cato is framing you for a crime that you didn't commit. I can't stand the man to begin with. But I've admired you, sir. I think you are a fine officer, and so do many others. Aulus says your secret organization will pay me well for helping you now. So, here I am. I am deserting the legion with you. Your senator friends better be true."

"It's all true," Varro said without hesitation. "I will guarantee it with my own life. I swear it to you."

"A new guard shift begins soon." Aulus guided both Varro and Falco by their arms out of the pen. "We can go into deeper explanations when we're away from here. But if we don't flee soon, we'll be lying beside these four unlucky men, but not unconscious."

Falco snorted, then spit. "They're lucky, all right. If I had a weapon, I'd cut their necks. Their Longinus's things. I can't even call them soldiers."

Aulus held up his palm. "Let's not give Cato more crimes to work with, sir. It was difficult to get four sacks, leather strips, and enough rope with no one asking questions."

Lars held up a small sack that sagged with weight. "We made our own saps. Seemed only right to beat them the way they planned to beat you tomorrow."

Varro smiled in appreciation. "Well, you gave them a hard beating. You better hope they survived it."

As if in reply, one of the knocked-out guards rolled to his side with a groan.

Aulus pointed to Gaius and Lars. "Use the last of the rope to tie their feet."

While they cooperated on this, Aulus drew both Varro and Falco together.

"I have your daggers here. Your swords and shields are with our horses. I've got your horse, sir. Centurion Falco can ride with you. I wasn't able to get much else. Recovering the pugiones was the best I could manage."

Falco chuckled. "If you only knew how often we've had to get Varro's back."

"Sir, that is why a tattoo is better. You should get one that you can reveal when you need to." Aulus then handed out the two pugiones.

Varro accepted the comforting weight into his hands. While the pugio was sheathed, he had no harness to hang it on. They had stripped him to his tunic and not even allowed a cord belt. "Where did you leave our horses?"

"We couldn't get them out of camp," Aulus said. "Not without notice. I thought it best to rescue you first, then retrieve them. We've got them picketed at the edge. I was sure to pull up some spikes there after it was inspected and loosened a few others. We'll grab the horses, jump the ditch, and be away. No one will be the wiser."

"You've just cursed us," Falco said.

After binding the guards' feet, both Lars and Gaius joined their huddle.

"We have to get Curio." Varro pulled out of Aulus's grip. "I don't believe he's Cato's pet. In fact, I think he's probably headed here to conduct his own rescue."

But Aulus bit his lip and lowered his head.

"I'm sorry, sir. He was with Cato this afternoon. I don't know what they discussed, but he came and went with no guards."

"That means nothing," Varro said, his voice hardening. "He has what we need to prove not only our innocence but also to keep Cato from charging all of us. We must get him away or else we'll have no leverage to bargain with Cato."

Before Aulus could protest, Falco broke in.

"Forget who Curio is working for," Falco said. "Let's just grab him and be on our way. If he really joined with Cato, we'll beat sense back into his thick skull later on."

Gaius held up both hands. "Sir, we're all deserters now. So I'm forgetting rank and telling you that's not what we planned. I'm not going into camp again. We're out and now we're getting you out. Centurion Curio can deal with his own problems."

Varro shook his head. "Gaius, I am forever in your debt. I won't ask you to follow me into any more danger. Get out of Iberia and find Senator Flamininus. Tell his household guards you're from Servus Capax. It will get his immediate attention. He'll take care of you, I'm certain. Same for you, Aulus and Lars."

Lars nodded, but gave a sly grin.

"Right, sir. I've never been afraid of a fight, though. And if you're telling me I can crack Centurion Curio on the head, then I'm with you. Since we're all outlaws now, I don't mind saying he can be an arrogant prick."

Falco covered his mouth to squelch a laugh. But Aulus sighed.

"We're running out of time. If we're doing this, then it must be now."

"I'm not doing it," Gaius said. "Maybe Centurion Varro thinks I'm a coward. But I'm being practical. Centurion Curio is in the middle of the camp surrounded by his men. If you go there, you'll be caught. There won't be a trial then."

Varro warned Gaius to silence with a look, then turned to Aulus. "What is your plan from here? Where do we run?"

"There is a secluded spot among the hills north of here with a nearby stream and plenty of game. We should be able to hide there while we work out a deal with the locals. They'll help smuggle you to the Ilegertes, and from there I'm certain they will get you on a ship for Rome. After that, it's on you to reach Flamininus and explain the situation."

Falco folded his arms. "The Ilegertes are Roman allies. They're legally bound to hand us over to Cato."

"No," Aulus said flatly. "They may be of a different tribe from mine, but all tribes live and die by their honor. Albus will not forget what you did for him, nor will his father. In fact, they will be relieved to dispense with their debt to you. For they owe you more than they can repay."

"You're quite clear on what we've been doing," Varro said. "We have much to discuss when this is done. But I agree we are wasting time here. Let's get to camp. Gaius, you can scout ahead and wait for us in the foothills."

The former tubicen turned to look at the black humps of the forested hills, then looked at Varro with an expression of utter terror.

"I can't go out there myself. I'll get lost. There might be wolves."

"Then come with us," Aulus said. "Hurry, the guard change is soon and then our chances of escape will plummet."

They gathered the triarii spears, though Varro wished for a sword. He and Falco stripped off their harnesses, then fit them as tightly as they could to themselves. With help from the others, they were ready to head back to camp. One of the bound guards groaned as they fled the area.

A Roman marching camp at rest, even a reduced force of three thousand, was an awesome sight even by starlight. The perfect square of it bristled with sharpened wooden stakes and a ditch that would trip up horses and anyone foolish enough to charge. Neat rows of tents were faint gray patches under the night sky, but the straight lines and ordered paths spoke of strength.

"The guards on duty aren't especially vigilant." Aulus leaned into Varro to whisper. "But we are twice asking for Fortuna's blessing tonight."

They all drew to a halt and crouched low before the final approach to camp. Varro saw the torches over the two guards standing watch at the north entrance.

"We'll call on her many more times than twice." He scanned down the long line of stakes and his trained eye saw the gap.

"There is where we get inside. I can't believe no one fixed it. That's quite obvious."

"We picketed the horses with the baggage train on the end," Aulus said. "Our gear is prepared. If we weren't going after Centurion Curio, sir, we could be away this moment."

"You and the others stand with the horses. Falco and I will get Curio." He and Falco then handed their spears over. "Put these with our horses. Spears are unsuited for our work."

"Sir, is it wise to split us up?" Not only Aulus raised a brow to the idea but also Lars and Gaius.

"Falco and I know Curio and his habits better than you. We would know him even in the dark. You three wait here and if you hear the alarm sounded, then do as I said before. Find Flamininus. He will still reward your efforts, though without the proof that Curio has he might not do more for you."

Aulus leaned closer. "Sir, what is this proof?"

"He doesn't know," Falco said with a growl. "He's just guessing. But we need Curio no matter what. We've been through too much together. I won't let him make a mistake like this. Now, let's get going."

They crouched low as they approached the gap in the stakes. To Varro's trained eye it seemed like a mile-wide gap, whereas in fact only a single man could fit through at once. He and Falco left the others to pull out the remaining stakes to accommodate the horses while they rushed toward the concealment of the camp interior.

The open area before the tents was the most stressful part of the crossing. But they were swift and soon among the shelter of hide tents and the ordered rows of wagons of the baggage train. Slaves slept wherever they could find a spot. So Varro and Falco picked their way among them and skirted along the edge of the line.

They knew the exact set up of the camp and where Curio

would be. They knew the guards watched for exterior threats and a pair of guards guarded the camp crossroads for anyone out after dark. The tribune and the consul had their own guards, but Varro wasn't headed there.

As strange as it felt for him to creep like a thief among his own fellows, he took careful steps and paused at every sound. Falco, for all his size, maintained silence as well. They both had done this sort of work too often to be sloppy.

Curio's tent was at the rear rank and end row of his century. Varro and Falco both crouched behind it, listening for snoring or other signs of the occupants. Curio himself did not snore, but had a distinctive cadence to his nighttime breathing. Falco knew it better than Varro, but both strained to hear it through the tent wall.

Falco's heavy brows drew together and he shrugged. Varro did the same, not hearing Curio at all. He heard the shifting of someone struggling with a restless night. It gave him pause, for he did not want to awaken anyone but Curio.

They had not discussed a plan, Varro realized, as they both assumed Curio would gladly join with them. But if he resisted, they would do as Falco described. They would neutralize him and carry him out by force.

Falco pushed at Varro's shoulder, urging him to act. So they swept around the front of the tent to enter the flap. Curio liked to sleep on the right side by the wall. Centurions always took the front position to be able to exit ahead of their tentmates.

Pushing aside the flap, Varro's eyes settled on the sleeping men. The five were still as the dead. However, Curio seemed to squirm and wrestle within his blankets. Varro looked to Falco, who rolled his eyes.

Clearly, he was having nightmares for betraying his friends. Well, Varro thought, it's time to put an end to those bad dreams.

He glided inside while Falco followed. If Curio fought, he

would keep him quiet and Falco would grab his feet. They would wrap him in his blanket, then rush to the horses.

But no one else stirred and Curio continued to roll amid his gray wool blanket, covered head to toe. Varro put his hand on his body and the struggle stopped. Curio stiffened and let out a low moan.

"Curio?" he whispered as loudly as he dared. "It's me and Falco. You're coming with us."

He bucked harder under the blanket. Varro pressed him with a gentle hiss, then ripped back the blanket covering his head.

The face looking up at him was flushed, wide-eyed, and gagged.

And not Curio.

18

Varro had to squeeze his eyes shut twice before he comprehended what he looked at.

"What is it?" Falco whispered harshly. He leaned forward, then twitched back as if avoiding a viper's strike.

The man shuddering under Varro's hand was Curio's optio, Pontius. His sandy hair was mussed and a fresh scrape topped a bulge on his forehead. A leather strip held a cloth stuffed into his mouth. His pale eyes rimmed red, he implored Varro for help.

But he did not trust him to keep quiet and the gag did a fine job keeping him muffled. He looked over at the others to ensure no one else awoke.

The other bedrolls were empty. Sacks peeked out from the tops of blankets to give the illusion of sleeping men. A hot flash of anger spread through Varro and he snarled at Falco.

"Check the other bedrolls. I think we're alone here."

"What is this about?" Falco released Pontius's feet and crawled over to the other bedrolls and pulled aside the blankets. He cursed each time he flipped over a blanket that revealed a filled sack.

In the meantime, Varro turned back to the optio and peeled

back his blanket to reveal his hands bound at his back and his legs tied.

"If I didn't know better," he said under his breath, "I'd say Aulus was here tonight."

"These are all dummies," Falco said in disgust. "Bags stuffed with grass and sand. What is this all about?"

Varro leaned to the optio's face. He then drew his pugio and set the gleaming point under his chin.

"Listen, Pontius, I will not hurt you unless you force it. If you speak louder than a whisper or try to struggle, this blade will find its way to the back of your skull."

The optio pressed his eyes closed and nodded as much as he dared with the point denting his neck. Varro let the threat sink in. Falco joined him, sitting by the tent flap to keep watch on the outside.

After Varro cut away the leather tie and pulled out the cloth, Pontius gasped.

"Thank you, sir. By the gods, I can't breathe too well through my nose."

Varro noticed that it was crooked, probably broken and never properly healed.

"Where's Curio?"

"Aren't you going to free me, sir?"

"Free you?" Varro looked back to Falco, who gave a bland smile. "Let's see how helpful you are. Now, what happened here?"

Pontius licked his lips and once more pressed his eyes shut before answering.

"Everything was normal, sir. We were settled for the night. But Centurion Curio looked sick. I thought for sure he would throw up in the tent. So when he went outside, I didn't think twice about it. But he met someone out there."

"Who was it? What did they say?" Varro found him driving the point of his blade harder, making Pontius squirm. So he pulled back and softened his voice. "What do you think Curio was up to?"

Pontius rocked his head side to side. His brows crashed together and his eyes vanished into the wrinkles of his frown. "I don't know, sir. I didn't see who came to meet him. They were careful not to be overheard. I tried to get closer, but one of the boys grabbed my leg and warned me to mind my own business."

Falco gave a soft whistle. "He's got some balls to speak to an optio like that."

"That's what I thought too, sir. And it wasn't like him to be that way. It felt like a warning, not a threat." Pontius stopped and stared up past Varro as if seeing something in the tent's dark roof. "Then someone hit me on the back of the head. I fell onto my bedroll. I saw the gods, sir, bright lights and strange sounds. Someone hit my head again as I turned over. I don't remember what happened after."

Varro withdrew the pugio and looked to Falco, who drew a heavy breath and turned away to peer outside.

"But I did wake up, sir." Pontius said brightly. "I was tied up and gagged with my blanket thrown over me. Everything echoed and I felt like I was on a ship in a storm. I could hear what they were saying, though."

Now Falco crawled to sit beside them while Pontius stared eagerly between them.

"You'll free me, sir?"

"Tell me what you heard." Varro patted the optio's arm. "Then we'll consider."

"Of course, sir." Pontius's expression faded to disappointment and he once more pressed his eyes shut to concentrate. "It's not really as clear as I thought. I remember Centurion Curio. He sounded exhausted. He said something about having everything now, and that he was sorry to endanger someone. Maybe it was the others?"

"The rest of his group," Varro confirmed. "Since they're all gone, it makes sense. What else did he say?"

"He did say more, sir. But I can't think what it was. The memory is just there, but I can't recall. Anyway, it just happened a few moments ago. Surely, he must be nearby, sir. You could catch him if you hurry."

Varro looked to Falco who shared his dubious expression. From his own experience, he knew men who took hard blows to their heads often did not recall time correctly or remember events associated with their injury. Pontius might never remember what happened. Even in the dim light from the tent flap, he could see Pontius's eyes were dilated. Curio or whoever hit him had delivered a hard blow.

"You've been here longer than you know," Varro said. "What watch is it now?"

"First watch, sir." But Pontius's smile faded when Varro and Falco both shook their heads. "I thought it was just a moment ago. I don't remember them leaving or tying me up for that matter. Centurion Curio told me something, though. It was about you, sir."

Varro leaned closer, returning his pugio to its sheath. Terrorizing Pontius would not help him recall something that might have been knocked out of his head forever.

"Listen, Curio has evidence of something Consul Cato does not want found out. It's for the good of Rome that we learn what he has discovered. Think hard on what he said."

Pontius closed his eyes and bit his lip as if he were lifting a boulder overhead. While he struggled, Varro sat up and whispered to Falco.

"See if Curio left anything behind."

"I doubt he'd be so stupid, but I'll give a look about."

Opening his eyes, Pontius gasped. "Sir, it's just right there. He was whispering to me. He wasn't angry, just weary. But I can't remember more."

Varro offered the optio a consoling pat on his shoulder.

"All right, maybe you'll remember when your head recovers. We've no more time to spend here. Falco, did you find anything?"

"Just this, and I don't know it means anything. It was pressed into the ground."

Falco extended his hand. A dirt encrusted silver denarius gleamed even in the faint light.

"Just dropped from someone's purse," Varro said. "We've got to go."

He retrieved the cloth from beside Pontius's head, then stuffed it into his mouth. The optio struggled and tried to force it out. But Varro refastened the leather strip over it.

"Sorry, Pontius. For whatever reason, Curio did not include you in his circle."

Falco shifted up to him. "Don't feel bad. He left us out, too, and we're his best friends."

The optio tried to shout and his eyes went wide. But Varro pressed a firm hand to his forehead.

"Cato will not believe you're uninvolved. He will to want to hear your story as well, and I can't let him know any of it. Besides, you know he'll use interrogators on you."

That made Pontius cease struggling. His dilated eyes opened wide.

"That's right," Falco added with exaggerated relish. "Curio didn't do you any favors leaving you behind. Cato will flog the skin off your back and roll you in salt."

Pontius moaned and Varro waved Falco to silence.

"We're taking you with us. Both for your protection and because you might remember what Curio said and did before tonight. So be still while we carry you out of here."

Before Pontius could protest, Varro yanked the blanket over his head again. Falco then peered out the tent flap and waved forward to signal the outside was clear.

"I've got his feet," Falco said. "Nice of Curio to leave him all tied up and gagged for us."

"I doubt he believed we'd come looking for him," Varro said. "Last he knew about us, we were going to be executed tomorrow."

As Falco hefted the squirming optio by his legs, he cocked his head.

"That's right. So, he was just going to leave us to die?"

Varro shook his head and let out a sharp sigh. He grabbed Pontius by the shoulders and together they lifted him off the ground.

"Don't fight us," Varro whispered. 'If we're caught, you'll be killed one way or the other. I'm not giving you back to Cato, and you don't want him helping you remember things. Cooperate and we'll eventually make you whole."

"That's right," Falco added. "Otherwise, Cato will kill you when he's finished asking questions."

So Pontius went slack as Falco backed out of the tent with him. Once outside, Varro scanned around the area. Tents stood in neat rows in the darkness, at peace and undisturbed. The sound of snoring came from the one beside theirs. Now that they were outside again, both would maintain silence. Falco knew to carry Pontius over his shoulder even without asking.

He grunted as Varro helped settle the wrapped-up body over Falco's burn-scared shoulder. Setting his feet wide, he steadied himself before indicating he had the optio under control.

Now they rushed from cover to cover, Falco unable to stoop while bearing away Pontius. Varro led them, checking every corner and pausing at every noise. He thought back to all the times he had crept through camps under the cover of darkness. His old centurion Drusus had always known his absence, but never asked where he had been. Even under so much pressure tonight, the memory of his old centurion's scowl made him smile. What would he say to all this skullduggery? he wondered. Life in the legion had been far different for him, and Varro felt a pang for those simpler days.

They reached the edge of the camp where their horses were picketed. Aulus and the others hid behind their mounts, looking the wrong way as Varro approached. He let out a low whistle to draw their attention.

Aulus and Lars peered through the darkness at them, but Gaius jumped with a muffled shout.

"You got him, sir!" Aulus joined Falco to help him with his burden.

"Not quite," Varro said. He went to find Thunderbolt, who snorted in greeting and carried saddlebags filled with Varro's gear. They had set out a wicker shield and gladius which he attached to his harness.

Falco set Pontius over the rear of a horse, then sneered at his own gear. "That's a cavalry shield. What am I supposed to do with it?"

"That's all I could arrange, sir." Aulus helped steady the groaning optio on the horse. "Who is this?"

They gave a brief explanation and then mounted their horses. Falco leaped up to ride with Varro, and each of them had a triarii spear besides their own weapons.

"It feels good to be properly armed," Falco said.

"Lead the way," Varro said, pointing to Aulus.

Even now upon their mounts, their profiles etched against the faint light of stars, they trotted across the space to the trench line with no one raising the alarm. In some ways, it disappointed Varro that these men were so derelict in their responsibilities. While they only guarded the entrances, it took no effort to look down the line. Then he recalled his own long nights standing watch and remembered sleeping on his feet while cricket songs lulled him into a trance.

The stake gap was now widened to fit the horses single file. They did not even need to jump the ditch, but walked their horses carefully through it until they were away. Now their profiles vanished into the blackness of the hills guarding the horizon. Aulus went in front with Pontius tied to his mount as they strung out with Varro and Falco in the rear. Falco gripped Varro by the waist with his free arm and whispered.

"That was easy," he said. "Where do you think Curio went? Why didn't he tell us anything? It makes no sense."

Varro sighed as he guided Thunderbolt along. But his horse was eager to follow Gaius's, and so he did not need encouragement.

"It all made sense to Curio. He is clever, but not too good at planning what comes next."

"He's made a mess of this. How are we going to find him? We're going to have three-thousand infantry on our heels by tomorrow."

Varro chuckled. "I don't think that will happen. I think Curio knows we would escape. Maybe he noticed Aulus's mark and guessed we'd have help from him. If he has something Cato does not want revealed, we won't have an army at our backs. Besides, Cato has a very real Bergistani rebellion to handle. I wouldn't be surprised if he just let us go. Curio is his real prize now."

He felt the hot breath of Falco's sigh on his neck as they rocked along with the horse. Aulus set the pace, and a steady trot would attract less attention, not to mention anything faster would risk the horses' footing in the dark.

"I guess so. If we show up in public again, we'll be declared deserters and that'll be the end of us."

"But not if we can get what Curio has discovered into Senator Flamininus's hands. He will protect us from Cato and his friends. Whether or not we like it, we're fighting a faction war now and doing nothing for the greater good of Rome. That's an old story, and one we're never likely to hear again. We were cheated, Falco. Servus Capax might advance Rome's interests. But those interests belong to certain senators only."

Falco growled. "When we see Senator Flamininus again, we're going to get a clear answer. I don't care who we're serving and for what reason. Doing it for Rome made me feel better. But if it's just to make some senators richer than they are, so what? As long as I come out better than before, right?"

"Those must be the same sentiments my father had while he helped steal farms from the widows of dead soldiers."

"Oh shit, sorry about that."

"We've got to be in this for something better than enriching a few rich men. I can understand some senators might oppose the aims of Servus Capax. But I won't abide criminal dealings. If I find out that's what we're doing, then I'm taking what I can and fleeing to Numidia. I'll go live in the mountains with honest people."

"We might have to do that, anyway."

They both chuckled as they rocked atop Thunderbolt's back, following the line set out by Aulus. The slow pace and calm night could fool him into thinking they were in no danger. He closed his eyes to indulge in the fantasy, letting the breeze soothe his skin and comb through his hair.

When he opened his eyes with his next breath, the fantasy died.

Aulus pulled up the line, and in the gloom ahead of them a horseman stood at the front of eight men on foot. The feathers on the helmet of the rider marked him as Roman, and Varro did not need to guess at who blocked their path.

Centurion Longinus kicked his horse forward. His face was ensconced in shadow, but his smile caught the gleam of starlight.

"I suspected there might be trouble out here. So I led the shift change myself. You don't disappoint, do you, Centurion Varro?"

"Not half as much as you do." Varro rode his horse to the front beside Aulus.

The eight men had fanned out to block them. They were nothing but shadows even at such a short distance. He noted only half carried spears, meaning the other four must be the triarii guards they left tied up and whose spears they possessed.

Longinus lowered his face with a smile.

"You're a cunning man to have come so far. And you must tell a great story to have brought these others into your scheming. But I've got you here, Centurion."

Varro lowered his spear at Longinus.

"You're the only one here who has to die tonight. The rest of you should step aside and let us pass. We've no desire to hurt a fellow Roman."

One of the triarii gave a bitter laugh, but Longinus answered.

"No, Centurion Varro, no one at all needs to die tonight. You saved my life. Truly, I would not be here if you hadn't dared so much to rescue me."

Falco's hot breath puffed against Varro's ear as he whispered, "I told you that was a bad idea. Should've let him die."

"I would have dared nothing had I known you to be a liar and a snake." Varro used his knees to angle Thunderbolt at the mounted Centurion Longinus. Both horses snorted as if they shared the same animosity as their riders.

"It is not in your nature," Longinus said. "You are a good man, Centurion Varro. In fact, that is why we are even talking right now rather than just taking you off that horse and placing you back under guard."

Aulus gestured to Varro's left, just out of sight. Lars and Gaius both brought their horses forward to widen their frontage. Varro appreciated this, as even eight men could not stop them all. With four of them weaponless, they had even less hope of blocking an escape. But Varro was wary of any tricks and kept his spear lowered.

"I will not listen to one of Cato's lackeys. Tomorrow you're prepared to put your lies in the official record in order to kill me and Falco. Why should I trust anything you say?"

Longinus seemed to stare at the point of Varro's spear.

"I'm sorry about how the consul dealt with you. You need to understand him. He does not trust easily, and so he wanted a guarantee that you would remain committed to him. But you are making a mistake, both you and Centurion Falco. Curio was far more practical than either of you. He could see what you two refuse to see. You work as spies and killers for a group of men you don't know and for a reward that you cannot even describe."

"Out of the way," Varro said. "I've heard all this before."

"But not from me," Longinus said. "Consul Cato has made mistakes and he is a hard man to serve. But he is honest and deals forthrightly."

Now Falco burst out with a laugh.

"Threatening us with the fustuarium for not joining him is honest? You must think we're daft. His idea of a reward is to let us live at his pleasure. You know what? Fuck him!"

"You're worthless to your masters now," Longinus said. "Please, don't turn aside the only chance you have to prosper. I came out here tonight because I owe you my life. I wanted you to have once last chance to make the right choice."

"One chance before your filthy master frames and then kills us." Varro echoed Falco's bitter laugh. "That's no choice at all."

"What if I could offer proof Flamininus will betray you?"

Varro did not even consider it.

"One lie follows another."

Then he kicked Thunderbolt forward.

"Charge!"

19

Varro charged with his spear lowered at the man whose life he had saved only a week ago. At the same time, Falco tightened his arm around his waist and raised his own spear.

Longinus darted his horse forward but to the side. Varro's spear thrust into emptiness, but Falco threw his spear as Thunderbolt sped past.

The wet thump of the spear striking flesh was clear over the shouting men. Longinus's horse screamed with terror and pain as Varro bounded away.

"Got his mount in the side," Falco shouted with triumph. "Fuck him and Cato!"

The triarii on foot were wise enough to dive aside as all four horses charged straight ahead. A triarius called after them.

"Cast your spears! Don't let them escape!"

Varro urged Thunderbolt forward and Falco twisted with a curse to bring his shield around to the rear. They fled into the night, hooves thrumming out the beat of their flight. Varro prayed Thunderbolt would pick a path clear of ruts and rocks, either of which could break his leg. But the scent of blood and violence seemed to terrorize him into a gallop.

Spears sailed out of the darkness. They had only just passed through the thin line of footmen, but night provided a black drape to mask them from attack.

One spear caused a horse to scream and then crash. Another spear thumped on something Varro could not see.

"Who was struck?"

Falco struggled and turned behind him as they fled into the night. But he eventually put both arms around Varro's waist.

"I can't see. We lost someone, but the other two are keeping up."

"We can't go back," Varro said. "If we do, we will risk getting pulled off our horses.

"Sir," Aulus shouted. "Keep riding. They'll sound the alarm."

Before Varro could agree, he heard the brilliant notes of a bucina behind them.

"Well, that'll bring the cavalry," Falco said. "We can't stop now."

It took all of Varro's effort to calm Thunderbolt from his terror. Otherwise, the blind run would end in disaster with both him and Falco thrown from the saddle. Aulus and the other had veered off and it seemed both had the same issues steering their mounts.

"Get back to formation," he shouted across the dark. His voice sounded like a thunderclap in the night, certain to bring the world's attention to himself. They had to get away, but not in a headlong flight. Any cavalry would have the same issues they did with footing. So they could move at a less dangerous pace.

It seemed half a night's work to bring them all together again, but in reality it could not have been even a fraction of that time. They had fled across the fields into the cover of trees that spread out before the foothills. Varro could no longer see through the trunks to where the camp lay. But he did not need to see it to imagine the scores of torches bobbing along in the dark to answer Longinus's alarm.

Thunderbolts's sides heaved from his effort. He needed water and Varro hoped a stream lay nearby. Gaius was the first to arrive with his horse whose sides also gleamed with sweat.

"So it was Lars that fell," Falco murmured from behind. "Damn, I liked him."

He and Varro dismounted and Thunderbolt seemed thankful for it as Varro stroked his neck, promising feed and water soon.

Aulus emerged behind Gaius, his horse ambling with its head down. Aulus, too, seemed defeated and slouching in the saddle. For a moment, Varro worried they had struck him with a spear.

Then he saw Pontius.

His body was still wrapped in a gray blanket, but a spear now ran up the length of it. The wrap was black and heavy with blood at the bottom, which ran in sweat-diluted streaks down the flank of Aulus's horse.

No one spoke as Varro and Aulus removed the slain optio's body from the horse. Varro unwrapped him to confirm his death. He found the spear skidded up his body then lodged under his neck and up into his head. Its point buried itself somewhere in his brain.

"He didn't deserve this," Varro said.

"Sorry, sir," Aulus said. "I should've done more to protect him."

Falco patted Aulus's shoulder. "It was just an unlucky throw. It happens like this. We'll bury him here and mark his grave so the boys will find him"

"What about Lars?" Gaius now spoke up, looking frightfully over his shoulder at the trees they had passed through. "We're just leaving him there?"

"Was he alive when he fell?" Varro asked. "If we turned back for him, we would've been dragged down and overcome."

"I don't know how he fell other than his horse went down. We could've gone back and fought off the guards," Gaius said. "But you just left him."

"We left him," Falco said, emphasizing the inclusiveness. "That's what happens in a mad run for freedom. Lars was another unlucky man. Hopefully, he wasn't struck and only his horse got it. Though if the gods have mercy on him, they'd have broken his neck in that crash."

"You can't turn back now," Varro said, guessing at Gaius's state of mind. "But you don't have to remain with us if you'd rather find your own way."

"What?" Gaius straightened up and looked at the others. "I didn't say I wanted to leave. I just, well, you would've left me behind too, right?"

Falco now put his arm about Gaius. "Right, and you'd have left me. It's the only choice we have. We are running for our lives. You have my promise. If I can save you, I will. But if I can't, you've got to save yourself. We couldn't have saved Lars, even if we fought. Longinus would have called the camp up and they'd be on us too fast to make an escape."

"We're still too near, sir." Aulus surveyed the darkness ahead. Varro wondered at what he could see that no one else could. The way forward was all darkness but for stars above. "We can still make for that camp tonight."

Varro shook his head.

"We cannot go there. We have to assume Lars survived that crash."

Gaius rubbed his chin. "Lars wouldn't give away our plans."

"Of course he would," Falco said, still keeping his arm looped about Gaius's shoulder and giving him a gentle shake. "The interrogators would just need to twist his broken bones, or worse. He'd start talking."

"What other places can we use to hide?" Varro joined Aulus in staring at the indigo darkness, not sure what he was looking for.

"We need to stay near water, and Cato's men will know that. I am familiar enough with this area, but I'm not a local guide. So we should push north, then loop east to reach Ilegertes territory."

"We'll have to go farther north than Cato will go," Varro said. "But he will dispatch trackers to find us, or else put a handsome bounty on us."

Falco snorted at the idea. "We'll deal with whoever comes along, if they can find us. We'll lead them on a chase they'll never forget. We learned a few things in the mountains of Numidia, eh, Varro?"

"No doubt," he said, drawing a heavy breath. "But I'm unsure how useful those techniques are here. In any case, the immediate need is water and feed for the horses. We'll have to press the locals for that. Now, let's bury Pontius and move on before we lose any advantage we have."

Aulus had packed their horses with tents and trenching gear just as if they were joining a legionary march. With four of them working together, they had Pontius in a hole deep enough to prevent wild scavengers from digging out his body. It had been arduous work. But the night was cool and silent. They used the stones dug up to mark the grave and Varro scratched the optio's name into one, hoping it would be legible in daylight.

"Looks like they're waiting for dawn to pursue," Falco said as he put his small spade into the saddlebags.

"More likely they've captured Lars and will learn our plans."

"So Cato will be alerted to everything," Falco said, his heavy brows joining. "Not just where we are going, but also about Curio and the proof he has. If he wasn't sure before, then he will be now."

"I think it is best to assume that Cato knows everything we do." Varro batted his palms against his thighs, then looked down on Pontius's grave. "Our best plan should surprise even ourselves."

"That's comforting," Falco said in a tone that suggested otherwise. "Look, we've got one task now and that's reaching Flamininus. He'll set this right."

"What about Curio?" Varro couldn't see much of Falco's expression in the dark. But his friend drew a sharp breath.

"He didn't want our help. So he has to figure it out himself." Now Falco looked at Pontius's grave. "Or else he gets what he earned. I guess he found others better than us to help him. Besides, what can we do for him now?"

Varro nodded, recognizing the same feeling of betrayal he felt himself. But unlike Falco, he could see possible reasons for Curio striking out alone. Voicing this now would only exacerbate Falco's mood. So he turned to Aulus and Gaius, and they mounted their horses to leave the unfortunate optio's grave behind.

They located a stream for both themselves and their horses to drink from, but then pushed on until they reached the foothills. Aulus declared it a suitable campsite. No one else knew the land as well as a native, so it made sense that Aulus assumed that role. They had two tents between them, and enough supplies for a few days of travel. Exhaustion claimed all of them. Varro was the last to sleep. With so little left to the night, no one took a watch.

The next morning, as they ate bread and drank wine from their limited supplies, Varro looked closer at Aulus. The owl tattoo seemed obvious now, but most of the time they were together he wore a helmet with cheek pieces that concealed it. They both sat on flat rocks across from each other, with Falco and Gaius flanking them. Everyone chewed in silence, with only early morning birdsong and the snorting of their horses to break it. Varro cleared his throat.

"Let's hear it, Aulus. How did you join Servus Capax?"

Falco had a mouthful of bread, but he added his own question.

"And what do they make you do? Who do you report to?"

Gaius looked between all of them, his face full of bright innocence.

"Can Servus Capax really make me a tribune?"

Varro and Falco both sat back in shock, but Gaius was earnest. Aulus held up both hands, his face shading red.

"It's not that complicated, honestly. When I was a child, Scipio came to Tarraco and won his great battle there. My family was all killed in the clash between Rome and Carthage, though we did not fight for either side. I have no memory of it other than being taken from my home and seeing my mother lying on the ground outside the door. Nothing bloody, just as if she had fallen and could no longer stand."

"You were made a slave, then?" Falco asked as he continued chewing on his bread.

"No, sir, a Roman took me away to his garrison and I lived there ever since. I still kept in contact with my old tribe, as we were aligned with Rome. I did menial tasks for the soldiers, and I was always free to leave. But I had no family and only a few friends in my tribe. Besides, I liked garrison life. It felt safe and the men treated me like I was a little brother. The one who took me in was a centurion, Lucian. He became the garrison commander and had me in the ranks before I was seventeen. When Centurion Lucian joined Servus Capax, he recommended me. We met with a man from Rome who did not give his name. I swore my oath beside the man who was like an older brother to me."

"What rank was the man from Rome?" Varro asked.

"He only said he represented Scipio and Centurion Lucian advised me not to ask too many questions. We'd both be rewarded with land and riches for serving."

Varro smiled, remembering the promises offered to him. "And Centurion Lucian? Is he alive still?"

Aulus shook his head and looked up at the hills.

"He died in battle, sir. Against the Turdentani, about eight years ago."

Varro looked at Falco, who finished his bread and now sat with his head resting in his palm.

"So that explains why you hate them. But what did you do after joining Servus Capax?"

"I personally did not do much different, but Centurion Lucian changed a lot. They promoted him, as he described it to everyone, but no one understood what this new rank was. He never explained. His posting took him out of Iberia. When he returned a year later, he had new scars and smiled less often."

Falco gave Varro a blithe smile. "I can guess why. So, Aulus, what did you do while he was gone?"

"For that year, I served as an interpreter for the new commander. When Centurion Lucian returned, he refused to speak of where he had been, but promised me he had seen enough. We were in the right place, he said, and was glad I joined him in Servus Capax. He thought it was useful that I could stand in two worlds, Iberian and Roman. Not long after, we joined a skirmish against the Turdentani and he was killed. A javelin got him in the liver. He kept fighting but soon fell and never stood again."

Varro hated these kinds of stories that reminded him how a lifetime of valorous service could abruptly end on a pointed stick cast by some unwashed barbarian during a pointless skirmish.

"Sorry for Lucian's passing, but what did you do after this? You say someone issued you an order regarding us. So, who was it?"

Aulus rubbed his tattooed face. "Sir, I got a letter before Consul Cato's arrival. No one signed it, but the papyrus bore the owl mark. I was ordered to join his legions as an interpreter and to look after three Servus Capax that members would arrive from afar to serve the consul. I was to not reveal myself to you until needed. But I was excited for you to arrive, for I might learn more about whoever sent me the letter. It's my first order from Servus Capax, except for serving Centurion Lucian, that is."

Falco stood up and stretched. "So you knew about us from the start? Where were you for that whole mess with the Ilegertes? Could've used your aid then."

"I'm sorry, sir. But Tribune Galenus would never let me go. He was so focused on glory and making his name. We had to be at the front of every patrol or skirmish. You know how he was. Besides, you two are officers and I thought that if you needed help, you'd find me. So when Centurion Varro met me, I was shocked he did not recognize the mark I wore."

Varro smiled. "The tattoo is a nice touch. Maybe we'll get one and not worry about our pugiones so much."

"Do you know why they use the pugiones, sir?" Aulus's eyes sparkled as he leaned forward on the rock. "It's because Servus Capax started here, sir, in Iberia. Centurion Lucian said it was from when Carthage still owned these mountains. The original members were here to bring tribes to Rome's side before Scipio arrived and to carry out covert attacks on Carthage's holdings. The Romans liked our swords and daggers so much that they stole them, as you well know."

Falco grimaced. "I wouldn't say we stole anything. I admit the design is similar. Anyway, thanks for the history lesson. You don't know shit about anything going on. That is really what you want to say."

"Sir, that is true." Aulus leaned back on his rock. "But I've worn this tattoo since I was a boy, and have dreamed of the day it would mean something. Now here I am."

"A traitor to all," Falco said, spreading his hands. "Except to us, that is. But you take my meaning. Anyway, come with us to Flamininus. If you stay here, you'll end up dead eventually. There will be a bounty on our heads."

"Thank you, sir. I would like to see Rome at least once. But I want to die here. This is my home."

Varro stood and dusted the crumbs from his tunic.

"Death in Iberia is forever possible after last night. No matter where we go now, it will always be hostile territory for us. Do you still believe we can secure local aid in smuggling us to Albus and King Bilistages?"

"Wait," Gaius shot to his feet beside Varro. "You lied to me. You don't even know who's giving you orders. You can't help me advance."

"And if you stayed behind," Aulus said. "You'd be facing the interrogators instead of sharing bread and wine with me on this fine morning."

Varro chuckled. "We are going to Senator Flamininus. He will help you."

Gaius's panicked expression remained unchanged. "But what if Centurion Longinus was right? What if Senator Flamininus is done with you?"

Falco clasped both hands atop his head. "I'm done thinking about what might be. Longinus and Cato are manipulators. So fuck anything they have to say. Let's focus on what is. We've got to escape Iberia. Varro's right. This is hostile territory, and as long as we're in it we're hopeless."

Aulus at last took up Varro's question.

"Sir, if we press north until we reach the base of those mountains, I expect we will find people willing to help. It would be better if we had something to trade for it. Do you think Albus would part with some wealth? Livestock would be better than coins. But maybe we could persuade them otherwise."

Varro shrugged. "We'll never know what these local people want unless we find them. So let's move out."

They headed north following Aulus's lead. Varro was glad to focus on the next moment rather than wonder any more about what could be. He shared Falco's frustrations. The longer they traveled the more he could not help but wonder at his purpose in coming to Iberia. Certainly, there was basic soldiering work. But why had Flamininus recalled them to serve what has turned out to be an enemy? The more he wondered the more chilling Longinus's offer of proof became. Had he been too rash in dismissing it?

These thoughts vanished when Aulus pointed out they were being shadowed.

"Sir, there along that ridge. I've spotted men keeping low, trying to steal a glance at us. They've been at it for a while now, and now I am sure they aren't just curious."

Gaius groaned at the news, but they all paused their mounts to look up the ridge. They were sticking close to trees and low ground to hide their profiles.

Varro watched until almost out of patience, then saw a dark head pop up from behind a rock. Though impossible given the distance, Varro was certain they locked eyes.

"Aulus, we are in Bergistani territory now, aren't we?"

"Most certainly, sir."

"And the Turdentani are allied with them."

Without another word, Aulus urged his mount ahead at a trot. Varro and the rest matched the pace.

But then the shapes crested the rise upon seeing them flee. At least a dozen mounted men showed and Varro heard their lusty battle cries carry over the distance.

"Show the way, Aulus, and fast. We've got to lose them or we're done for."

20

Thunderbolt raced ahead at Varro's urging. They traced the open grassland beside the wall of pines to their left with Aulus leading their three-horse column. With Falco holding onto his back, Varro sensed Thunderbolt's flagging stamina. Gaius and Aulus both outstripped him and both turned back to urge him on.

Behind them, the hoofbeats of the closing Iberians pounded out an urgent rhythm. Their whoops and calls bounced off the trees and hills.

"I can't fucking stand another horse chase!" Falco shouted from behind. "This isn't the flat desert of Numidia. My knees are going to break."

Varro could only nod agreement as he focused on guiding Thunderbolt. Thankfully, he was loyal to Gaius's horse and followed her lead. Otherwise, Varro doubted the beast could keep the pace any longer.

"They're gaining on us," Falco shouted again. "And we're losing the others."

"Shut up!" Varro urged Thunderbolt with his heels, and the

horse strained to meet the demand. But his sides were already heaving against Varro's legs.

He wouldn't outstrip the Iberians with the extra weight that his pursuers did not suffer.

"Dump the baggage. Throw off your shields and anything you don't need."

"Can I talk now?"

Despite Falco's banter, his voice quivered with the fear. He wrestled with the saddlebags, punched Varro on the back so that he would shift away as he worked, then dropped them. His shield and Varro's flew away next.

"I hit one!" he shouted. "Good idea!"

But Varro could not turn about to enjoy the chaos of dropping obstacles into the Iberians' path. He heard their shouting turn to curses, but otherwise had to focus on the way ahead. Gaius pulled forward and Aulus now mounted a slope and headed for sparse tree cover. The reduced load allowed Thunderbolt to gain speed, but Varro knew it was not enough.

"Falco, you're killing my horse."

"Well, forgive me for not keeping my spare horse in my fucking pack!" Varro felt him twisting again. "This isn't working. They're coming into javelin range."

Varro did not hesitate in his decision, but yanked hard on the reins to point Thunderbolt toward the trees. He protested and pulled against the reins.

"You'll meet your girlfriend later," he shouted as he drove his horse faster. "Go to the trees."

For the moment, Thunderbolt heeded him and ran for the dark shelter of the pine trees streaking by on the left. This would provide cover from javelins, though he could not get too deep into the woods. It would also separate their pursuers, as some would continue to chase Aulus and Gaius.

The brush and branches slapped against Varro's naked head.

He had forgotten he was not wearing armor or a helmet. As Thunderbolt smashed through branches and into the shade of the trees, pine needles showered over Varro.

The trees were sparse enough for a horse to pass if it could pick the path. A gentle slope lit with a thin spread of yellow light raised up in the general direction Aulus had picked.

Thunderbolt dodged trees and cried out in protest. But Varro pushed him as fast he could go.

"Falco, get the spears, then jump off with me."

"What?"

Varro launched himself off Thunderbolt's back. The constant practice he had with this in Numidia saw him land on his heels and then collapse into a roll to break the momentum. He tumbled into bushes and low rocks, cursing the rough ground.

Falco thumped to the ground shortly after him, and Thunderbolt continued to run ahead, dancing in between the trees. Varro blinked away the pine needles and dirt as Falco crawled toward him.

"By the gods, I just do whatever you say. You better not be getting me fucking killed. I swear, I'll haunt your dreams if you do."

"If you die, I die," he said breathlessly, pulling Falco into the underbrush he landed in. "Thunderbolt will lead them on a chase. He'll try to get back to Gaius's horse."

Falco frowned at this, but said nothing as he handed over one of the captured triarii spears.

"So, an ambush?"

"Probably. Let's see who comes after us."

They both ducked down as the sound of the pursuers crashing through the trees followed. Their horses slowed and they called to each other in short, frustrated shouts. Varro peered between the bushes as he counted four horses pushing in the general direction.

Thunderbolt continued up into the trees, crushing branches

and bush under his hooves. The Iberians cried out when they spotted him.

The horsemen now passed in a line. As they drew near, he saw they were unarmored but carried round shields and spears and other gear hanging from saddlebags. He and Falco crouched low behind the trees as they trotted past, more careful about their horses' footing than Varro had been.

There were six men and the last two followed on stout brown mounts that puffed their exhaustion.

Varro whispered as these caught up to their fellows. "Take out the riders. Leave the mounts."

Falco's heavy brows drew together in grim determination and his knuckles turned white around his spear shaft.

They let the Iberians trot past. One leaned down to comfort his horse. Varro pointed to that one for himself. Then he and Falco broke out of hiding.

The sudden explosion of leaves and crunching branches startled both horses and their riders. But Varro held a Roman spear, one that felt like an extension of his own arm. He cocked back, then let it sail up into his target's ribs. It skewered him, knocking him from the horse to collapse on the man beside him.

Unfortunately, this frightened the other horse and it bolted, heedless of its rider. Falco's spear arced into empty space and he cursed.

The riderless horse, now equally terrified, ran ahead.

But Varro's desperation lent him speed. He seized its reins and hauled it aside. It was well trained and knew a firm hand. It calmed enough for Varro to mount into the saddle.

The other rider, however, had also regained control of his horse. Falco drew his gladius and charged. Varro knew he would try to kill the mount, which would be easier than reaching the rider.

Varro spun the horse to face Falco's opponent, then kicked him forward.

With enemies on both sides, the Iberian seemed unable to decide on a facing. Varro blocked his joining with his friends while Falco stabbed his horse in its side.

The horse reared up and the rider toppled out of the saddle. Varro now turned to see the other four pursuers. They had ranged ahead, but not so far that they were out of hearing. Through the trees, he could not see their expressions, but saw them turning their horses.

Falco fell on the man he had unhorsed and rammed his gladius into his side. He let out a scream that ended any hesitation for the other Iberians about what had happened.

"Get your spear," Varro said. "And keep moving. I'll lead them off."

Turning his stolen horse, he pushed deeper into the woods. His pursuers followed, but he held a short lead.

He hated woods and forests for their treacherous footing and the ghosts that haunted them at night. But now he was glad for the crowded spaces and low branches that made a fight from horseback impossible. The Iberians, however, seemed to insist upon it. They pushed through the trees, cursing as they rode and brandishing long swords.

Varro led them in a circle back toward Falco, certain to pick the most restricting route and force them to string out. The Iberians were not fools and sent two of their number to cut off Varro's intended route. But he smiled, for Falco waited for them.

He turned his horse and dropped behind it, using it like a mobile wall to hide behind. Numidian riders showed him how they could hang off the side of a horse to hide from javelins and sling shot. He had marveled at their dexterity and knew he could never do such a thing without years of practice. But the same principle applied here. Between the trees and the horse, the Iberians would have to face him on the ground.

The first rider broke through the trees into the small clearing Varro had selected. A fallen tree long covered with moss barred the best way out. He slid out of his saddle and his sword flashed the light falling between the overhead branches. The second rider called to his companions as he too dropped from his mount.

They rushed him, and Varro hauled his horse around to face its rump toward them. Then he stabbed it below its tail.

The beast screamed and kicked back into the Iberian charging the short distance. The bucking horse struck him. His head made a wet clomp as his body flew back into the brush. The horse then bolted away, leaping over the fallen log to vanish into the trees.

But Varro did not hesitate and counterchanged his attacker. The Iberian held up his shield, but Varro was both bigger and stronger. He threw his weight against it before the Iberian could strike. He collapsed against a tree, and Varro's gladius found the Iberian's guts. They stared at each other as he gasped out his last curse.

Withdrawing his sword, he heard Falco's struggle ahead. The last mount shied away from Varro, and so he instead rushed through the trees toward the sound of battle.

Falco had killed a horse, and its rider squirmed and cursed under it. But he wrestled the other Iberian who had grabbed his spear. The two staggered around, shoving at each other, smashing against trunks and branches, until Falco spotted Varro through the trees.

Then he hauled backward, taking the Iberian's momentum, so that both fell to the ground. This exposed the Iberian's back, and Varro stabbed the unsuspecting enemy through his kidney. Falco shoved him aside to let him writhe and die in the underbrush. His sweaty face beamed up at Varro.

"Would you be angry if I told you I had him even without your help?"

Varro extended his arm. "I didn't know you enjoyed dancing with barbarians. I'll remember to let you have your fun next time."

After he got Falco to his feet, both dusted off twigs and dried pine needles. Beside them, the last Iberian struggled under his dead horse. Falco's gladius stuck out of its belly. He put his foot to it and dragged it out with a sucking sound. More of its blood gushed onto the rider below, who cried out in rage.

"All your friends are dead," Falco said over the horse.

"We've got a prisoner for questioning." Varro said.

Falco snatched up his spear, then frowned.

"Really?" He looked over at the trapped Iberian. "Did your tutor teach you Latin? What? You were too busy studying etiquette and philosophy to bother learning proper speech? Well, I should've realized."

Varro put his hands on his hips as the Iberian cursed Falco in his native language.

"Let's see if this will teach you what your tutor did not."

Varro saw Falco cock the spear in one hand and stepped forward.

"Don't! I want to find out what he knows."

"And I'm just teaching him Latin."

Falco plunged the spear into the Iberian. Varro could not see as the horse blocked the view. But he heard flesh tear and the Iberian wail.

"Do you understand me now?" Falco drew the spear up. But before Varro could do more, he slammed it down again. The Iberian stopped screaming. Falco twisted the spear and his victim groaned at the sounds splitting flesh and grinding bone. "He doesn't feel like talking."

Varro sighed and looked between the trees to glimpse the remaining horses.

"We've got to catch up to the others. We'll use these horses for now."

"What about Thunderbolt?" Falco asked as he wicked blood from the spear over the ruined corpses of horse and rider.

"I don't dare shout out for him. I think he might have gone a bit higher up the slope before slowing down. We don't have time to search for him."

They tried to approach the Iberian horses, but they fled when Varro or Falco neared. In the end, they were forced to search for Thunderbolt, and after a brief search located him standing amid trees. For once, the horse seemed happy to see Varro, immediately coming to him and enjoying Varro's patting his side.

"We need to find Gaius's horse," he said soothingly as he took their dangling reins. "Will you take Falco again? It won't be much longer."

"He better," Falco said. "We've lost too much time looking for a horse that will accept us."

Once they were both atop Thunderbolt, Varro let him pick his way to the edge of the trees. The brightness ahead revealed nothing and it tensed Varro's stomach. He had made a snap decision to split their group, which usually was not a good idea. But today it had allowed them to defeat half of their pursuers. He hoped the other half had given up the chase.

They regained the open grassland and following the churned-up ground was simple enough. The trail led up toward the tree line where they had last seen Aulus.

"He would've tried to lose them in difficult ground," Varro said. "Just like we did."

"And their horses?" Falco asked. "You think they could've remained mounted?"

Varro lowered his head, knowing what Falco meant. They would have done something similar, but less foolhardy than what he had done. If they evaded the Iberians, it meant they gave up their horses and went into hiding. Their supplies would've gone with the horses, leaving them with only what they carried.

Falco snorted. "Right. I don't think Thunderbolt can take four riders."

"Let's find them before we worry about the horses."

They found Gaius first. His corpse splayed facedown in the grass halfway up the slope with two javelins in his back. His legs appeared to have been trampled by horses, shattered and pressed into the ground. Flies had already gathered to feast on the blood congealing in the grass. They rose in a small cloud when Varro dismounted and approached.

"That would've been us," Falco said as he slid off Thunderbolt. "Good thing we ducked into the trees."

Varro crouched down and touched Gaius's shoulder.

"He wanted to be a tribune."

Falco stood behind so that his shadow fell across the corpse.

"That would've been a stretch. But he was a good man, a brave man even if he complained a bit. He saved our lives."

"And we failed to save his."

"Don't start down that road," Falco said. "He knew the danger he faced. Aulus dazzled him with promises of a rank he'd never possess. I'm as grateful as you are for his help. But he and Lars both volunteered out of greed. So don't start crying because they reached too far and paid for it."

"I'm not crying," Varro said, then stood. "I doubted his bravery once. Even if he was greedy, I don't anymore. Aren't we all?"

"Varro, stay with me." Falco grabbed him by both shoulders. "Philosophy is for some other time, hopefully a time that will never come because it's so fucking dull. Right now, what are going to do?"

Varro sighed and looked up-slope. The churned-up grass created a trail that continued on into the trees.

"Gaius got picked off his horse. If we can find her, we might recover some supplies and rations. Then we can either search for Aulus or move on."

Falco released Varro's shoulders and folded his arms. The two of them stood in silence while birds sang in the trees. It meant that the animals nearby saw no threat, and Aulus had led his pursuers away.

"You know," Falco said in a low voice. "We should probably use the distraction he has created to get away."

"True," Varro said. "But do you know where we are? Can you speak to the natives, who won't see Romans as friends?"

"They will not see Aulus as one, either."

"But he can speak to them and explain things. All we can do is hold up our palms and pray someone knows enough Latin to bargain with us."

"We do not know where he went," Falco said, but returned to Thunderbolt who was cropping the grass away from the bloody scene.

Varro followed him. "We'll follow the trail, and at its end we find him or not. If he escaped, he will find us. He's a woodsman, at least a better one than you or me."

Leaving Gaius where he fell remained an unspoken decision. Both realized they had neither time nor tools to dig in the rocky earth. Nor did they want to leave proof of their passing. The Iberians would certainly return for his body, if only to parade it for their fellow tribesman as a trophy. Better that the enemy should not suspect their presence here and search the woods where they had had last been. It was an unfair ending for a brave soldier, and Varro regretted it.

They kept close to the tree cover as they followed the trail. Falco watched their surroundings for trouble while Varro steered Thunderbolt along the path. They climbed into the trees where lack of space made finding the hoof prints harder. Freshly broken branches aided in keeping track. But eventually, the trail petered out into the denser woods. They exited on the other side of it, facing a steep climb up into rocky ground.

"He went there," Varro said. "Unless they captured him without a fight."

"You think he let his mount go and climbed up into the rocks?" Falco asked as both slipped off Thunderbolt's back to let the horse rest. "We didn't find any blood along the trail. We didn't find his horse, either."

"The Iberians didn't climb after him. But maybe captured his abandoned horse," Varro said. "If they had gone into the hills, then their horses would be down here with someone to guard them. So they probably circled back to link up with those who chased after us."

"So there's a better way than going through the trees to leave this hill," Falco said looking around.

"Which means there's a faster way to get here when they find all their companions dead. We need to move."

It was as if his words called the Iberians to return. For in the next instant, the distant sound of pounding hooves thrummed along the ground.

Varro leaped onto Thunderbolt's back and hauled Falco up. Then he turned the horse in the opposite direction.

"Time to flee again, Thunderbolt!"

21

They sped along a natural road created by the steep incline to their left and the stand of trees to their right. The ground bulged upward and Thunderbolt huffed as he struggled to meet the demand for greater speed.

Falco, hugging Varro's back as they careened forward, turned behind.

"Shit, it's them!" He grabbed Varro tighter, his shouting loud in his ear. "How did they get here so fast?"

But Varro did not answer. He drove Thunderbolt up the ridge toward an outcropping of rocks. He hoped for something better behind it, open ground or else a chance for them to climb into the rocks and deprive their enemies of their horses.

Varro launched into the air. Falco's arms yanked against him and broke free as he had the strangest sensation of weightlessness. Were the gods lifting him to safety?

A beautiful blue sky with rolling, puffy clouds now passed over him. A gauzy white haze rimmed the edges of his vision. He realized he heard nothing at all, and had somehow gone deaf. This cloudy disorientation seemed to suspend him in blankness for what felt like hours.

Then the horrific sounds and pains roared into him as he felt himself plowing through grass and rocks. Thunderbolt screamed and thrashed below his feet. He realized he was on his back and facing the sky. The hooves of the pursuing horses thrummed through the earth to shake against his back. Falco lay in the grass beside him, on his side with his back to him as if he had curled up for a nap.

The pain came next. The shoulder he had injured in his fight against Iberian slingers now blazed up in hot pain. Fresh pains came from old wounds. His joints had never been the same after Sparta, and now each one of them burned and throbbed.

Hooves suddenly slammed all around his head. Reflexes triumphed over pain and he balled up to keep from being stamped to death. Riders called triumphantly overhead, their shouts maddening amid the terror of horses pounding the earth around him. He pressed his eyes shut, as if doing so could make him smaller.

Once this terrorizing attack ended, Varro felt someone land beside him.

He reached for his pugio and flipped to the side. But his enemy had straddled him, and only had to widen his legs to keep upright.

Varro's shoulder protested the cross-body motion and created enough of a delay that his enemy raised his spear to bring it down over Varro's chest.

But he stopped short.

Varro yanked his pugio free of the sheath, but in the same instant a sandaled foot stamped down on his hand, pinning it and breaking open his grip.

The pained shout he heard was his own. Awareness of the last few moments rushed back to him as he listened to Thunderbolt thrashing and screaming. He had caught his hoof on something and tripped. Varro had launched over his head with Falco holding on from behind. He twisted enough so that he landed on his back, but he struck his head hard. The throbbing pain was just now pulsing through the haze. Falco was dead or knocked out beside him. The Iberians had caught up, then encircled them, and now seemed ready to kill but for something that made them pause.

Varro heard the distant voice. The man poised over Varro twisted to look up into the high rocks, but his spear point dangled just over Varro's neck. He shouted something loud and guttural back to that voice. But Varro instead turned his head to see Falco. They had flipped him onto his back with another Iberian disarming him. A bubble of blood issued from his nose and it pulsed with his breathing.

"Thank the gods," he muttered. His captors did not hear him, but continued shouting up at the other voice.

At last, the Iberian straddling him, a bald man with a massive black beard, stepped back. He had swirling tattoos across his head and face, much like Aulus's. He frowned as the other men yanked Varro upright.

"Sir, I've told them you're an important prisoner."

Aulus shouted from the ledge above. Varro gave him a wan smile as his captors manhandled him toward a horse. Aulus raised both of his hands and climbed down out of the rocks.

Varro now looked about at his captors. These were the six others he had hoped to evade. They glared at him, seething hatred plain on their tattooed and scared faces. These were no mere scouts, but veteran warriors. Two of them threw Falco over the rump of a horse. He groaned and twitched, but was not any threat in his battered state.

The bald Iberian wrenched Varro's arms back, then tied them with a length of cloth. Once Aulus descended the rocks, they did the same to him.

Thunderbolt had stopped thrashing, but his cries of pain still echoed off the trees. Since the suffering of another horse visibly upset the other horses, one of the Iberians drove a spear through Thunderbolt's neck. He spasmed and thrashed, then fell quiet.

Varro closed his eyes, twisting at the agonizing death of his loyal mount. Another needless casualty brought about by Cato's scheming. One day, he promised himself, when he escaped this debacle, he would ensure Cato paid for all of it. He would return all his grief to Cato tenfold.

The Iberians now dragged Aulus toward their mounts. With his arms bound and his weapons confiscated, he seemed to have shrunk in size and an embarrassed flush colored his face.

"I'm sorry, sir. They would've killed both of you."

Before Varro could thank him for saving his life, the bald Iberian flipped his spear around and slammed the shaft into Aulus's head like he hoped to bat it off his shoulders. He collapsed to his side, and the Iberian continued to batter him while the others laughed.

Instinct drove Varro to reach for his sword, forgetting his hands were bound and a barbarian held him from behind. Despite being weakened and dizzy from his fall, he wrestled against his captor. The bald Iberian continued to savage Aulus with the butt of his spear. When he at last relented, Aulus had a swollen face covered in blood. With his hair sticking to the gore and all his tattoos, Varro couldn't even tell if his face remained.

Others dragged Aulus off the ground, hands bound at his back, then threw him over the rump of a gray horse.

When the Iberian holding him from behind tugged Varro toward his mount, he did not resist. Someone had to remain whole if they ever hoped for escape. So he lowered his head in shame as the Iberians jeered at him. One spit on his face as he passed, the foul and slimy juice crawling down his face. He gritted his teeth and counted his luck compared to Aulus. He could endure spit better than a savage beating.

They rode along the edge of the slope back the way they came. Then they picked a path up into the hills that had been well hidden. It was narrow and shadowed with sharp corners that blinded Varro to both forward and behind. But soon they exited from the pass and rode into a village where people of every age and description came out to see them.

Most of them either stared or cursed at Varro and the others as they passed through the huts and dilapidated structures of this scruffy village. But others, women and old men, ran up and down the line in desperation, calling out names and getting nothing but shaking heads in answer from the riders. These were the relatives of the men Varro and Falco had killed. Seeing their sadness turn to hatred, Varro grew sick with fear. There might be no time to escape if the riders handed them over to the villagers.

They came to the largest dwelling, a house of weathered black wood. Ravens stared down from the roof, turning their heads side to side as if they had never seen a Roman before. Varro took it as a bad sign. The barbarian village was poor compared to the one he had raided in the mountains, and the inhabitants dressed in faded tunics in as much disrepair as their homes.

The riders dragged Falco and Aulus off their horses and let them fall to the ground like two sacks of grain. Varro was last, and the bald Iberian who had thought to kill him now held Varro up by his shoulders. He was unsteady on his feet, but he tried to meet his enemy's glare.

The Iberian spoke in short, fierce words that meant nothing. He narrowed his eyes and shouted what sounded like the same things. Varro thought about spitting in his face. While such an act might satisfy the urge for revenge, the price would be too high.

In the end, he shoved Varro into the custody of others and went to drag Aulus off the ground. He hefted Aulus over his shoulder and dragged him to Varro. He then repeated all his threats and shook Aulus as if he had fallen asleep.

Raising his head, Aulus tried to open his swollen eyes. When he spoke, his teeth were stained red and showed a fresh gap where a tooth had been knocked out. His voice now had a strange whistle to it.

"Sir, he said they will kill us for what we did today. They are going to flay us to learn what we were doing and learn what Cato's plans are. Then they will burn us alive as a sacrifice to the gods."

"What did you say about us?" Varro expected he would have no more chances to speak to Aulus and needed to know what leverage he might have.

"Sir, just that you were both important officers with knowledge of Cato's plans."

The bald Iberian realized his mistake in bringing them together. He roared at Varro, then shoved Aulus away into a waiting man's grip. Then he jabbed his thick finger into Varro's chest as he drew eye to eye with him. He smelled of garlic and his breath of cheap wine. His greasy nose touched Varro's as he growled out some threat in his native tongue.

Varro gave no reaction. This seemed more unsettling to the Iberian than if he had spit in his face. He renewed his threat, but Varro simply stared back. At last, he turned away and went into the shabby house while Varro stood under guard outside.

The entire village kept a wide semicircle around them. One woman's sobbing reached a crescendo and it sounded as if someone led her away. Falco and Aulus both were now made to stand, with Falco beside Varro and Aulus on his other side. He whispered as they stood facing the dilapidated building.

"Am I lucky to not remember how I got here?"

"You are. We're to be interrogated, flayed, and then offered to their gods on a pyre."

Falco was about to offer one of his quips when their guards shouted at them and slapped the back of Varro's head. They both fell to silence.

As they waited, the crowd grew bolder in its agitation. People called out, no doubt begging for the spectacle of their deaths. Their guards did not respond, but did nothing to discourage the growing anger. Varro felt his back prickle with the glares of his enemies as stinging as a scourge.

The bald Iberian emerged from the doorway, then spoke commands. Their guards herded them inside, drawing angry shouts and wails from the crowd behind them. Varro was first through the black doorway. Inside smelled like sweat, wet animal fur, and mold. But smoke from the hearth that smoldered against the left wall added a tolerable sweetness to the air. A white haze seemed to divide the room, where a dozen barbarians lounged on the opposite end.

These men wore green tunics with a decorative stripe on the bottom hem and carried spears. They surrounded their leader, who sat on a heavy wooden chair at their center. He was a ponderous man, though under the fat there seemed to lurk great muscle. His graying hair was short and curly and his face sad but resolved. He too wore a green tunic but also silver chains around his neck heavy enough to choke a mule.

The leader waved them forward, and Varro's guards shoved him ahead.

Their guards pushed them down to kneel, and while they all resisted, they also all ended up on their knees. Varro's shoulder throbbed from the slam of a spear butt that drove him down.

This defiance seemed to entertain the leader, who now ordered his silver cup filled. A servant scuttled from a dark corner to pour him wine, which he drank deeply from before turning to his captives.

Varro expected him to speak Latin, for he wore his hair like a Roman patrician. But that was the extent of such imitation. He prattled on in a stern voice, speaking mostly to please his listeners.

But then he looked to Aulus, and his guard encouraged him with a jab from his spear butt.

"Sir, his name is Virlus, and he is chief of this village. He has heard of what we've done and wants to know why we are here and what are our plans. He demands you answer him or he will flay us as we were just told."

"Tell him we are Cato's personal agents and he sent us to gather intelligence on the Bergistani in the area. Cato would pay handsomely for our return, and we are better hostages than dead men."

Aulus translated, but Varro wondered how true it was. For with every word, Chief Virlus's mirth seemed to increase, as did that of his followers. Soon, they were all laughing. Falco grumbled, and Varro looked inquisitively at Aulus.

"They think we are lying because we look too poor and are too few to be Cato's agents. Also, they had been following us for a while and thought us lost. He has guessed that we are deserters, sir."

Virlus then stood and sweepingly announced something that seemed to please half his men and caused the other half to turn aside or cover their mouths. When he finished, he looked down at them with sheer disgust as he waited for Aulus to translate.

"He said that they will deal us with after they settle the burial of those we killed and after he feasts his Turdentani allies who will arrive today. He says our interrogation might be excellent entertainment for their feasting."

With this settled, Varro found himself swept off his feet and spun around to face the rectangle of yellow light entering from the opened doorway. His guards marched him and the others back out to the crowd, which had closed around the building. They exchanged shouts and curses with the bald Iberian who once more assumed custody for them.

He lowered his spear and the crowd parted as he forced a path for Varro and the others to be led away. As they passed, some threw rocks or cursed them. Varro kept his shoulders squared and stared at the back of his bald captor's head. He would not afford them the pleasure of bending him, no matter how terribly he felt.

Their guards delivered them to three narrow cages of rusted iron not far off the open ground surrounding Chief Virlus's hall. Forced in at spear point, Varro closed his eyes when he heard the cage door rattle shut and the crude lock click. He turned around to see a ring of guards set around him and the crowd dispersing back to their chores. Many lingered before more moving off and looked longingly at them. Varro guessed these were the kin of those he killed earlier.

Falco groaned. "It smells like they kept animals in here. Gods, my head hurts."

The Iberians had positioned their cages just far enough apart that they could not reach each other through the bars. But they were close enough for speech.

"Sir, I don't see an easy way out of this." Aulus slumped to the ground in his cage. It was so tight that his knees pressed to his chest.

"Don't give up," Varro said. "Believe it or not, Falco and I have been in worse positions before. Just stay alert and don't let fear blind you to opportunity."

Falco gave a snorting laugh. "It's a sad thing when you can look at us now and truthfully say this is not as bad as we've seen. But it's not a great position, either. Aulus, are you still glad your friend got you mixed up in Servus Capax?"

"Sir, Centurion Lucian was like my brother. I am glad I can honor his memory, even with this small service."

"This is no small thing," Varro said. "You've twice saved our lives. That's more than honoring a memory, but worthy of honor in its own right. When we get out of this, I'm going to reward you. Whatever you want, if I have the power to grant it, then I will."

A smile appeared on Aulus's face, and the bloody gap in his teeth whistled as he spoke.

"You are quite positive, sir. Is this part of your training in Servus Capax?"

Varro looked to Falco who was too tall to even sit inside the cage. He gave a weak smile before answering.

"In a manner of speaking. Our service has brought us desperate moments, and if you survive enough of them, you can learn to keep your head in times like these. But it doesn't mean I'm not afraid to die. We've no weapons and no hope of being left unguarded to make an escape. There are no more allies to come to save us. Worse yet, the Turdentani are coming, and only the gods know what they'll do to us if they figure out who we are. The situation is bleak, but I refuse to accept death as the inevitable outcome."

"That's right," Falco said. "It's just the likely outcome. So don't waste your strength feeling gloomy, Aulus. At least we've still got our skin on our backs."

Aulus gave a fleeting smile and set his head back against the cage. Varro could just shimmy down the cage to sit on the hard ground. The village seemed to return to normalcy, with people crossing back and forth as they went about their chores. Their circle of guards chatted, hardly ever looking back at them.

While he sat and waited for something to happen, he picked at a torn hem in his tunic. He idly realized the only things he owned now were this tunic and his caligae. Both had been issued from the legion and it was all that remained to mark him as a soldier. He tried to look at the condition of the caligae, twisting his foot so that he could inspect the hobnails. Certainly, some had fallen out, but the iron bars confined him so tightly that he could not twist enough to see the bottom. It did not matter, but with these sandals being all that he possessed he wanted them in good condition. A foolish smile came to his face as he imagined asking for hobnail replacements so he wouldn't die with improper caligae on his feet.

Both Falco and Aulus remained with their own thoughts. Falco had to stand since the cage was too narrow and he wrapped his hands wrapped over the bars. Aulus seemed to have fallen asleep. It was hard to tell from his swollen and blood-crusted face.

The Turdentani eventually arrived to sounding horns and lines of villagers rushing to greet them. Chief Virlus emerged from his crumbling hall to greet them. The lead elements were on horseback and footmen trailed behind them. Varro could not see the details between people and buildings in the way. It seemed several hundred Turdentani had arrived, though Varro could never tell one tribe from another.

They set up their camp and seemed to melt into the overall activity of the afternoon. Varro and the others remained under guard but forgotten.

But when the sun hovered just over the western horizon, messengers came to talk to their guards. Aulus lifted his head off the bars and summarized their conversation.

"Sir, they've come to take us to the feast. We're going to be tonight's entertainment and tomorrow's sacrifice to the gods."

22

Varro tested the manacles on his wrists once more. They were old and rusted, chafing his skin with each pull. Yet for their condition, they held up against his efforts. He focused on trying to work free while all around him barbarians spoke in loud, boasting voices while seated at long benches and tables set out for a pleasant evening of feasting. Children chased each other through avenues created by the arrangement. Dogs followed them. It was a merry scene, for the barbarians, at least.

"You're not strong enough to break them," Falco said. He held up his own manacles. "Even rusted iron is too much. Where did they even get these?"

Varro shook his head and continued to fight against the manacles.

"I'm not trying to break them. They're just locked with a pin. If I can work it out, I'll be free."

Falco laughed, and it blended with the boisterous merriment surrounding them. "Then what will you do? Sprout wings and fly back to Rome? Our guards are right here, you fool."

Indeed, their spear-armed guards stood watching Varro's

struggles. Even without knowing their language, he knew they called him a fool. Releasing himself from the manacles would earn him nothing. In fact, the six men holding him, Falco, and Aulus, aside from the celebration, seemed interested if he could do it.

"I need to know if we can get these off," Varro said. "They're all watching me right now. If you and Aulus can work out of yours, then we might do something. These manacles were meant to be closed permanently. So once the pin pops out they just fall away."

His struggle was born out of desperation for their last moments. Earlier Chief Virlus made a welcoming announcement to his much more regal counterpart and Aulus explained he intended them as pre-dinner entertainment. The visiting Turdentani were especially pleased at this promise, and Aulus said they would be equally pleased to eat Roman livers as well. From harsh experience, Varro knew this was not an empty threat.

"Even if they don't take them off," Falco said, "our feet are free. Let's just kick them in the nuts and run. We'll probably die with javelins in our backs, but it's better than being cut to bits for the crowd. So, are you ready?"

The Iberians were within a spear thrust of them, and could run them through before Falco could ever land a kick. Hundreds of warriors who came to the feast armed and ready for battle also surrounded them.

"Sir, neither plan will work," Aulus said through his broken teeth. "Every eye at this feast turns to us, waiting for our blood to flow. Even if we killed these men outright, they would surround us no matter what we do. The time to fight back is past us now."

"Fuck!" Varro dropped his arms and his explosive curse made the guards laugh and point at him. "Is there nothing we can do?"

Falco's voice was soft and resigned. "It doesn't seem like it, old friend. Time to pray to Fortuna for a stroke of luck. She likes you best, so ask a favor for all of us. There's no other way."

Varro shook his head and looked past their ring of guards, who now seemed disappointed he had resigned himself to the manacles. Chief Virlus and his Turdentani counterpart sat at the head of the long table rows. They were behind a large and twisting tree that stretched its long branches out as if offering a blessing. The open field was a wide grass field with smaller, similar trees dotting the area. It was a fine place for a celebration, but a horrid place for escape.

If they broke free and ran, no doubt a thousand drunken Iberians would enjoy chasing them down. Nothing in any direction offered a hiding place. The nearest hope was the collection of buildings that formed Virlus's village. There was no escape on foot. As Falco had joked, he would need wings to lift himself from the circle of enemies.

The sun cast long shadows while the Iberians built up a bonfire against the oncoming darkness. Varro thought back to the dead Romans hanging from the gibbets with their livers cut out. They hung around a similar bonfire.

A lone figure approached from where the two Iberian chiefs presided over the feast. He was an older man with a heavily lined face and a long, pointed nose. As he addressed the guards in a low whisper, his watery eyes constantly glanced at them.

"I can't hear them, sir." Aulus's voice whistled through his broken teeth. "But he is a holy man. They are probably going to begin their entertainment by offering one of us to the gods."

"That is correct." The old Iberian spoke up in answer to Aulus's guess. His speech had a thick accent, but his voice was firm and commanding. He pushed through the guards to look over his captives.

Varro thought of using his manacles to attack this holy man. He might become a hostage he could use in trade for Falco and Aulus. But their guards were equally aware of this possibility, and they lowered their spears as they closed the circle.

The holy man sneered at Varro, then Falco, and finally settled on Aulus.

"You are a traitor," he said. "You think you are a Roman? You think Rome would accept you?"

Though Aulus's face had been ruined and was covered in dried blood, he stood straight and spoke clearly.

"I have sworn my sword to my brothers. I have betrayed no one."

The holy man gave a slow nod.

"The Romans hate our people and lust for our land. You who were born here and raised on its riches would give it all to Rome. You serve the one called Cato. He murdered all our people in the mountains, leaving not even a child alive. The blood of their mothers stains you. Today, traitor, we return that misery to you. You shall die as you caused our people to die."

Even through Aulus's swollen face, the whites of his eyes stood out. Panic gripped Varro as he realized two of the guards had already grabbed him by an arm each, and another touched a spear to his back. Two others shifted behind Varro and Falco. The cold prick of a razor-sharp spearhead jabbed into his flesh.

"The gods watch over you both." Aulus tried to look over his shoulder as his captors led him away and the holy man followed.

Varro wanted to call out to him, but the spear set against his spine warned against it. The third spearman positioned himself in front of them, so that if either tried to break free they would be impaled from both sides.

"If we're fast," Falco said. "We can get away."

"Freedom for our last heartbeats," Varro said. "Then we will be run through."

"Fuck, Varro, what are we going to do? I don't want to die here."

"I don't want to die anywhere," Varro said. "But we're not being offered choices."

The spearmen at their rear urged them forward once Aulus

was far enough ahead. The Iberians had all stood from their benches to either curse Aulus as he passed or cheer his impending death. They did the same for Varro and Falco as their captors herded them to the edge of the crowd. Some hurled their wine cups at them. One struck Varro's injured shoulder and exploded thin, sour red wine over his face.

The Iberians took Aulus to one of the trees dotting the field. A row of young men stood opposite it, lined up javelins in the ground.

Falco groaned. "This looks familiar."

Varro blinked in astonishment. Truly, the gods would punish him for his cruelty on that day in the mountains. These Iberians were going to lash them to a tree and throw javelins at them until they revealed all they knew about Cato and his plans.

"I have no more loyalty to Cato," Varro said. "Let's just tell them what they want."

"Yes, but you've loyalty to the legion and to our boys. You will not say anything and neither will I."

Aulus kept his head up as his guards ran rope around him to bind him against the trunk. Across from him, the young men walked through their casting form. When secured, the guards backed away and the holy man addressed the crowd.

It was a fiery and angry speech, and by the end of it Varro felt withered from all the hateful glares cast on him. Many times during his speech the holy man pointed to Aulus, who remained silent and did not struggle.

When the holy man ended his tirade, he then daubed Aulus with something Varro could not see from his distance. He sprinkled him with water and then arranged pine branches into his bindings before stepping away.

Into this almost reverent silence, Aulus shouted something in his native tongue. Then, when the holy man extended his palm to the first of the young men lined up across from him, Aulus gave one last shout in Latin before the first cast.

"Long live the Republic!"

In answer, a javelin soared across the field in a perfect arc, its thin shaft turning amber in the final light of the day. It plunged down with expert precision, nailing Aulus's leg to the tree trunk.

He arched his back and clenched his teeth against a long, growling moan. The young caster raised his fist in triumph and his friends congratulated him.

The Iberians leaped up in joy, clapping and shouting while raising their cups overhead.

Tears stung Varro's eyes. Both for Aulus's suffering and his valiant last words. He whispered to himself, "Go on to the Elysian Fields, my friend. You have earned your place among Rome's heroes."

But the Iberians were not prepared to send Aulus to his death so soon. The next caster let his javelin fly, immediately hushing the crowd while it seemed suspended in the air. It sliced down to sink into Aulus's left shoulder.

He again bucked back and howled in agony. This sent the crowd into a frenzy. For an instant, Varro felt the hot tip of the spear against his back ease as his guards cheered Aulus's suffering. He had the instinct to run. But now he could only run into the field. Behind him surged the jubilant and bloodthirsty crowd.

A third cast missed, and the caster rested his hands on his knees while his companions shoved at him playfully and the crowd jeered at him. He waved apologetically as the next man took aim. In the meantime, a young boy ran up with a fresh armful of javelins.

These men were certainly their best, at least as accurate as Roman velites and perhaps better. Aulus suffered for it. Thin white shafts hung out of his legs, arms, and torso. Fresh blood rolled down over the dried blood and gleamed with the decaying sunlight. The crowd celebrated every cast and Varro endured watching the entire spectacle. As much as the torture turned his stomach, he had caused this fate for Aulus by his own failings as a leader. He should've taken the time to question the Iberians and offer them incentives beyond reprieve from torment in order to secure their aid. But he had rushed to save Centurion Longinus, a man not worth the mud stuck between his hobnails.

"He must be dead," Falco said, his voice weak. "But they won't be satisfied until he falls apart on that tree."

It seemed their goal, for Varro likewise suspected Aulus was long dead even as more javelins thumped into his body. Yet his lack of reaction did not diminish the crowd's enthusiasm. Yet the spectacle ended when all the javelins had been cast. The same young boys who had resupplied the casters now ran up to the tree to gather any salvageable javelins.

Varro did not watch what came next. The holy man brought out a long, curved blade that certainly had no practical use in cutting Aulus from the tree. So he closed his eyes as the crowd calmed when the holy man and his assistants stood before Aulus's corpse. The crowd had gone so silent Varro could hear the wet slicing even at a distance.

"By the gods," Falco hissed. "I wish I closed my eyes for that."

Varro's remained shut but he heard the holy man shouting and the crowd murmuring in reply. Eventually, he guessed the spectacle had ended and opened his eyes. They had removed Aulus from the tree. He glimpsed the holy man holding up a glistening, bloody organ to the crowd before placing it into a wicker basket. His assistants then carried away Aulus's body.

Before Varro realized it, the spear pressed against his back and two men grabbed him by each arm. They dragged him into the field toward the killing tree, which was slathered in Aulus's blood. More men waited with blood-drenched ropes to tie him in Aulus's place.

"Varro!"

He couldn't look back but heard Falco's struggle erupt behind him. His shouting washed away on a tide of jeers and curses. Varro's captors kept his arms held tight and the spear in his back threatened to sever his spine if he resisted.

"I will not die as your spectacle!"

He pulled free of one man and stepped forward to avoid the spear striking at him. The blow glanced off his cheek as he punched the Iberian in the face. He cursed, but easily wrestled Varro around into the grip of his companion. The captors laughed as they regained Varro's free arm and wrestled it down. The spearman reversed his spear and thrust it under Varro's jaw to snap his head back. The violent jerk caused him to brown out and collapse between his two captors.

They wasted no moment of his grogginess, dragging him to the tree where two men pinned him as others ran around him with rope. He could hear Falco shouting his name amid the cheering crowd.

Across from him, the young men were once more lined up and stepped through their casting form. They gave him evil smiles and several gestured to their crotches, as if threatening to impale Varro through his manhood. By the time he had recovered enough to resist, he was bound tight to the trunk. Aulus's warm blood slithered down his leg. A jagged scarlet spray glistened on the grass before him.

His captors jumped away from him as the first caster prepared to throw. Varro's throat closed up and he felt faint. His thoughts raced out of control and his breath came hot and short. But he recalled Aulus and how bravely he had faced his end. He could do no less.

"Long live the Republic!"

The first cast soared up to vanish into the glare of the setting sun. It reappeared as it arced down and Varro braced for the searing pain.

The shaft slammed hard between his legs and exploded into fragments against the trunk that stung his flesh. The broken shaft embedded just beneath his crotch in the tree, missing its target by a thumb's width.

The caster shouted in rage as the others laughed at him. Another man pushed him aside as he held both hands over his head in defeat. From how the next man strained to set his aim, Varro could tell he planned to make the same throw. He couldn't move his legs enough to protect himself, though he fought against his bindings.

He clenched his teeth and squeezed his eyes shut against what must come next. But no sooner had he done so, a great shame raced over him. He must die like a Roman soldier, brave and without shame. So he flicked his eyes open to watch his doom soar out of the sun.

Yet it did not come.

The casters had lowered the javelins and stood aside with their heads bowed in deference. A man strode across the field, and from his broad shoulders and the heavy silver chains clasping his muscled neck Varro knew him for the Turdentani chief. His commanding and confident bearing set him apart from common men. As he passed the line of casters, he extended his palm and received a javelin.

He continued to stride forward as the crowd fell to a confused silence. Only Falco's shouting continued in the distance. But Varro could not look to him, transfixed on this king of death sweeping across the field at him. His long hair had turned gray at the temples, but his eyes seemed to burn with youthful blue fire. He came close enough that Varro saw the twisted smirk on his face.

This kingly man raised the javelin as he walked, then skipped forward to let it fly.

It flew with such speed and so level to Varro's sight that he didn't see the javelin until it slammed into the tree between his left ear and shoulder, and less than a finger's breadth from his throat.

The crowd gasped, for from their angle it must seem as if the javelin had struck him. But the Turdentani chief did not slow in his approach, though his smile flattened. Next, he drew a dagger from a sheath at his hip. It was a sharp wedge of bronze with a white edge to it. It gleamed in his powerful hands as he approached.

His clear eyes stared hatefully into Varro's. However, he had resigned himself to death and did not fear speaking.

"You will eat my liver, then? So be it. Live like a dog, eat like a dog."

The chief cocked his brow and spoke in clear Latin.

"You consider yourself food for a dog? I thought you would hold yourself in higher esteem."

"A pig cannot tell slop from a feast. Cut out my liver, pig. Gods willing, it will poison you."

"Well, perhaps I should." The chief's blazing eyes shifted to the shaft beside Varro's neck. "But the gods have already chosen to let you live."

That statement caught Varro's retort in his throat. His astonishment must have been plain, for the Turdentani chief gave a wry smile as he placed his dagger's edge against the rope binding him to the tree.

"You wonder why, Centurion Varro?"

"How do you know my name?" He strained to recall where he had met this man. His sole distinction was the lack of tattoos on his face so common among his people, though swirling blue lines crawled up his neck from beneath his tunic.

"I only learned it now. It seems I owe you a small mercy, the same mercy you took upon my son."

The Turdentani chief twisted to the side and let Varro see behind him.

Servius stood with his arms folded triumphantly. The scar on his shoulder that Varro had given him was bright pink but narrow. The doctor had done well in stitching it up. He smirked, but said nothing.

The chief stepped back and sawed at the ropes around Varro's body.

"You were a valuable instructor to my youngest son. You wrote your lesson on his shoulder. Good work. A harsher teacher would have ended the lesson with his life. So, in gratitude, I now spare your life and give it to my son. You will be his slave and his teacher. For despite his trials, he has not learned all his lessons yet."

The rope broke free and uncoiled at his feet. The crowd in the distance moaned, but it seemed they knew better than to challenge the decision.

Feeling tingled back into his hands as he pushed away from the tree, aware of the razor edge poised to slice his throat if he did anything foolish. More men had come up from where the chiefs sat, bringing the manacles once more.

"What about Falco?" Varro asked. "The other centurion. You will spare him as well?"

The chief sniffed and frowned in the general direction of the crowd.

"I've not heard his name before. I need only one Roman slave. He shall die."

23

The night was dark, and a chill breeze carried across the fields to make sleep impossible for Varro. Once again held in a narrow cage, he could not have slept even without the shiver of the deep night teasing him awake. He was too saddened by the empty cages next to him.

His so-called rescue by the Turdentani chief had soured the celebration. But he was Chief Virlus's superior, even if only an ally to the Bergistani tribe. Virlus was poor and had half the number of men that the Turdentani had brought. He was a leader, but not a king. So when the Turdentani declared the casting competition over, Virlus was quick to silence his own people's objections.

Varro had manacles slapped on him, set once more with a pin, and dragged back to the cage. Falco seemed to have vanished into the crowd along with his captors, and Varro worried about his fate. Since they took him back to his cage, he did not see the end of the festivities. But he assumed someone would come by to taunt him with Falco's corpse, or part of it. Since none had done so, he expected Falco lived.

But both he and Falco had intelligence the two chiefs would

want. So Falco might be the first to receive their attentions. He thought of Virlus's threat to flay them. Yet if Falco endured this excruciation, wouldn't his screams reach into the night?

Even with the addition of the Turdentani warriors, the village remained at peace. The feast had continued and the glow of the dying bonfire stained the dark sky beyond the rooflines of the village. Yet only crickets sang and an owl hooted in the distant woods.

So his mind churned on all the chaos of recent days. He drew a line back through all of this to Consul Cato. One day, he would have revenge. Only now it seemed impossible that he could ever enact it. With manacles and a cage, he was doubly trapped. Not to mention, by tomorrow they would brand him as a slave and carry him off to an uncertain fate.

"Army deserter and marked slave," he said to himself. "At least I cannot fall any lower now."

While he worried about Falco, he also could not block images of Aulus's last moments. It occurred to him that both he and his mentor, Centurion Lucian, died from javelin wounds. Such a coincidence smelled of the gods meddling, though Aulus's fate had been many times worse than his mentor's. It was a cruel ending for him. He thought of Gaius, who also met his death by javelin, and then Lars who at least had been picked off his horse by a Roman spear.

"Doesn't anyone die by the sword anymore?"

Then he knew beyond any doubt that the gods toyed with him.

As if answering his question, two young men emerged out of the darkness. Despite the chill of the mountain air, they wore only their tunics. Both men were red-faced and wobbling on their feet. Varro recognized them as two of the young men who had killed Aulus.

They glared angrily at him, and each carried a javelin that they waved as they spoke to each other. It seemed these young Bergistani men were unhappy with their sport ending prematurely. Varro knew it just from their sharp, angry gestures.

He shoved back against the iron bars and cowered. They were drunk and not thinking what their actions would mean for them when the Turdentani chief awakened to find his new slave stuck with javelins. A sober friend might warn them off their foolishness.

But Varro could not communicate with them. The best he could do was call for help.

So he began screaming. "Help me! They're going to kill me!"

He could've shouted poetry to the same effect. No one would understand him, and no one would come to his aid. He did not even have a guard assigned.

But the drunk young men did not feel the same. Their red faces turned white and they seemed to realize their mistake. But being drunk, their thoughts were muddled. They both raised their javelins and cast them anyway before fleeing.

Varro pressed back as one sailed wide of him and another javelin clattered between the cage bars then cracked. The iron rang out and vibrated with the impact and splinters stuck close to Varro's eyes. He turned aside, and when he looked back again, the two men had vanished.

Varro snickered at them. Two fools, if ever there was, he thought. But now at his feet was a perfectly fine javelin head and a hand's length of shaft still attached.

He scooped the broken javelin between his legs and crouched over to hide it even with no one near. With his hands still manacled together, he would not be a threat to anyone. Yet now he had a means to undo them as well.

"Thank you," he repeated over and over as he worked. "Thank you for drunk, dull-witted boys!"

He held the javelin point between his feet. His inner thighs burned, but he was limber enough to brace the javelin fragment.

The manacles were set with a pin. To use them properly, a blacksmith would weld the pin in place. But his captors had not done so, thinking to reuse these manacles. Now Varro had a pointed edge to pop the pin from the manacles.

He made several failed attempts, but he had time, as no one came to answer his calls for help. If those boys hadn't been drunk, he would've been stuck with javelins. Yet again, had they been sober they would not have come out for mischief.

"Thank you for drunks!" he repeated gleefully as he patiently lined up the pin and javelin point. After slipping twice more, the pin at last popped up high enough that Varro could work it free with his teeth. It tasted like rust and iron, and he spit it out as soon as he felt the manacles release.

He hissed, the only way he could express his joy at freedom. Rather than fling the manacles away, he set them open and to the side. If anyone did come to him, he wanted to appear as if he were still bound.

Now he slouched down to admire the javelin point. It was not a great weapon for close fighting. If he struck armor or a shield, he stood a good chance of dropping or ruining it. But then he didn't plan to take it to battle. Rather, he now had a way to seize an opportunity if any arose.

Of course, he had been given his opportunity already. His captors had feasted and got drunk, forgetting to post guards around him. Then the gods sent him two stupid boys who threw their weapons at him before running home to hide under their blankets. Any more opportunity had to come from himself.

So he looked up at the night sky, hoping he would see the answers in the stars.

And while the stars revealed nothing to him, looking overhead did.

With only starlight and the glow of a distant bonfire for illumination, he strained to see the details of the bars overhead. Despite the narrowness of the cage, it was high enough that he could raise his arm overhead to touch the top bars. It seemed as if these were more corroded than the other bars.

He stared up, the stars gleaming through square holes wide enough to fit both arms. Brushing his fingers against the bars, he felt gritty rust flake off onto his face.

Now he grabbed the bars with both hands and pulled up. His heart raced as he expected the corroded metal to give way. Yet the bars remained firmly in place, and he dropped back down. The hobnails of his sandals gave a muted chime when he fell. He blew out a long breath of frustration.

Yet he wondered what had caused the top bars to rust worse than the sides. He clapped the rust from his hands as he studied the cage more closely. As he did, he discovered the cage door hung from a new set of hinges. He confirmed it by finding the remnants of the old hinges on the opposite side.

The cage had been flipped over and the door rehung so that the lock would be at the correct height again.

"These Bergistani are too frugal for their own good." His whisper was full of excitement for this discovery. Just as they had reused their manacles, never welding them closed, so they reused their iron cages. Virlus was a poor chief and so were his people. They probably acquired these cages long ago and lacked the means to maintain or replace them.

This cage had sat in the mud and its bottom bars rusted faster than the others. Rather than repair the cage, someone realized they could flip it and rehang the door so that fresh bars now formed the bottom and therefore extend the useful life of the cage.

So now Varro got to his knees and examined the bars he had been sitting upon. The cage had sunk into the dirt over the years and even in the faint light he saw red stains in the earth.

They had not remembered to flip this cage again and the corrosion was far worse than the overhead bars.

Within moments of his discovery, Varro jumped against the side. No one was nearby and this was his chance. He threw himself from one wall to the other until he discovered the two sides that held the most hope of dislodging the cage. His shoulders ached as he butted up against the corroded iron, but soon the cage rocked with his jumping.

He thrashed back and forth until the cage dredged up from its sunken moorings. Then he climbed up one side and leaned into the cage's tilting momentum.

With a jarring clang, the iron cage collapsed on its side among the other cages like a soldier falling out of line. Varro looked down between his feet and saw the bonfire light shining through the ragged holes still clogged with dirt.

Now he set his sandals against the bars. His enemies had thought they had stripped him of everything Varro might use against them. But they clearly had no experience of the Roman caligae, which Varro had used in battle to finish off enemies on the ground. The heavy soles were perfect for his work now.

Since his panicked screaming went unanswered, it emboldened him to slam on the bars with all his strength. The clank of hobnails did not draw any attention. Each blow bent them out, straining the last of their already weak resistance. At last, he kicked open a hole nearly as wide as the entire cage bottom. He shimmied out of it and stepped back into freedom.

Even though he knew the village lay in drunken slumber, leaving his cage left him feeling exposed, as if everyone realized he had escaped. But he knew better and set aside that fear as he gathered the broken javelin and manacles. He briefly searched for the other javelin, but could not find it.

He needed to save Falco, and he knew exactly where he would be.

Crouching low, he dashed to the outskirts of the village and used the cover of night to move effortlessly toward the bonfire light. A dog barked at him from inside a building as he flitted past. Other than startling him, the dog had little effect. He passed without issue through the village into the wide field on the opposite side.

The sound of cricket song faded under the droning snores of scores of men passed out at their tables or curled up under their cloaks in the grass. If Varro had not known otherwise, it looked as if they had all died of poisoned food. As much as that fantasy entertained him, he knew to be careful while passing among them to reach the flickering bonfire on the other side. Not all of them would sleep deeply. However, he figured most of these were Bergistani warriors who had no home to return to here, meaning one patch of grass was as good as any other. They would be tired from their march, and the drink would ensure they stayed down until roused by the dawn.

So he padded carefully among the tables, passing powerful men fast asleep with empty cups in their hands. As he did, he searched the orange halo spreading from the bonfire. Virlus lacked the wealth and means to create a gibbet, so Falco stood tied to a post in its glare. His head hung to his chest, and even from a distance the cuts and bruises of his beating were clear. But his blood-stained tunic had no slits around his liver.

He paused when someone stirred near Falco. A figure emerged from behind the bonfire and lifted Falco's head by the hair. His voice carried only faintly, but Varro heard the threat. Falco did not seem to react, but he must have said something. The man forced Falco's head down and spit on it before moving back out of sight.

So they had set a guard for Falco, but had assumed Varro was well in hand. He smiled at their miscalculation and glided out from between the long tables. Since the bonfire was low but its stark light still strong, he had to loop back into the night and approach his target from the darkness.

His nerves tingling with the thrill of escape, he strode with confidence back into the field and circled around to where he found his mark sitting on a bench. A spear rested against it. The man leaned forward, scrubbing his red hair with both hands.

With ginger steps, Varro approached him. He raised the manacles in both hands. In the final moments before reaching his target, the clink of the manacles caused the Iberian to twist around.

Varro slammed the heavy iron across the back of his head, knocking him off the bench and flattening him to the ground. He groaned as he lay dazed, but Varro jumped the bench and landed on his back.

He drove the javelin point into the enemy's neck, forcing it through tense muscle until the shaft vanished into his flesh. The other side of his neck bulged with the point. Little blood flowed out of the wound, but the Iberian gurgled and gasped. Varro flipped him over so that he would choke on the blood rather than let it spill in the grass.

While the Iberian writhed in the last agonizing moments of his life, Varro confiscated his dagger and grabbed his spear. When finished, the Iberian lay still with both hands folded over this neck and staring at the stars.

He now approached Falco calmly, so if anyone was in a twilight state their attention wouldn't be drawn to him. Even though the bonfire had died down, its heat still painted Varro's back with sweat. He realized that Falco had probably been much closer to the flames when first tied here.

If Varro hadn't grown up with Falco, he would not have recognized him. His face was slick with blood that dripped onto his chest in runny lines. The fire had slicked all of his bruised flesh with sweat, causing the blood to run freely. His cheeks were cut and bruised and one eye was swollen shut so that his entire face was distorted.

"Are you alive?" Varro whispered as loudly as he dared. "Can you walk?"

Falco raised his head. How he could see through the swelling amazed Varro, but he gave a red smile.

"Sure, I can walk. They were most interested in my face tonight. They were going to start cutting off my toes in the morning."

"Fuck, this was too close," Varro muttered as he used the stolen dagger to cut away the rope bindings holding Falco to the wood post.

"How many times is this, now?" Falco asked as the ropes loosened.

"You mean rescuing you? I can't count so high. You're such a bother, Falco. Next time I ought to leave you."

"Really? Well, you've enjoyed several rescues yourself. Seems like we should stick together for now. You know, not run off like Curio."

When the ropes fell away, Varro jumped in front of Falco to catch him. He collapsed against his shoulder and Varro held him in place.

"Can you really run?"

Falco patted Varro's back and then squeezed him.

"I thought that bastard put a javelin through your neck. I'm so happy you're alive."

Astonished at the uncharacteristic emotion, Varro gently pushed him back.

"You take the dagger, and I'll take the spear. We've got a few hours before sunrise before they start looking for us. We need to find a hiding place."

"We're fucked, you know." Falco accepted the dagger. "We don't know shit about where we are or where we're going. Even if we stumble across a hiding spot, they'll dig us out. But at least then we can die like soldiers."

Varro stared at his battered friend. Somewhere under all the blood and bruised flesh he saw a mischievous gleam that made him remember the boy he grew up with. He smiled back.

"That's right. As soldiers. Now, let's head for the trees."

They pulled back from the bonfire and used its glare to mask their flight from the slumbering revelers.

Then they found their way blocked by three shadows. One stood forward from the rest, holding an iron horn in one hand and a short sword in the other. He was short, only a boy in a tunic that revealed a shoulder with a fine pink scar that ruined a blue tattoo.

"You think to escape, slave?" Servius gave a thin smile and raised the horn as if threatening to sound it. "I've been watching you. Good work, but no more playing around."

The two other figures, men with long spears, stepped forward and lowered them to charge.

24

Varro snapped his spear out at the first man to challenge him. To his shock, the spearman flinched back as if unsure whether he should strike. However, at his right, the spearman didn't hesitate to attack Falco, who carried only a dagger in his defense.

With the skill of vigorous practice, Varro shifted to the other spearman who lurched forward from Servius's side.

"Wait!" Servius shouted.

But Varro's spear jabbed under the spearman's arm and into the soft flesh. He recoiled and screamed as he fell to his knees. Blood flowed between his fingers as he gasped.

Despite his battered condition, Falco used the confusion to dash behind Varro at the other spearman.

"No, no, no!" Servius raised both hands, seeming to forget he held an alarm horn.

But Falco growled in anger as he slapped aside the shy enemy's spear and slid down its length. At the end of the motion, he slipped the dagger into his enemy's gut.

Varro now wheeled around at Servius, both hands on the blood-slicked spear, and struck for his neck.

Servius ducked away and crashed to the ground, both hands raised.

"No, they just wanted to scare you! Stop!"

Varro blinked at Falco, who hovered over the groaning man at his feet, dagger poised to finish him. His bloody teeth clenched tight and his ruined face contorted with rage.

"Fuck him!" He plunged the dagger into his enemy's neck, causing his back to arch in one last spasm.

Varro looked at the spearman fallen in the grass, his hand clamped under his arm and shivering in his last moments. He was hardly older than Servius, a youth of maybe fourteen years.

"No," Servius moaned. "I told them you would help us."

Rising to his full height, Falco stepped toward Servius as he kneeled in the grass. "You should've told them we'd kill all of you. Get his horn, Varro."

Whatever the situation, Falco's command made sense. He kicked Servius flat, then stepped on his arm until the horn fell out of his grip.

"Don't kill me! I want to leave with you."

"Really? We're headed toward death," Falco said. "So we'll send you ahead."

"Hold on." Varro held up his hand, but kept the spear at Servius's throat. If Falco had his own spear, he might slip it under Varro's guard. But he pulled up short.

"It's true," Servius said. "My father treats me like a fool. I will never be king. My brother is a monster. I cannot stay with them."

Falco chuckled. "Well, Aulus sure taught him how to speak."

"I learned from a slave since I was a boy," Servius said. "I just pretended not to speak when I was with you."

"You want to come with us?" Varro looked back to the orange

glow of the bonfire, then to the stars. Soon the sun would rise to expose their escape. "Can you take us to a hiding place?"

"Fuck, Varro, if we take him everyone back there will come looking for us."

"And if we don't," Varro said, "half of them will find us looking for a bolt hole in the rocks. Maybe Servius knows a place nearby?"

"I'm not from here," he said. "But my friends were, and you killed them."

Varro let his spear tip rest on the ground. "Don't wave spears at armed men if you want peace. I don't understand you, boy. If you hadn't run in the first place, then you'd still be with me."

"As a slave?" Servius crawled away from the spear and rubbed the arm Varro had stamped on. "Never. But now you need my help, and I need yours. I did not recognize you until they tied Aulus to the tree. At that moment, I begged my father to spare him. I wish I could've saved him."

"No more talking," Falco said. "If he's coming with us, then he better keep up. We can find out what he's about later."

"My friend said there is a cave in the ground nearby. It's not well known, but he has been there."

"Last time we found a cave in the wild," Varro said, thinking back to his experience in Macedonia, "there was a bear in it."

"Not this one," Servius said. He looked sadly to his friends in the grass, their blood reflecting starlight. "It's a safe spot for boys and girls to meet."

"Then it can't be far," Varro said. "Lead the way, and if you try anything foolish, you'll regret it."

"At least take their packs," Servius said, looking away from his fallen friends even as he pointed to them. "We brought some supplies once I guessed what you were doing."

Both he and Falco exchanged confused frowns, but Varro would not question his good fortune. Servius led them to the trees and plunged them into total darkness. They held hands to keep from separating and moved at a crawling pace. But when the eastern horizon stained white with the oncoming dawn, they emerged into the hills. From there, they sped higher until Servius declared the crevice must be nearby.

They could find nothing until the sun rose high enough to reveal a landmark that Servius had learned from his fallen friends. After that, they found the thin crack in a wall of reddish stone.

"If we carried any gear," Varro said. "We'd never fit through that space."

"Send the boy in first," Falco said.

"I'm not a boy," Servius said as he squeezed into the crevice to vanish into the darkness. "Oh, it's smaller in here than I thought."

Falco's swollen face looked horrible in the morning light. But he rolled his one open eye then pointed with his head. "You go next. I'm probably not going to fit."

Varro slipped through, sucking in his gut to press down the gap until he popped out into a low black space. Before Falco cut off the light trying to press inside, Varro glimpsed a wide, circular space with a low ceiling. Certainly, two people could sit comfortably, but Falco would crowd them. He popped through the gap with an exasperated gasp, then surveyed the narrow space.

"Just like the tents we slept in back in our recruit days," he said as he stretched out on his back. "We'll be sleeping face to face."

"Your face has expanded to twice its size," Varro said. "They broke your nose."

"And probably my cheek as well," Falco said. "I feel like someone is gouging out my eye with every breath. My back tooth is loose too. What I wouldn't give for a skin of wine right now. If I ever get to pay them back, they'll get worse."

"We should sleep while we can," Varro said. "We'll travel by night. Servius, how badly will your father want you back?"

"He didn't search for me when you captured me the first time. He said I was a fool and deserved my fate."

"But now you are running away." Varro lay back on the rocky ground. "I'm sure that is different. His pride will be hurt and he'll want you back just to keep his face before his people."

"Don't worry," Falco said. "They can't waste their time with us. They've got to meet the other Bergistani to fight Cato."

"Gods, it's hard to remember there's an actual war on right now." Varro cupped the back of his head in his hands to ease the pressure of the rock floor. "You're right. He might sweep the area or leave men to seek his son. But the main force has to continue on to the battle or else Cato will have it easy against a divided army."

"Cato aside," Falco said. "I hope our boys rip them to bloody shreds."

Servius remained quiet, as if trying to sink into the stone walls. Light did not reach far into the cave, but enough of it bounced around to describe their outlines. Varro hoped no one looked inside as he drifted off to sleep. The weight of all he had endured finally pulled him into a cold and silent darkness all his own.

He awakened to the sounds of voices. Falco's head popped up at the same moment. Both of them were too on edge to sleep through danger. Bright daylight flowed into the crack, and thin shadows flickered beyond it.

Without a word, Varro gathered his spear and crawled toward the entrance. Falco placed his hands on Varro's back as he followed with his dagger.

Someone spoke outside the cave, and his voice seemed to echo down the crevice. Varro lifted the spear to brace it for the first man who entered. But there was no other exit from this cave. He was simply ready to kill as many as he could before they smoked him out or else overwhelmed him.

The man outside spoke animatedly, and his shadow blocked the light as he tried to fit into the crevice. Varro held his breath, but the intruder made little progress. Someone beyond him laughed.

It seemed the first one pulled out and then another tried, only to discover he was too wide to fit through as well. The third man, however, forced his way into the crack and shimmied down its length.

Varro and Falco both pushed back to the far end of the cave, hoping to hide in the shadows there. But they ran into Servius, who awakened with a start.

Falco immediately clamped his hand over the boy's mouth, but the shadow in the crevice paused as if listening. Questioning voices spoke from beyond, and the shadow crawled froward again.

The sound of his body scraping against the stone was the sound of coming death. Sweat beaded on Varro's forehead as he sat on both knees, the stone floor digging into his flesh. He held the spear tight to his side, ready to strike when the man emerged.

But he paused at the end of the crevice, likely sensing the open space beyond. His shadow made strange shapes against the light as he tried to guess what he might find. He extended his foot to test the space ahead. His own shadow probably obscured his view, not to mention the rock walls pressing his face.

Varro understood his wariness, since without knowing where he stepped he might fall into a hole or else anger a viper or other vermin hiding in the cave.

The sudden inspiration hit him. He stabbed the spear forward, its tip just pricking the searching foot before he retracted it just as fast. To Falco and Servius it must have seemed rash. But Varro knew the man feared the unknown. That painful jab would become a snake bite or the nip of a wild beast in his imagination.

The man screamed and retreated. Varro held his breath as the shadow vanished from the crack. For a moment, he heard nothing. Yet the shadows of men outside continued milling around the entrance. There were murmured conversations before all fell silent and the shadows vanished.

They waited a long time before relaxing. Varro at last let the tension out of his gut and lay back on the cold rock. They did not dare speak, but from Falco's glare he knew he did not want to search outside.

So they waited all afternoon, and sleep came fleeting and fitful. But Varro's ruse had kept the enemy away. The Iberians had moved on, as expected. By nightfall, they sent Servius outside to inspect. He was the smallest of them, and a good stand-in for Curio. In fact, while he was outside, Varro said as much to Falco.

"I'd rather not hear that name again, to be honest."

"Don't give up on him," Varro said. "I believe in Curio. He did what he did for reasons we don't yet understand."

"They're gone," Servius said as he pressed into the crevice. "You scared them off."

"I just helped them realize their fears," Varro said. "They defeated themselves. Now, can you show us the way to Ilegertes territory?"

"That's easy," Servius said, backing up as both Varro and Falco emerged from the cave into the young night. "We travel toward the coast and we'll find them."

"Then show the way. But we must avoid the battle. Do you know where your father intended to lead his army?"

"My father has treated me like a stranger since I found my way home. He didn't tell me anything. All the important things are for my brother, not his weakling son."

"You're only a boy," Falco said. "Don't expect to be treated as a man."

"I'm sixteen years old." He squared his shoulders and scowled at Falco. "Don't you both stare at me like that. I had a fever when I was young. It kept me from growing as tall and broad as my brother."

"You're twelve at best." Falco said, waving his hands as if to dismiss the matter. "You don't even have the start of a beard. How can we deal with you if you're going to lie?"

"I'm not lying." Servius spread his hands wide and his voice cracked with frustration.

"No matter your age," Varro said, waving Falco away. "I need to understand a few things. What about your two friends? Will their fathers also seek revenge?"

"Both were my brother's slaves. Romans aren't the only ones to make slaves of our people, you know. We do it to ourselves."

Varro shrugged. "Such is the way in all the world. Now, what do you expect coming with us will achieve?"

"Aulus convinced me I was lucky to have been captured by you." Servius's youthful face brightened in the late afternoon light. "He told me his own story, and how he had become part of a secret company of soldiers who would one day rule the world. If I served you well, he said, then you might make me part of that. I will have nothing if I stay with my father. In fact, my brother will eventually kill me to make sure I cannot challenge him."

Falco smirked. "Well, you're a bit on the small side to challenge anyone."

"I almost killed him," Servius said, pointing to Varro. "He just got lucky."

Varro's eyes flicked wider and Falco burst out laughing, but Servius continued in earnest.

"I could challenge my brother and my father. You know, if people listen to me, they see I'm not a child. I have men who would follow me. That's how I gathered my own war band when my father would not let me fight you the first time."

"So, we have battled your father before," Varro said. "It was a horrible defeat for him."

"Because he doesn't think anyone is better than him," Servius said, shaking his head. "Only what he thinks is the best plan, even if it's not. My brother is the same, except he does whatever our father wants."

Varro collected their meager gear. "Yet you ran back to him. Why didn't just ask me for what you wanted?"

"Well, Aulus forbid me from repeating what he told me. Besides, I would not be any man's slave, and I thought I might still be welcome at home. I thought people would see me as brave for having defied Roman captivity. But that was not true. Everyone hates me now for having been made a slave. If it had been my brother, everyone would call him a hero. So when I saw you had escaped the cage I wanted to follow. You know, I would never keep you as a slave. That was my father's idea. We were both going to escape when the time was right."

Raising his brows, Varro looked to Falco. "Then it is best I did not wait for your convenience. Very well, Servius, I owe you my life and need your guidance through this land. We are going to Rome. If you will stay with us, then you are leaving your home forever. While you have my gratitude, be certain Rome is not welcoming of foreigners. Nor can I guarantee you anything other than I will offer what help I can. You chose a hard path to follow."

"Harder than having my brother find a quiet way to kill me if I remain here?"

"Harder than finding a new group of your own people to follow you," Varro said. "But I suppose you can always return here. In any case, we've delayed long enough. We must make the best use of the light remaining and then travel through the night more carefully."

They set out with Servius acting as guide and scout. The similarities with Curio were striking to Varro, and he knew Falco felt the same. It hurt to think that they headed away from their old friend now. Varro had to get back to Flamininus and clear their names. But he was not done with Curio. He would return here to find him again. If Flamininus had other plans for them, he would convince the senator that locating Curio had to be made a priority.

"He's not the same," Falco said, as if reading his thoughts.

"No one replaces Curio," Varro said. "But we need a guide and this one happens to be small and slippery just like our old friend."

"Too slippery for his own good," Falco said. "He should've said something to us. Anything at all would've been better than this."

They traveled through the night, and when they paused to rest, Servius filled in the details of his escape both during the initial Turdentani attack and later when Varro sacked their village.

"They were a strange folk," he said. "And lived differently from others of our tribe. I was happy to leave them, to be honest. They housed me with a woman who thought I was her dead son. I think the chief wanted me to take that boy's place. So when your attack started, I escaped through a secret way my new mother told me about. She went with me, too, but I left her behind. I feared for my life with her."

Servius proved to be a lively young man with interesting thoughts about his place in the world. Varro could see how he had the charisma of an influential leader. However, the misfortune of being in a stunted body ensured his warrior-minded people would never follow him.

Yet the stories were simple diversions from the harder aspects of traveling by night. The few supplies Servius and his companions had grabbed only lasted a day. By the third day, they were ravening with hunger, but had at least slaked their thirsts while following streams and brooks out of the mountains and through the plains.

They saw the dust of Cato's army on the march. Servius paused them at the edge of a forest to let them see.

"They go to Bergium where my father will join the high king of all the Bergistani. So both tribes will try to hold against Rome. I think they will do it."

Varro and Falco watched the brown clouds of three thousand men, only a portion of Cato's might, heading for the stronghold of Bergium. They shared knowing glances, but neither discouraged Servius's misplaced pride. He had never witnessed Roman war machines tear down fortress walls like ripping away rotted cloth.

"At least Cato and all his lackeys are behind us now," Falco said. "It feels good to see them going one way and us another."

"It's not how it should be," Varro said in a near whisper. Falco knew it too, and they both lowered their heads. "If we must put this behind us, then let's do it quickly. We must reach the Ilegertes before they are summoned to this battle, if they haven't been already."

So they passed the distant column of their former companions heading to battle and traveled east toward the coast until they came to Ilegertes territory. Servius found directions to the fortress where King Bilistages and his son, Albus, lived. They arrived at the smudgy outlines of the castle on a gray and blustery day.

With Servius to translate, they made their names and desires known at the gates. The answer came swiftly, and it was good tidings for Varro and Falco, who expected Albus must be pleased to welcome them.

They were led through the settlement where people went about their days in peace, though there were still the burned ruins of buildings left over from the siege. Several people recognized them as they passed, and they were met at the hall by Prince Albus himself.

He greeted them with mumbled praise and eyes that would not meet theirs.

It made Varro stand back and his own smile fade.

But Albus and his men whisked him, Falco, and Servius into the hall with promises of a special welcome.

And right to Centurion Longinus along with twelve legionaries all seated on benches around an empty table.

The stout centurion's beard had darkened considerably and the white scar on his cheek flexed with his sincere smile.

"Varro and Falco," he said while expanding his arms. "No need to chase you around Iberia when anyone could guess where you'd end up. Your countryside sojourn is over. Now it's time to return to camp."

25

Falco was first to reach for the dagger at his hip, but with one eye still swollen shut the Ilegertes warrior at his side easily seized his arm. Varro did not even attempt to fight, knowing it would avail him nothing other than more suffering. The man at his side snatched away his spear. Servius squealed like a girl, but as he was behind them Varro did not see what happened.

Instead, he locked eyes with Centurion Longinus who observed their disarming with smug satisfaction. He relaxed at the table beside his twelve soldiers who all seemed to enjoy the shock and surprise of prey walking into their trap.

As men wrestled his arms behind his back, Varro's eyes shifted to Albus who stood inside the door, his head lowered. He still wore his platinum hair long and flowing. He was a giant of a man, with an eagle talon tattooed on each of his hands. As Varro listened to Falco struggle uselessly, he accepted his capture. He leaned forward to Albus.

"How soon you forget the good others have done for you."

But Albus simply shifted aside to let Falco and his guards stumble through the door. His guards disarmed him and his swollen face was red with rage. But he shoved his guards around as they struggled to secure him.

Servius tripped along after him, a strong Ilegertes warrior pushing him.

"Thank you, Prince Albus," Longinus said. "Do not listen to the words of deserters and thieves."

"I have done as you asked," Albus said, his voice weary like a man who had just carried a heavy burden uphill. "You have the men you came seeking, and you have enjoyed the hospitality of my table for days. Now, I ask you to go."

"Of course," Longinus said as he stepped away from the table. His dark eyes gleamed with delight. "Consul Cato was clear that these deserters be returned to him at once. Just give me time to prepare the prisoners for travel."

Longinus stepped up to Varro, and he clapped his shoulder.

"You should be glad it's me who the consul sent to fetch you. I haven't forgotten what I owe you."

Varro narrowed his eyes at him. "Your life? Don't hold me to my mistakes."

With a gentle squeeze to Varro's shoulder, he stepped back and folded his muscular arms.

"We'll talk on the march. There is an easier way to do this than what's waiting for you back at camp. Look at Falco's face. You can still tell it's him under all the bruises and swelling. That won't be your condition, Varro. It'll be a lot worse."

When Varro did not answer but glared into the shadow at the end of the hall, Longinus gave orders to secure them for travel while he and some others gathered their gear.

Albus left the hall in care of his men, more of which showed up with spears and shields.

"What about me?" Servius asked as his guard lined him up with Varro and Falco. "I did nothing that they did. Set me free. I am the son of a king!"

In the end, all of them were tied together by their necks. They secured their arms at their backs and their feet tied together to restrict their strides. Nor did the legionaries do this by half measures. Varro could barely breathe through the rope cinching his throat.

Falco could still speak. "Any of you bastards part of the guards we knocked out?"

No one answered him, and Falco laughed.

"I guess you'd not admit to being a failure. Anyway, if any of you were, I'm sorry I didn't kill you the first time. But I will if I get another chance."

The soldiers only looked at each other. They were not triarii, but not recruits either. It seemed they might have been ordered to refrain from interactions, but one with light hair and light eyelashes could not help himself.

"A big threat coming from a man with a face like a bowl of blood soup. Keep your fat mouth shut, or I'll finish what the last man didn't."

Falco did not back down, but stepped forward as far as his rope allowed.

"Release me and we'll settle that threat. Anyone can defeat a tied man, except a milk-skinned lily like you."

The soldier punched Falco in the face. He staggered back but did not cry out no matter how bad it must have hurt him. For an instant, it seemed he might pass out. Then he leaned forward and spit blood onto the floor. In it was the yellow chunk of a tooth.

"Ah, that's better. It was driving me mad just dangling back there. Thanks for the help."

"Be silent!" Their guards pulled the rope around their necks and tugged them into line.

Varro led the group and turned to give Falco a confused frown.

"Invite no more pain," he said. "These men aren't important. They're just following orders."

Falco's eye now swelled such that it seemed ready to explode. Blood dribbled down his mouth onto his chest. Varro marveled at the amount of punishment his friend could withstand. But he could not afford any more blows to his face or he might go blind.

The legionaries led them out of the hall, following the same path they had just walked moments ago. Only now, confused or expressionless people lined their path. No one said anything as they filed through the town. Varro felt the heat on his face, both from the shame of their condition and for becoming entrapped.

He should have realized Cato would guess his destination. Even if he had not, Lars would have exposed their general plan. Varro had thought the time that had passed since their escape to arriving in Albus's hall might have convinced Cato they were not seeking aid from the Ilegertes. But Longinus was right; they had no other choices left.

Varro had expected Albus to be more welcoming of them. After all, they had saved his life and his father's fragile kingdom. But it was not so. Albus was a politician first. Soldiers like Varro were just useful pieces on his game board. Now that he surrendered them, he had Cato's favor again.

Aulus had been wrong about Iberian pride. Every place in this land was hostile to them. He and Falco had no friends. Even Servius, as tentative as their relationship was, begged to disassociate from them. As they filed along the dusty paths back toward the gates, Servius prattled on at the rear about being innocent and not part of whatever crimes "those two" committed.

They gathered into a small cluster, and their guards surrounded them. Servius eyed his captors with a mixture of fear and hatred. Falco kept his head down as blood drooled in long strings onto his chest. Varro could not see his own condition, but guessed he would appear as pathetic as the others.

After what seemed an age, Longinus and the rest of his men joined them. The sky was thick with gray clouds and a flat glare cast a diffuse light on the dreary scene. The gathered Ilegertes watched in silence from a distance. To Varro, it felt as if he were a ghost watching the living through the veil of the spirit world. Everything felt dampened, from color to sound to the burning roughness of the rope tied around his neck.

Neither Albus nor King Bilistages came to see them off. No doubt, they did not want to confront their own perfidy. In the end, the Ilegertes opened the gates and Longinus led out the long marching column with his prisoners strung out between him and a rear guard.

They marched down the slope toward their remnants of the lines Diorix had arrayed against the Ilegertes. Vestiges of those fortifications remained as charred logs and pits decaying into the earth. As they crossed these, Varro mourned for all that had gone before. What had he achieved here? He marched toward a death that meant nothing to anyone and would not advance any cause, never mind advancing Rome's influence.

Yet Curio was out there still. With every step forward, he expected him to arrive with horsemen to free them at the last moment. Yet the afternoon passed and no one came. Before they headed into a woodlands track at the edge of Ilegertes territory, Longinus called a halt to the march.

"Rest up," he said. "We're going to double the pace here on."

The soldiers moaned but took their offered break. Their guards tied the rope with its string of prisoners to a tree trunk. Varro noted it was not well bound, but the soldiers dropped to the grass only a javelin throw away.

"Run now?" Falco asked in a low voice.

"You'd run right into a tree," Varro said, staring up at the glare spread out into the clouds. "You can't even see me from this side."

"You could hold my hand."

It was not an especially funny comment, but Varro laughed. It was an overwhelming emotion. They sat on the cold ground, tied by their necks and bound to a tree, with what should have been their infantry brothers guarding them. Torture and death awaited them at the end of the march. But Varro could not stop laughing.

Falco joined him, shaking his head.

"Sorry, I can't feel my hands. I forgot they were tied at my back."

The soldiers gave them dark looks, but also turned to Longinus. In his tireless manner, he patrolled the line of his men even after offering them a break. He raised a brow at their laughter, but said nothing. The soldiers shrugged, then relaxed in the grass.

"What is so funny?" Servius asked. "What did the two of you do?"

"It's nothing we did," Varro said. "But something we didn't do."

"That's right," Falco said. "We didn't flip on our backs like feet-licking dogs. But, Varro, we should rethink that decision. Unless you've got another crazy plan to escape, we're done."

The laughter faded away and Varro looked back up at the sky. A single black bird glided across his view, then an entire flock suddenly sprang up from the trees nearby.

"No more plans," he said. "Bound by hands, feet, and necks, we've no hope."

Falco grunted agreement. "These are good knots, not some half-witted barbarian rope twist. We're not getting out of these unless someone cuts us loose."

"What are they going to do with me?" Servius asked, his face pale. "I have nothing to do with your crimes. I'm innocent."

"So you've been shouting," Falco said. "You're a fine example of a typical Iberian."

"But I did nothing." Servius leaned against his rope. "I helped the both of you come here. You said the Ilegertes were friends to you."

"So I had thought, and Aulus believed they would help." Varro watched the flock of blackbirds wheeling away into the glare of the afternoon. "Anyway, you're bound for the same camp you escaped from, and I expect you'll be sold into slavery as you should've been before I selected you for lighter work. If you're extremely fortunate, Cato might ransom you back to your father."

This quieted Servius, but Varro expected Cato would have him silenced then throw his body into the forest for scavengers to devour. He would just become another casualty in this pointless game played with all their lives.

"We cannot join Cato," Varro said. "Curio is still out there."

Falco remained quiet long enough for Varro to realize he disagreed. The three of them sat in awkward silence while Longinus and his men rested before the last push for the day. He likely wanted to clear the woodlands and find a campsite in the clearings beyond.

Longinus shouted his men back to their feet, then approached Varro and the others. He wore his disarmingly friendly smile.

"I see you enjoyed your rest. Had a pleasant laugh, yes? Listen, both of you. When we get to Consul Cato, all you need to do is recognize that you've made a poor decision. I will support forgiveness for both of you. The consul would be far happier if you worked with him rather than against him. We all understand how valuable you are. It is a waste of your talents to serve Flamininus."

Varro felt Falco's presence beside him, but his friend kept his mouth closed and head bowed. Servius's eyes were wide and fixed on Longinus.

"I can serve," he said. "I know all about my father's plans and where his people live. I hate all of them. You can kill them. Just not my mother."

But Longinus ignored Servius and awaited Varro's reply.

"I thought Curio had made that sensible choice." He tilted his head back and sneered. "But that was a lie. He's gone and took his command group with him. I'm certain Consul Cato wants him back. Do you think we would aid him in hunting our brother?"

Longinus's smile did not falter. Instead, he dipped his head in acceptance. "I see your point. But Curio is a separate matter. Don't let his bad choices cloud your own. You've got time on the march to consider things. What about you, Falco? Varro's not your master. You've got your own mind."

Falco rolled his neck along his rope bindings. "I'm trussed like a goat for the slaughter, and your hand has the knife on my throat. Fuck you, First Spear. I'm not stupid. You'll kill us after you've used us for all you can get."

Longinus shook his head like a father who could not understand his willful children. He turned back to his men and ordered them into ranks. The light-haired soldier untied their line from the anchoring tree, then led them into place. He would draw them along as Longinus set a pace into the trees.

The darkness settled over them while the deep greens of underbrush and densely packed trees pressed on both sides. The overcast day was already cool, but now in the forest Varro's exposed arms and legs pricked with the chill.

Longinus kept a strong pace, but he had gone only a dozen strides into the trees when Varro saw the figures poised on either side of the track.

They were ghostly, shrouded in gray and green cloaks with hoods that hid their faces. Their spears were tied with branches to obscure them from view. But their hands held them ready for the call to battle.

Longinus bent forward at the march, oblivious of the trap.

Varro looked back to Falco, unable to say anything. He used his eyes to guide Falco's only open eye toward their sides. But he was not sure if he could see anything in his condition. Their ghostly sentinels were waiting for a signal, and when it came Varro and the others might have their moment to escape.

The cloaked attackers came screaming out of the heavy brush lining both sides of the dirt track. They bellowed war cries and charged with lowered spears.

Longinus and all his soldiers were caught unaware. But they were experienced men who reacted with greater speed than their heavy shields and armor would suggest possible. Their own shields and swords flew up in defense before the enemies could reach them.

At the front of the column, a man on a black horse bounded out of the forest to cut off progress.

Then Varro felt the rope slacken.

He turned to find the fair-haired soldier hunkering behind his scutum as spearmen charged from his right. But in the next moment, another enemy charged from his rear. The spear sank into his back and he screamed in agony as he collapsed forward onto his attacker.

Though still bound hand and foot, Varro and the others were freed.

Both before and behind the column, dozens of cloaked attackers joined the battle. None targeted them and indeed seemed to ignore them.

"We can run!" Falco started forward, but the rope tying them together hauled him back.

"We can't," Varro said. "Not through the trees. These ropes will catch on everything."

Servius started screaming something in his own language. But Varro turned to the man lying dead on the ground. His gladius lay just out of his hand, while his attackers had moved farther ahead.

"I hold his sword firm," he said. "And you can cut the bonds on your hands."

"What?" Falco looked around him. "We don't have time!"

Now Servius started laughing. "No, don't worry! They're Ilegertes warriors. Listen to them!"

But all Varro heard was the sharp clang of metal on wood, the screams of the wounded, and the curses of the combatants. The entire column milled with spears rising and falling, mutilating the Roman defense and driving them down to slaughter.

The brightly colored scutum shields now lay in heaps like the shed scales of a snake. Perhaps thirty Ilegertes in long, flowing cloaks made swift work of the outflanked and surprised soldiers. Varro and the rest stood at the center of the devastation, with corpses spread in both directions from them.

The ambush finished with the same startling speed as it had begun. Surprised and outnumbered, the Roman column collapsed under the swift brutality. At the former head of the column sat a rider on a black horse, and he looked down from his mount with a long, bloody spear pointed at a soldier on the ground.

"They dress as Bergistani," Servius said. "But speak as Ilegertes."

Varro could not distinguish between tribes, but he smiled at the ruse nonetheless. The rider at the front signaled the end of battle by raising his shield. His warriors raised their spears and cheered. They immediately fell to stripping their defeated enemies of their gear.

Though Varro held no love for his captors, he disliked the looting of his former companions. Yet he remained bound by his neck and feet, and so could not protest.

The rider pulled back his hood and called out over the line of dead bodies to his men. Three stood up from their robbery to attend Varro's bonds along with the others.

"Centurion Varro, that is how you defeat an enemy with proper warriors. Not with sticks and dented helmets."

Varro recognized the face and outline of the man on the horse.

"I am grateful for it, Samis," he said as he turned his back for a warrior to cut away his bonds.

He had first met Samis as part of the emissaries that petitioned Consul Cato, and later he worked with Curio to defeat Diorix behind his fortress walls.

"You seem to need my help often enough," Samis said. "That gratitude should come with a bit of gold, yes?"

Once freed of his bonds, Varro rubbed his rope-burned wrists and neck and stretched his legs. Falco and Servius both fell to massaging their limbs.

"You will have to be patient," Varro said. "For the moment, I have little more than thanks to offer."

Samis laughed then waved him forward. "Come, I have another gift for you. You will owe me doubly for it."

All of them picked a careful path through the dead bodies and bloody puddles, avoiding the Ilegertes stripping the Romans down to their tunics and piling up their spoils beside the track.

Centurion Longinus sat on the ground beneath Samis, his shield lost and gladius shattered. A rend in the mail on the shoulder of his sword arm flowed with bright blood. His face was pale and sweaty, making his dark jaw stubble darker by contrast.

"The only survivor," Samis said. "He fought well. But I was glad to return all the insults he offered to my prince during his unwelcome stay."

Longinus scowled up at Varro. Though he was disarmed and injured, his eyes radiated threat.

Falco clapped his hands. "Let me have the first blow on him."

"He's in hand for now," Varro said. "I'd first like to hear why Samis just named Romans as enemies."

"A manner of speech," Samis said, his spear still dangling before Longinus's face. "My prince wishes you to know he has not forgotten what he owes you three. Though I miss Curio. Where is my old friend?"

"Fuck all if we know," Falco said.

Samis shrugged and continued.

"When Longinus came with his demands, Prince Albus knew you had fallen afoul of your treacherous consul. We have longed to return his treachery to him. Our people do not suffer that sort of treatment. So, he determined to aid you. Indeed, the conduct of this one and his men made it quite easy to decide on this ambush."

Longinus's scowl deepened and he glared at Samis on his horse.

Varro pieced together the rest of the plan. "So, Prince Albus had to show his people that we were taken captive. But then sent you ahead to free us in this woods away from prying eyes."

"Spies are everywhere," Samis said. "And we must remain at peace with Consul Cato for now. But he tests our limits. All he will know about today is his men vanished in woods known for banditry. It is a time for war, too. So who can say what befell Centurion Longinus and his men? They will find no bodies."

Varro shuddered and looked back at the line of warriors now stripping the Romans naked.

"Take your pick of their belongings," Samis said. "Prince Albus has begged a merchant to delay long enough to take you aboard and send you back to Rome. He would also tell you he has settled his debt to you. He remains your friend, but he owes you nothing more than hospitality if you should ever dare return."

"You're making a mistake," Longinus said. "All of you. The Ilegertes will pay for this, and, Varro, you will regret today."

"So what about this one?" Samis jabbed with his spear at Longinus.

Falco again stepped forward. "Give me that spear and I'll ram it through his heart."

But Varro raised his hand. "No, he has valuable information. We will take him back to Rome for Flaminius to deal with."

"What? He's too dangerous to keep as a prisoner. Who knows what trouble he could make for us? Let's kill him now and be done with him."

Yet Varro knew he was right. Longinus could unlock everything and so was too valuable to kill.

"Samis, please bind him as tightly as he can stand. We're taking him home."

26

The merchant captain was a reed-thin man with eyes permanently narrowed from a lifetime of peering at the horizon. He filled his fat-bellied ship with trade goods secured by rope and nets to the deck, spilling up from an overflowing hold. He was happy for two more fighting men to serve as deckhands and guards, though Falco's injuries limited him on both counts. But when confronted with the bound and gagged Centurion Longinus, he balked.

"I don't want trouble," he said. "Not in Rome, especially. No one said you'd have a prisoner."

"We represent Rome," Varro said smoothly. "And we're on official business. He is an important prisoner."

But whatever Albus had arranged with the merchant outweighed his fears. "Just keep him below deck and out of trouble."

They set off, leaving Samis with promises of repaying him one day and asking him to thank Albus on their behalf. Also, they were once more dressed as Roman soldiers and they reduced Longinus to the appearance of a common man. It felt good to once more carry a scutum and gladius, as well as wear a helmet and harness. While they both had a way to go before clearing their names, they both agreed they felt restored.

Servius accompanied them with great reluctance for someone who had only hours before tried to trade the lives of his family and people for freedom. Varro was uncertain how useful he would be, but for the time Servius had nowhere else to go. "I will see Rome," he said. "My tutors spoke about it so much. I will see if it is as grand as they claim."

The merchant ship would not travel directly, but make a detour to link up with other merchant vessels on the same course. The waters in the middle of the sea were safe from piracy, the merchant said, but less so as one approached Rome and civilization.

The peace of being at sea and away from the dangers of Iberia left Varro feeling numb, as if he had just emerged from a storm that had buffeted him for weeks on end. He did not know what would happen next, but Longinus would be key.

They held the centurion below decks and kept him bound and gagged unless he had to eat or relieve himself. He refused to say anything, and Varro refused to beat more out of him.

"We will not kill him," Falco said. "Let's just find out for ourselves. If we give him over to Flaminius, we might learn nothing more."

"If I keep resorting to torture and violence for everything, I will become a monster."

Falco rolled his eyes, but did not argue. "Here comes the old Varro I thought I left in Macedonia. Fine, but we should do ourselves some favors for once. I'd beat him if I didn't already know the fuss you'd make."

"Thank you for understanding."

But Falco probably did not understand. No one would, but Varro regretted he had drifted so far from where he started. He felt obligated to get back to his principles, even if the work he chose for himself directly opposed them. A balance had to exist and he would find it.

After four days at sea, they would arrive in Rome the next day. They had passed an uneventful journey, but for a night of heavy gusts and high waves that made Varro and the others vomit from the motion. The sailors laughed at them for it, but Varro did not mind. Knowing Rome was but a day away lifted his spirits.

The night before they were to arrive, Varro settled down in the corner of the hold where he, Falco, and Servius were assigned. It was little better than a space between crates and amphorae, but given all they had endured it felt like a feathered bed from Rome's finest dwelling.

A sailor roused him from sleep, his eyes wide in the darkness.

"Your friend and prisoner are escaping."

Varro was on his feet before he understood what he had said. Falco, too, lurched upright and cursed. Beside them, Servius's place was empty and his belongings gone.

They raced after the sailor and up to the decks to find a crowd where the ship's boat had been racked. The merchant paced with his hands on his head. When he saw Varro, his teeth flashed in the moonlight.

"You! He killed one of my men and stole my rowboat! It's your fault!"

Varro shoved him aside and pushed to the rails.

The ship's boat bobbed on the water as Servius and Longinus wrestled with the oars. For their frantic rowing, they hadn't made tremendous progress.

"Can you turn the ship around?" Varro asked.

The merchant spluttered. "She's not meant for tight turns. Yes, we could turn, but we're in formation in dangerous waters and I don't want to leave the company of the other ships. I'm not chasing after your captives! Show me proof of your authority. Ha! We both know you're deserters who I was foolish enough to accept for promises that might never be fulfilled. Ah, but I am a cursed fool! No, they stole the ship's boat and killed my man. I am done with all of it!"

Varro realized the mood of the sailors surrounding them. They turned from the loss of their boat to glaring at Varro. A sailor's body lay against the gunwales of the ship with his throat cut. Someone had tried to stop the bleeding from the red-stained cloth plugged under his neck. But the sailor stared up with glassy eyes.

"All right, we will accept responsibility." Varro used his arm to bar Falco from protesting. "When we arrive in Rome, I will repay you for the boat and compensate for the slain man. But I will need time to get my money."

The merchant growled and pounded his head with his knuckles. The crew started to mumble about bad luck and dumping them overboard. Varro had to deflect that sentiment before it took root.

"That man out there killed your shipmate. If you won't turn to fight him, then you cannot blame us. I would drag him aboard and cut his throat myself. He is one injured man accompanied by a boy. We can easily handle them. Look to your captain if it angers you to miss avenging your brother."

Now the merchant captain's narrow eyes opened as wide as two wine jugs.

"But you all know the dangers. If we turn now, we'll be on our own. Do you want to be Carthaginian slaves? Or Numidian slaves? It's just a boat and we won't get back the life lost."

This seemed to mollify the crew, but Varro knew fresh anger could sprout over the next day.

"They are beyond javelin range. Does anyone have a bow?"

The crew turned to each other and shrugged, but one sailor held up his fist.

"Here is my sling and some shot. I use it on gulls, mostly."

"Can you make that shot?" Varro asked, but he was already taking the sling and bag of stones from the sailor. "I am not certain I can. I played with a sling as all boys do, and I've drilled with slingers before. But nothing substitutes for practice."

Varro stood on a crate and fed a smooth, heavy stone into the sling. He then twirled it overhead and let it fly.

A white splash plunked close to the rowboat as it rocked along the waves. It did not seem to alert either Longinus or Servius.

"Falco, put that aggravating voice of yours to good use. I need Centurion Longinus to stand up, please."

"Of course, sir!" Falco leaned over the rails cupping his hands to his mouth as he shouted. "Longinus, you're a dead man. I poisoned your wine. You're going to roll over tomorrow morning unless you come back for the cure!"

Longinus's faint laughter echoed over the waves, but he continued to row frantically. Falco did not stop.

"If you wanted time alone with the boy, we would've traded him for information. You didn't have to do all this."

This got laughter from the crew and struck Longinus's pride.

He sat up straight to shout his retort.

Varro had kept the sling spinning throughout. He released the instant Longinus popped up.

The stone struck the top of his head. Despite the lowly status of slings and rocks as weapons, nothing was more devastatingly effective. Longinus's skull shattered with a hollow pop, still audible over the distance. Bone and brains showered on Servius, who screamed and fell flat to the hull.

Longinus wavered and extended his arm as if he held a sword and then toppled over the side into the water. His body made a short, white splash before it was lost to the night.

Varro stepped off the crate and held out the sling and bag of shot.

"Anyone who wants to try to hit the boy is welcome. The man who killed your shipmate is dead."

Someone snatched the sling away and loaded it. The other sailors jostled for their chance and soon many were betting for or against Servius's escape. Varro did not wait to see the outcome, but simply affirmed his agreement with the merchant with a curt nod. Falco joined him as both returned to their spot below deck.

Falco sighed. "So that little bastard Servius was not worth the mud between my toes."

"I suppose I'm not the judge of character I thought I was," Varro said as they sat against the wall of their sleeping area in the hold. "I think he's made his last escape. If the sailors don't get him, blood in the water might draw sharks that could tip his boat."

"Or pirates will get him," Falco added brightly. "But I hope he starves to death. Where were they going, anyway?"

"I don't know," Varro said. "I guess Longinus probably talked Servius into some sort of deal when we weren't around. That boy couldn't decide on what he wanted."

"No wonder his father hated him."

Varro chuckled and rubbed his face. "And here I was just thinking I must stop resorting to violence as my first choice. I could've let them go and probably nothing would happen to us. The gods should hand out justice and not me."

Falco snorted and shook his head.

"Better that you did it. The gods aren't always watching. Longinus got what he deserved. And you shut down the crew from blaming us for their friend's death. Someone had to do it or we'd be swimming to Rome."

"Well, it is done now," Varro said. "I'd have liked to have learned what Longinus knew."

"It doesn't matter," Falco said, scratching his head. "It was never our plan to take him back. Just an opportunity that didn't work out. Are you really going to pay for the boat and that dead sailor?"

"I intend to," Varro said. "But that depends on what awaits us in Rome."

"We'll be there tomorrow," Falco said in a whisper. "I really thought we wouldn't return this time."

Both sat in silence, listening to the laughter above deck and the creak of the boards beneath them. The rocking of the sea reminded Varro that he needed his sleep. Yet that was lost to him now. Though he had escaped Iberia, threats still lurked there. And maybe even worse, threats awaited in Rome. He did not know.

"I can't believe we did it," Falco said. "We left Curio behind. He's really gone."

"He will find us again," Varro said. "Or more likely, we will go back for him."

"We will?"

But Falco was smirking, his one opened eye gleaming with mischief.

Varro folded his arms and tried to get comfortable against the hold wall.

"I'm sure of it. We don't leave our brothers behind. Let's get straightened out with Senator Flamininus and then plan our next campaign in Iberia."

Falco stretched out beside him. "I can hardly wait."

So they dozed as the night passed with the merchant ship rocking on the waves. When dawn came, a sailor above deck shouted he had spotted land.

Varro's eyes flicked open. They were back in Rome.

He turned to Falco resting against the hold wall. They shared a long stare, then Varro nudged him.

"Come on. We're home at last."

27

Curio crouched in the underbrush with his gladius clutched under his gray cloak and hood pulled overhead. The man squatting over the trail in front of him was an experienced tracker. He prodded the ground, probably finding the light impressions of Curio's sandals. Then he looked up and touched a bent twig beside the trail.

Gritting his teeth, Curio held firm. He was not to attack until the signal. This would be the second tracker they faced today. From the tracker's patient observation, Curio guessed he was unaware that his partner was dead.

A sudden motion from the opposite side was Curio's signal. He leaped up with his gladius poised to strike.

In two strides, Curio reached him and punched forward with his gladius. But the tracker was unencumbered with armor, unlike Curio, and twisted aside.

From his rear, however, a dark cloaked figure emerged and swept over him.

This time, the tracker could not twist away.

Curio stepped back as the tracker screamed and fell toward

him, clutching at his throat where blood flowed freely between his fingers.

He collapsed at Curio's feet, looking at him upside down with wide eyes and begging for life. But Curio let him writhe and choke out his last breath as blood flooded his throat and spilled onto the mud track.

The other cloaked man now stood over him, hissed, then drove his gladius into the tracker's heart to end his suffering.

"You've never seen a dying man, Centurion?"

Curio blinked and shook his head without answering. He turned away from the scene and headed back toward the others. He had seen plenty of death. But that was one of his own, a velite most likely, and he did not deserve to die like this. How long must his fellow soldiers be his enemies?

"Hold on," the voice called from behind.

He stopped and closed his eyes, letting the sounds of the forest fill the silence. Then a firm but gentle hand pulled him around by the shoulder.

"It's hard, I know."

The voice was raspy but strong, full of commanding power. It had captivated Curio from the start, and it held him firm now.

"I might have known him."

"Maybe. But if he gets back to Cato with our location, then we're all in trouble and everything we've worked for will be ruined. You don't want that."

"Of course not," Curio said. He had only been gone from camp for a day and already trackers were in pursuit.

"Are you starting to doubt me, Centurion Curio?"

"I am afraid for Varro and Falco. They're in a lot of trouble."

"They're in excellent hands. Aulus will take care of them and get them out of the province. We need them to lead Cato away from us. For now, he's not sure which of us to pursue. It won't be long before he realizes he's chasing the wrong men. But it will give us a much-needed lead."

"I'm sure they would've helped," Curio said, then clipped off his next words.

"They are helping. Trust Aulus. He is like a son to me. It will all work out. Now, let's get the boys moving again. When the scouts don't return, Cato will know which way to probe. I want to lose our trail in the mountains."

So they returned to where Curio's former command group waited with the wagon and mules. One was tightening the cover over the wagon bed, and the corners of the boxes underneath bulged through the cloth. They saw the blood on Curio's legs and blinked.

"We've eliminated the trackers," he said. "But that will just tell Cato we're out here. So, we need to keep heading south like we planned."

They broke camp and hitched the mules to the cart. Curio dragged his feet throughout, wondering what Falco and Varro would think of him.

The same firm but gentle hand seized his shoulder once more and drew him away from the others into the trees edging the camp.

"I know that look," he said. "Servus Capax demands everything from its members. But it gives back as much as it takes. In time, you will know. Rome will rule all of Greece and Macedonia, all of Iberia, and one day all of Carthage and even more. The Seleucid and the Ptolomey will crumble. Servus Capax will make sure it all happens. And men like Cato will have to stand aside or else find themselves forgotten to history."

Curio bit his lip. "I'm not even sure I know all those names, sir. I just wonder if we couldn't have done this differently. Varro and Falco are amazing leaders."

"They are. But they have other work to do. And I needed your skills more than they did. It is better they do not know the details. With Longinus on their trail, they stand a far better chance of being captured than we do. But they have proved to be resourceful, and Aulus is with them. They will turn up fine."

Curio sighed. He had accepted that he might have to deceive his friends for a short time. But now it seemed like he was abandoning them to the care of an Iberian he hardly knew. He should help them escape, not Aulus.

"Very well, sir. I will do as I promised."

"I know you will. You are every bit equal to those two. You've undersold yourself for years, Curio. Now, you will have your part to play."

"Sir, if we are going to do this together, then you must be honest with me. Your name is not Placus, is it?"

The old soldier gave a gap-toothed smile.

"It has been one of my names. I've died more times over the years than I care to count. It's easy to do. Just lie down in enemy blood and pay the orderlies to count you among the dead, or else threaten their lives to do the same."

"So what is it, sir? You carry the gold mark on your pugio. According to Varro, that's only for important men."

The man pulled up his hood and turned Curio to face his command group gathered around the cart.

"If it means so much to you, then I'll give you my name. I've been in Iberia a long time, and it was the first place where I had to die and take on a new name. At that time, I was Centurion Lucian. That's the truth."

"Centurion Lucian," Curio repeated. "Then that is what I will call you from now on."

Patting Curio's shoulder, Centurion Lucian nudged him forward.

"Come on, we've got miles to go before we're safe."

28

HISTORICAL NOTES

Following Cato's victory at Emporiae (also known as Emporion or Ampurias), the driving force of the Iberian revolt had diminished but not extinguished. Uprisings continued in pockets throughout the province of Near Iberia. Not wanting to lose momentum, Cato marched his legions around the province and crushed rebellion wherever he found it. None of these battles reached the same scale as the one at Emporiae. Cato adopted a hardline policy for tribes that would not cooperate. He would demolish their towns, tear down their walls, and sell rebels into slavery. As his fearsome reputation grew, he would only need to threaten action to achieve compliance.

With matters settled for the moment in his own province, Cato turned his attention to requests by the praetors Publius Manlius and Appius Claudius Nero in Further Iberia to the south. While they had their own provincial armies to lead against the defiant Turdentani, they were panicked by the Turdentani hiring ten thousand Celtiberian mercenaries.

Cato marched his forces south, encountering and skirmishing with Turdentani war bands. These skirmishes were lopsided victories for Rome in all cases. The praetors welcomed Cato and entreated him to take swift action.

However, Cato could be a practical man. He reasoned mercenaries work for pay, so they could also be paid not to work. He first tried to convince the Celtiberians that they were on the wrong side and should join him. But when this failed, he simply bribed the Celtiberians to stand aside, which they did.

Seeing that the praetors now had more than sufficient forces to handle the Turdentani, Cato left them the bulk of his legions and took about three thousand of his men back north. The Bergistani were a small tribe, but the moment Cato left they fomented rebellion. Cato would not stand for this a second time.

Upon his return, Cato confronted the Bergistani in their stronghold of Bergium (current day Berga in Catalonia). He made swift work of destroying the fortress and shattering the Bergistani along with other allied tribes not wise enough to have learned the measure of Cato's abilities as a legion commander.

After this, Cato would remain in Near Iberia, organizing silver and iron mines and bolstering their revenues. At this point in history, he had quelled further rebellion. To the people of Rome, Cato was a hero. He would eventually be awarded a triumph as well as three days of public thanksgiving for his efforts.

However, the Iberians were never completely tamed, as they will demonstrate after Cato's eventual departure. Furthermore, Carthage played a part in encouraging rebellion and they would attempt to keep the rebellion alive even if any hope of real disruption was now long past.

Into this mix, we have Varro, Falco, and Curio facing enemies they cannot come to grips with in conventional battle. While they can stand firm against a line of enemy warriors, they struggle to meet the challenge of being soldiers in a longer and larger battle conducted away from the public eye. All of this is of course artistic license and not part of any formal history. But scholars have debated just whether Rome became an empire as an accident of history or as an intentional, long-term plan to subvert the known world to Roman interests. Of course, you have seen which side of the argument this series takes. Varro and company have a long road ahead of them yet.

Printed in Great Britain
by Amazon